MEN OF THE NORTH #0.5

FORBIDDEN LETTERS

Copyright © 2019
By Elin Peer
All rights reserved.
No part of this book may be reproduced in any form without written permission from the author, excepting brief quotations embodied in articles and reviews.
ISBN: 9781075055454
Forbidden Letters – Men of the North #0.5
First Edition
The characters and events portrayed in this book are fictitious. Any similarity to real persons or organizations is coincidental and not intended by the author.
Recommended for mature readers due to adult content.
Cover Art by Kellie Dennis:
bookcoverbydesign.co.uk
Editing: martinohearn.com

Books in this series

For the best reading experience and to avoid spoilers, this is the recommended order of the books.

Prequel:
Forbidden Letters # 0.5

First Generation
The Protector #1
The Ruler #2
The Mentor #3
The Seducer #4
The Warrior #5

Second Generation
The Genius #6
The Dancer #7
The Athlete #8
The Fighter #9
The Pacifist #10

Third Generation
The Artist #11
The Explorer #12
The Outcast #13
The Heir #14
The Champion #15

The books are also available in paperback and audiobooks.
For a full overview of my books and to be alerted for new book releases, discounts, and give-aways, please sign up to my list at
www.elinpeer.com

PLEASE NOTE

This book is intended for mature readers only, as it contains a few graphic scenes and some inappropriate language.

Trigger Warning.
This book mentions underage sex although there's no graphical description of it.

All characters are fictional and any likeness to a living person or organization is coincidental.

DEDICATION

To all the fans who asked for more books in the Men of the North series.

This book is proof that messaging an author pays off.

Elin

CHAPTER 1
Last Breath

Year 2236

Devina

What do you say to someone who is dying?

As a writer, I'm good with words, but not when my throat feels like an iron band is tightening around my neck and I can't breathe from the sorrow in my chest.

"Nana…" My voice broke and I could no longer hide the impending emotional breakdown that had been building up since I came back home three days ago.

My grandmother's eyes were hooded as she lay in her bed. "I know, my child." Her caress of my hand was slow and weak, just like her speech. "I hate to leave you like this."

With a loud sniffle, I buried my head against her gray hair.

"I know, sweetheart. I know." Her old hands patted my head. "If only they had developed the vaccine sooner."

Being twenty-eight, I hadn't lived with my family unit since I moved out seven years ago. There were no universities in our small rural area and I'd wanted to pursue a career as a writer.

Despite the distance, we were a close family and I had always talked to them daily. It had been only two months since my youngest sister, Maria, told me she wasn't feeling good. I'd teased her that she just wanted to be pampered for a day. With symptoms similar to the common flu, we had all thought Maria would get better, but then her school sent out a warning that it could be a potential epidemic and that kids should stay home.

At first, my sixteen-year-old brother, Justin, was excited to have some days out of school, but then the News began reporting about an outbreak and when a girl from Maria's class died, we all got scared.

Every day I called my family hoping for good news, but within a week, seven out of the eight of them had all contracted a fever and they made me promise to stay away.

The media named it the Triple D virus, which was short for Deceptive Death Disease. The Press came up with the name after a pattern emerged of victims showing signs of complete remission only to die of sudden cardiac arrest. Doctors specializing in infectious diseases spoke of the danger of infected people thinking they were well and going out to infect others. They theorized that the outbreak stemmed from a waterborne virus and kept promising a vaccine was close.

Most of the green area where my family lived was placed in quarantine, making it impossible for anyone outside the infection zone to get in and help. With hopeless despair, we were left to watch how, in the span of eight weeks, seventeen thousand people died. Among them were my three sisters, brother, dad, and both my mothers.

I waited seven hours in a long line to be among the first to get the vaccine when it came out seven days ago. Four days later the quarantine had finally been lifted and I'd hurried to my family's home up north. But by then, only my grandmother had been left

With all my heart, I wanted to believe I could heal her back to life, but her symptoms were different from the Triple D virus. From the sound of her strained breathing, it was a matter of time before I lost her too.

"Don't die, Nana," I cried.

"I gave everything." Her words were low, but I knew what she meant. Nana was a healer and trying to fight off the sickness of seven family members had drained her life-force. I'd seen her get tired after healing sessions all through my childhood.

"Take some of my energy," I offered even though I knew it didn't work like that. She closed her eyes as if she'd already given up.

"No, don't leave me alone." My speech was unclear from the sobbing.

"Devina, dear." My grandmother's voice was shaky and her cough made me lean in to support her head. Thinking these might be her last words, I sniffled hard and looked deep into her eyes.

"You shouldn't have come back here."

"I had to." Using the back of my free hand, I dried my tears to see her better. "The vaccine will protect me."

"Mmm... don't let our family die out." The dark circles under her eyes and the grayish color of my nana's skin made her look much older than her seventy-four years.

"Oh, Nana, let me save you. Tell me what to do."

She closed her eyes for a second. "I'm sorry."

"It's not your fault." I sniffled.

"A child..."

Her voice was so low that I had to move very close to hear her. "What child?"

"Your child."

I wrinkled my forehead, not sure what she was talking about.

"I don't have a child, Nana. You know that."

"Family. Is. Everything." Every word was forced out like her lungs didn't have enough air to both breathe and talk.

My head bobbed up and down in agreement. "Yes. Family is everything."

"Never forget us."

Raising her wrinkled hand to my heart, I assured her with my tears running down my cheeks, "I'll never forget any of you. Hannah, Maria, Caro, Justin, Mom, Dad, Mama... and you. You'll live in my heart forever."

Her eyelids kept getting heavier and there were long moments when she had to rest before saying a few more words. "Have a... child."

"You want me to have a child?"

"Mmm..." She gave a tiny nod and closed her eyes again.

It made sense that my grandmother would want me to join another family unit and be part of a community, but didn't she understand that I couldn't bear to lose any more family members? What if a new epidemic came? My soul was already in shreds from the massive grief that filled me.

"You must!"

I squeezed her hand a little.

"Children are the greatest gift. They bring new hope."

"But Nana..."

"Have a child," she repeated and coughed again. "Promise me."

I had no choice. Stroking her hair, I gave my dying grandmother a promise. "You have my word. I won't let our family die out with me. I'll have a child and if it's a girl, I'll name her Andrea after you."

The tiniest tug of her lip was the only indication that she had heard me. After that she closed her eyes and continued her strained breathing.

I sat with her, holding her hand, while Nana fell into a deep sleep. Several times, I thought she'd taken her last breath because there were long seconds between them, but then she heaved in another breath, and kept going a little longer.

I shared some of my favorite memories with her.

"Remember when you let me dress up in your clothes? You had that red dress that I loved so much and even though it was much too big for me, you said I looked beautiful.

"I'll miss your baking, Nana. The delicious smell of fresh baked bread and cakes that always made me feel loved and spoiled." My voice kept cracking as I spoke of childhood memories and my love for her.

Twenty-eight amazing years of my life, I had been loved by this woman, and then on this rainy day in July 2236, my beautiful, strong, and caring Nana took her last breath.

"Nooo," I let out my soul-wrenching despair in a desperate sobbing that made Nellie, our family dog, come and place her head on my thigh and whine herself.

The pain in my chest made it impossible to breathe, and I reached for Nellie and cried into her fur.

My family is gone.
They're all gone.

Just three months ago we'd been sitting in this house, celebrating Maria's twelfth birthday. My brother had given her a large and beautifully wrapped present and laughed hard when it turned out to be a tiny framed picture of himself. Justin had loved pranks and in his sixteen years he'd played a lot of them.

My body felt heavy, as if the sorrow of losing eight family members was measured in bags of lead that would be mine to carry for the rest of my life.

Lifting my arms or getting up from my chair was impossible. All I could do was slide down on the floor and cry my eyes out.

This isn't happening.
Please let me wake up from this nightmare.
Make it stop.

I was exhausted when I curled up in a ball wrapping my arms around my knees.

I need to call the authorities and let them know Nana died.

The thought of them removing her body and leaving me alone in this house made me cry harder. I would be all alone to sort through all the memories, and then what?

If only I'd died with them.

The thought was so strong that my crying slowed down.

It could solve my problems. No more grief, sorrow, or loneliness. What good do I have to look forward to anyway?

Nellie whined again, as if she understood my sinister thoughts.

Reaching out for her, I whispered. "I'll make sure you have a nice family before I leave."

And then my grandmother's last words came back to me. I had promised her that I wouldn't let our family tree die out.

Pressing both heels of my hands to my eyes, I cried again. Why in the world did I make that promise?

CHAPTER 2
Shining Object

Devina

I used to run through this forest and chase butterflies and fireflies with my siblings when I was younger. Back then my heart was light and my smile wide.

A memory of my sister Caroline pointing up and whispering, "Do you see the fairy?" made me walk a bit faster. It'd been four days since Nana died and it was like the ghosts of my family members were all around me.

Each room in the house was filled with memories, and after two days of packing things into boxes, I'd come out here hoping to get a break.

But there she was again, my mind's eye showing me Caroline as a seven-year-old girl running from tree to tree searching for fairies. She turned to smile at me, a beam of sunlight playing in her dark hair. "Come on, you slow snail. The fairies will be gone before you make it over here."

The pressure on my chest filled me with regret that I hadn't hurried back then. What I wouldn't give to share more memories with Caroline now, but with nine years between us, I'd been sixteen and felt too old for fairies. It was ironic, since today I was an author using my imagination to create my art.

In front of me, Nellie was panting. She was a protective old sheep dog and showed it by barking aggressively at a large group of crows who were flying around over our heads. The birds looked as black as my soul felt and the awful screams they made hurt my ears.

Another memory assaulted me of my sister Maria. She had been afraid of birds. Once when she was four, she'd been frozen in fear and unable to pass a tree because of two crows watching us. Birds never scared me and I would have ignored the noisy group today if it weren't for Nellie, who chased after them.

"Nellie, no, stay here." With a sigh of resignation, I trotted after her, trying to ignore the drops of rain on my head.

"Nellie, come back here," I ordered, feeling worried that she was running toward the border area because unlike me, she wouldn't be able to read the big signs saying "no trespassing," "danger," and "mines." "Nellieee." I was running now and felt relief when she stopped where the forest ended and the no-trespassing zone began. Her barking mixed with the shrill caws of the twelve crows that were surrounding a shiny object.

What is that?

My vision of the object was blocked by the birds fighting to be the lucky one to lift the thing with their claws.

It's a bottle.

I shooed the crows away, curious to see why the bottle was so sparkly. Most of the black crows took off, but the bravest two stayed and flapped their wings as if to challenge me for this incredible jewel.

Making a mock attack, I clapped my hands and shouted at them. Spooked, they hopped backward giving loud protests, but I ignored them and picked up the bottle, which was made of a thin, hard material and wrapped in a glittery surface. Turning it around, I studied it, wondering what kind of material it was made of. It was heavier than the biodegradable bottles we had here in the Motherlands. My eyes lifted to the wall in front of me.

Could it have come from the other side?

There weren't many brave enough to live this close to the Northern border. Not even the century-long peace treaty between our two nations could make people forget how the savage Men of the North used to hunt down and kidnap women here.

Except for a bit of trade there was no contact between the men living on the other side of that wall and us regular people living in the Motherlands.

From what I knew, our Council had meetings with their changing leaders every few years, but for the most part, it was like the world ended at that wall and it was imprinted in us to keep our distance.

I put the light bottle down again and stood back up. Still, my curiosity wouldn't let me back away from it. What if it really was from the other side?

Don't pick it up.

I looked around but saw no one.

There was a security camera on the wall. I only knew that because I'd walked here since I was a child and seen the wall before the thorn bushes overgrew the wall and camera. Now the whole area looked forgotten and neglected.

Nellie lay down next to me, her tongue hanging out and her eyes fixed on the two brave crows who were still on the ground watching us.

"We should leave the bottle to them," I told Nellie, who had been my sole companion for these last days. "Right?"

The only sound from her was her exhausted panting from chasing off the competitors to this foreign object.

"I think there's something inside it. Look." I pointed to the see-through bottleneck. "It looks like a letter."

For the first time in days, I wasn't thinking about my loss, but felt excitement at finding something unexpected.

"Okay, I agree. We should open it. It's not like the crows can read anyway."

Picking up the bottle, my hands shook a little when I unscrewed the lid and pulled out a rolled-up piece of paper.

To the Motlander who finds this letter,

My name is Wilma Green. I just turned fifteen.
I've always been curious about what it's like to live on your side of the wall. Will you please answer me? Just put a letter in this bottle and throw it over the wall. I live close by and will check every day, but hurry. In three weeks, I'll be moving. Not because I want to but because my bridal tournament is coming up. Large warriors will fight to marry me and I'll have no choice but to move to my new husband's house.

Wilma

A loud gasp escaped me. A child was being married off to one of those large scary men against her will.

"Nellie, this is awful." I stared at the wall, which had to be more than forty meters away from me and at least twelve meters high. How had a girl that young thrown a bottle this far? And what was she doing on that side of the wall anyway? Had she been kidnapped? Did she need help?

Three weeks... How long had the bottle been here? From the look of it, not long.

I wouldn't want to be stuck in the Northlands and I could feel my heart race as I reread the letter again. Wilma was the same age as my sister Hannah had been. The thought of her being forced into a marriage made me angry. It confirmed that it was still true: the Northlands was a place with primitive and savage men who abused women.

I studied the wall that had protected us from them for centuries. In school, we had learned about the awful years that followed after the Toxic War. In 2060 women had taken control of the world after power-hungry men almost annihilated humanity and destroyed most of our planet in that three-year war.

But not all men had been willing to accept the leadership of our all-female council and they had gathered up north where they fought among themselves for power. It had been a bleak time back then when the brutal men from the North would kidnap women to breed for them.

My family would have never dared live this close to the border if it hadn't been for the peace treaty of 2073. Now, sixteen decades later, we still supplied the boys that were needed for the Men of the North to sustain their numbers, but never girls. There were only two possibilities. Either Wilma was a descendant of some of the original unfortunate women who had been kidnapped or caught on the wrong side of the wall, or she had been kidnapped recently and needed help.

I bent down and picked up a stone, giving it my best throw, but it landed in front of the wall. There was no way I could get an answer back to the girl, unless…

"Nellie, come on." With quick steps, I began jogging back to the house while she ran ahead with her tail wagging.

In the corner of Justin's room under a pile of his clothes, I found what I was looking for. His slingshot catapult. When I bumped against his bookshelf, a bit of dust fell on my face and made me sneeze. If he had been here, I would have told him to clean his room.

But he's not!

I choked up again as I stood with the catapult in my arms. It was like a portal to memories of Justin glowing with pride when he showed me his project for school. He had made all of us come outside to admire how far he could propel test objects.

Tears were prickling just behind my eyelids, but I didn't have time to let my emotions go. Instead, I hurried down the stairs and placed the heavy catapult on the table.

An answer, I've got to write an answer to Wilma.

In this mess of boxes, I'd no idea where to find paper and I didn't have time to search. I turned Wilma's letter in my hand, considering writing on the back side, but no, if she had been kidnapped, I would need this as proof when I alerted the authorities. Opening the old cabinet, I bit my lips as I stared at the five books in there. One was a copy of the first book I'd ever had published. Not that it had sold many copies, but a book was sacred somehow. I couldn't tear out the last blank page to write on, could I?

Turning my head, I grabbed for the trash can that I'd filled this morning. One of my old drawings that I'd made for my grandmother as a child was on top. It would have to do. I wrote a quick reply to Wilma's letter and placed it inside the bottle.

Making my way back to the border took time, as I had to put down the heavy catapult several times. Once I got there, I was exhausted and decided that the catapult wasn't coming back with me.

At least, attaching the bottle was easy.

"Here we go," I muttered and stuck my tongue out in concentration. It wouldn't do to fail, because there was no way I was walking into the no-trespassing zone to retrieve the bottle when there were mines.

Communicating with someone on the other side of that wall was illegal, but I wanted to find out what Wilma's situation was before I alerted the authorities about her being caught on the wrong side of the wall. In order to do that, I had to get my message across that wall.

CHAPTER 3
Answer from the South

Tyton

"I got an answer." Wilma, my little sister, came running through the garden and grinned from ear to ear.

"Someone wrote you back?"

"Yes!" She stopped right in front of me with eyes bright with excitement. "Here, you can read it yourself."

Just as I reached for the letter she was holding in her hand, she changed her mind.

"No, I'll read it for you." Her eagerness to share it with me had me amused and I sat down on the large stone behind me.

"Let's hear it."

Wilma drew in a deep breath and steadied herself, "Okay, here goes."

Peace and Prosperity to you, Wilma,

Are you okay? How did you get to be on that side of the wall? Were you kidnapped or born there? What do you mean that they are forcing you to marry a large warrior against your will? My heart is bleeding for you, but dear Wilma, I will help you escape if you need me to. Just say the word and I'll alert the authorities.
I'll keep an eye out for your answer.

May you walk on a path of peace, abundance, and enlightenment,

Devina Baker

PS: I'm impressed that you can throw a bottle that far. I would have answered you sooner, but I had to use a catapult and it took time.

Wilma's eyes met mine. "Isn't it amazing? I have a friend on the other side of that border and she's worried about me."

"Why would she think that you're suffering and being forced to marry?"

"I'm not sure." She pinched her eyebrows together. "I only said that whoever found my letter would have to hurry with a reply because I'm moving soon. I don't remember writing anything about being forced to marry, only that I am forced to move from here even though I don't want to."

"Ah, she misunderstood you then." I reached for the letter and turned it to see a drawing that looked as if made by a child. "And why did she write on this? Don't they have normal paper over there?"

"I don't know, but I can ask her for you. I'm going to write Devina back right away."

"You do that, and make sure to tell her that *I* was the one who threw that bottle." My hands were dirty from my garden work, so I brushed sweat from my forehead with my forearm.

Wilma was tall and slim, and she wrinkled her cute nose. "Why? I don't mind if she thinks I'm strong."

When I laughed, my sister made that pout only a youngest daughter spoiled out of her mind can make.

I shrugged. "Here's the deal, either you tell her, or I won't throw your answer over that fucking wall."

"Then I'll build myself a catapult like Devina did. It works for her."

Watching her run to the main house of the estate I smiled with amusement, knowing full well that my sister wouldn't have the patience to look up how to make a catapult, gather the things needed, and actually build the damn thing. She would be back asking for my help in no time.

Bending down, I picked up more of the heavy stones that I was moving from this back area of the park to the front of the house where my mom wanted a pond with fish in it. I didn't mind the hard work. As the oldest son in the family, I was responsible for overseeing our massive lands of fields and forests, and I was no stranger to hard physical work. If a fishpond would make my mom happy, I'd make sure she got one.

"Tyton." It had only been fifteen minutes since Wilma ran to the house, but her voice was calling out loud and clear.

"I'm up front," I called back and kept positioning the stones I had gathered.

"Oh, there you are." Wilma held up the bottle. "I wrote my reply and I need you to throw it back over.

"What happened to the catapult you were going to make?"

She chewed on her lips. "If you don't want to do it, I can ask Dad."

"No, it's all right. I'll do it." I brushed my hands against each other to rub off the dust from the stones. "On one condition."

"What's that?"

"I get to read the letters."

Her hand holding the bottle went to her back. "Letters are private, you know."

"Did you mention me like I told you to?"

"Yes."

From the way her left foot rubbed against her right shin, I could tell she was lying. I held out my hand. "Show me."

With a sigh of protest, Wilma handed me the bottle and just to piss off my impatient little sister, I took my time opening it and pulling out the letter before reading aloud.

Dear Devina,

I'm so excited that you got my letter and replied.
Please don't worry about me. I'm fine and was lucky enough to be born on the right side of the border. Or at least that's what my family tells me, but I still wonder what it's like on your side.
How old are you?
Is it true that you hate men and that all women on your side have hair on their chests?
I'm so curious to hear what it's like in the Motherlands and I've often felt tempted to find a way to climb that wall just to see for myself. I know, it's a terrible thing to be so curious, but according to my mother, I was born that way, so I can't help it.

Here in the Northlands, people are happy. Or at least my family is. Well, except for my sister, Marni, but that's because her husband, Henry, is an ass. It's her fault though, since she chose him in her tournament. When I have mine in a few weeks, I'll choose more carefully.

I can't wait for my big day. It feels like, I've been waiting my entire life to get married, but I guess that's because I have. What about you? Do you like your husband?
My other sister, Claire, likes hers, but I think that's because Lucas is a good kisser. She didn't tell me so, but I'm smart like that and I've seen the way they smile at each other all lovey-dovey. I hope my husband looks at me like that too

when we've been married for eight years like they have. The weird thing is that they haven't gotten any children yet. Eight years is a long time to try, don't you think?

Write me back and tell me all about the Motherlands. That would make me very happy.

May you walk on a good road too,

Wilma

    I tilted my head. "You lied. You didn't mention me."
    "Okay, but I'll do it next time."
    "No, you'll tell her now."
    "Argh, seriously, Tyton, can't you see I'm in a hurry?"
    "The sooner you add it, the sooner I can get it to Devina."
    Finding a pen in her pocket, Wilma gestured for me to turn around and then she used my back to write against.
    "Happy now?" she asked and showed me the addition to her letter.

PS, it wasn't me who threw the bottle, it was my brother, Tyton, who is very bossy and nosy.

    I cocked an eyebrow at her.
    "Sorry, T, but you are."
    "What do you mean by 'May you walk on a good road too? That's a weird thing to write."
    "I know but that's what she said in her letter." Wilma found Devina's letter and pointed.
    I shook my head, "It says, 'May you walk on a path of peace, abundance, and enlightenment.'"
    "Yeah, but path and road are kind of the same thing."

Shaking my head, I rolled the letter and put it inside the bottle. "Let's send a letter to the Motherlands, shall we?"

Wilma gave a small shriek of excitement next to me and half ran to the border wall that was only a five-minute walk from the end of our property line.

"You have to stand right here. That's where you threw it the last time." Wilma pointed.

"Okay, are you ready?"

She nodded eagerly. Taking a few steps back, I raised my arm and used my whole body to throw the bottle in an arcing line over the wall.

Wilma was jumping and clapping next to me with the youthful enthusiasm that made her long brown hair wave around her shoulders. Her beaming smile showed off the small gap between her front teeth that I always found so charming. Her infectious joy was a sharp reminder of how much I'd miss my sister when she moved out in a few weeks.

"I'll wait here for an answer," she declared and sat down.

"She might not see your message until tomorrow or in a few days."

"Of course she will." Wilma gave me a look that said, you don't know what you're talking about.

An hour later, I was busy with the fishpond when Wilma came storming with a new letter held triumphantly in her hand. "Told you, she'd write me back right away."

"I'm impressed. What did she write?"

This time Wilma didn't talk about letters being private. She was too eager to share the excitement and began reading aloud again.

My dearest Wilma,

I wish I could talk to you in person and make sure that you mean what you say. It's confusing that you're contradicting your first plea for help. Is someone reading your letters before you send them?

For now, let me answer your questions.
1: I'm twenty-eight.
2: No, we do not hate men. Why would you think that?
3: This question made me laugh. I don't have hair on my chest and neither do any of my friends.
4: I'm not married and neither should you be if you're truly only fifteen. I'm crossing my fingers that I misunderstood something because surely it can't be legal for a child to get married. Marriages here are very rare. Personally, I've never met anyone who is married or wants to be, but I've read about it in books and know what it means. When you say that you'll choose more carefully than your sister, what do you mean? What is a tournament exactly?

Please thank your brother for throwing the bottle over the wall. If you'd like, I can give you instructions on how to build a catapult so you don't have to rely on a boy for help.

May you walk on a path of abundance and happiness,

Devina

I groaned and snatched the letter from her. "I'm no fucking boy and what's wrong with you relying on my help? Don't listen to her."

My sister skewed her mouth. "Why would she think I'm a child when I'm fifteen?"

"Because women are brainwashed on that side of the border. They always have been."

CHAPTER 4
Alerting the Authorities

Devina

The small woman in front of me had deep wrinkles and no make-up on. Her shirt was a few sizes too small and she kept pulling at it as if it would somehow make it bigger. "I assure you we have no missing person cases on a fifteen-year-old girl."

I pushed the two letters on the table toward her. "Please, Dolores. So maybe Wilma wasn't kidnapped, but she's in danger and we need to help her."

Clearing her voice, Dolores, the new official representative in our local town, picked up the second letter from Wilma and read it again. I watched her eyes moving from side to side until she lowered her hands and gave me a troubled look. "How do we know this is even written by a girl? What if it's a man trying to get your attention?"

"A man?" I hadn't even considered that possibility.

"Yes. This could be written by anyone. There's no way to know." She handed me the letter back. "Either way, there's nothing we can do about it since it doesn't relate to a Motlander."

"You're just going to let a child get *married*?" My tone was incredulous as I leaned back in my seat with disappointment.

"We don't have much choice. I wish I had all the time in the world to investigate your claim because honestly, rescuing a young girl sounds much more exciting than cleaning up after an epidemic. But..." She shrugged.

"Please, Dolores, couldn't you speak to a council member and have them negotiate with the ruler of the Northlands?"

Dolores moved some papers around on her desk. "The Council is under a lot of pressure and now isn't the right time. Besides, they don't have any authority in the Northlands.

"But we could send in someone to help her out, couldn't we?"

Three prominent wrinkles formed on Dolores's forehead as she watched me. "I don't know which old movies you've watched, my dear, but that's not how we do things these days. As long as the Nmen stick to the peace treaty and keep on their side of the border, we'll stay on this side and not bother them."

When I opened my mouth to speak, she held up a hand and continued, "I'm going to stop you right there because the truth is that we don't have the skills or the technology to break into foreign territory and rescue anyone. Back when they had hundreds of countries in the world, there might have been a need to spy on each other and get foreign intel, but after the first council got rid of countries and we all adapted to the same language, we haven't focused on that sort of thing."

"But there's still a border wall."

"Argh, yes, but the Northlanders are just ten million men compared to the rest of our one point five billion people. They are a nuisance of course, but before I came here, I'd thought they were nothing but a tall tale."

"You didn't believe the Northlands existed?"

"No. I'm from the brown area down south and I grew up believing that the world is a homogenous place. But I must say that the more I travel, the more I see how untrue that is. We might all speak the same language and call ourselves Motlanders, but there are vast differences in the culture around the world. It would be interesting to see what it's like on the other side of that wall, but as I said, I don't think the Nmen will listen if our Council makes protests about how they run their country. And sadly, we don't have the skills or the technology to undertake a rescue mission, which is a shame." Dolores drew in a deep breath. "Personally, I think there's something unnatural about our generation being less advanced than they were two hundred years ago, don't you?"

It was rare to hear an official criticizing our culture and it confused me.

"Think about how much we could have learned from the past if we hadn't been so quick to bury everything."

"We had to. It was a matter of survival to bury the dead and there weren't enough people left to rebuild the ruins of the great cities." I didn't know why I felt such a strong need to defend the survivors of the Toxic War. "And about our ancestors being more advanced than us... I'd say that we're more advanced. They invented technology to see what was possible, but we are more thoughtful and responsible in our approach." It was what I'd been taught by my teachers all my life.

"Yes, but this..." Dolores sighed and threw a nod to an electric typewriter on her table. "Before I was sent here, I worked in New Munich, where we all had computers. Nothing fancy but at least we all had access to Wise-Share. If I want to use a computer now, I have to walk down to the end of the hallway to the only one available to all four of us officials here."

"I'm sorry." I looked around her office, which looked like it hadn't been updated in at least a decade. "This region has always been behind the rest of the Motherlands. I think people here are afraid of Wise-Share getting corrupted like the old Internet did."

Men of the North – FORBIDDEN LETTERS

"Ahh, but Wise-Share is different since we have librarians to control all the content." Dolores pulled at her shirt again. "At least the rest of the country isn't as far behind as this place. Did you know that the council members use virtual reality when they meet up? That's pre-war technology right there, and the environmental engineers have advanced computers as well."

"I'm sure the Council wants the best for us." I didn't know what else to say.

Dolores softened her face. "Yes, I would like to think so too."

With the conversation coming to an end, I repeated my request. "Is there no way we can help Wilma escape her captors?"

"I'm afraid not."

"That's a shame." Standing up, I bowed my head to her. "May you be surrounded by light and positivity."

"Same to you. Let me walk you out." Dolores began small-talking as she led me out of her office. "How long are you staying in town?"

"I'm not sure. It's a big house and I'm sorting through everything."

"Do you have anyone to help you?"

"No. My friends are spread around and scared of coming into this area. I would never ask them to travel up here."

"Anyone local maybe?"

I shook my head. The Triple D virus didn't leave many behind and the few who were here had enough to worry about with their own tragedies.

"May I give you a bit of advice?"

"Sure."

Placing a hand on my elbow, Dolores gave me a maternal look of concern. "It's probably best if you believe every word in Wilma's last letter about her being happy where she is. That way you don't worry about her so much."

"And what if a savage was looking over her shoulder forcing her to write what she did?"

We had reached the exit and Dolores reached out her hands to me. "I wish I could help, but the only thing I can tell you is that thinking about it will drive you mad. Let it go and cease all contact with the girl."

"And if I can't?"

Holding on to my hands, she kept her eyes on mine. "I'm new to this region and I don't want to add on to the suffering that you and others are going through, but, corresponding with a person in the Northlands is dangerous and therefore illegal." She nodded toward my pocket. "Those are forbidden letters."

She was right and I knew it.

"I'm not going to take the letters from you or write a report about your correspondence, but I'm asking you to stay away from the border and forget about Wilma."

Even as she spoke the words, a strong voice inside me whispered, *Impossible!*

CHAPTER 5
Making Plans

Devina

Wilma had confirmed that someone was reading her letters before she sent them to me. I had her third letter in my hands and reread it.

Dear Devina,

Yes, someone is reading my letters, but it's only Tyton. You'll have to forgive him for being nosy. I'm afraid it runs in the family.

Do you have siblings?

Anyway, about your question. Bridal tournaments happen every time a woman turns fifteen and is ready for marriage. Mine will be on August 17th. It's a massive event this time because it's been three years since the last bridal tournament where Starr chose my brother Frederick.
The strongest warriors from our nation will gather to fight for me and I'll pick from the five champions. It's scary and exciting all at the same time.

Please tell me more about yourself. I'm so happy to have a friend in the Motherlands.

Have a great hike,

Wilma

Every time I read her letter, my frown lines grew deeper.

What hike is she referring to? I hadn't written anything about going on a hike. Could it be a hidden plea for me to come and save her?

My eyes drifted back to another word in the letter. "Scary." I tasted the word trying to decipher if Wilma was leaving hints for me to pick up on. *Is the word hike a plea for me to come and get her because she's scared?*

It was impossible to say without asking her face to face, but one thing was for sure: with the authorities unwilling and unable to rescue Wilma, it would be up to me to do it.

That thought is ridiculous. How would I save a girl on the other side of the border? It wasn't like I could walk over there and demand that the Nmen let her go. And besides, if I crossed the border, I could end up getting caught myself. And then what? The thought of being auctioned off in one of their tournaments made my skin crawl. Nmen were vile men who hated and abused women.

Am I willing to put myself in danger to save a girl I've never met?

The answer was in my chest, next to the longing for my lost family. Someone needed me. A girl the same age as my sister Hannah. I hadn't been able to help my sisters, but maybe I could help Wilma. No one could ever replace my family, but if I helped this young girl to freedom, I wouldn't be alone anymore. The thought was comforting and made it easier to push away my fear of all the things that could go wrong.

"Hmm," I muttered out loud and looked down at Nellie. "We just need a good plan. Right?"

Nellie looked away. Probably because she hadn't heard the words treat, food, or walk and therefore found the conversation irrelevant to her.

I spent my evening making long lists to get an overview of what I had to do. The first thing on my list was to make sure Wilma wouldn't be in danger from the Triple D virus. As far as I knew, the epidemic was over, but I still called the help line to make sure.

Next, I pondered about how to pull a rescue mission off. If I were to get Wilma to safety before the warriors began fighting for her, I had to find a way to get her over or under that wall.

Or around it...

I tapped my pen on the pad and tried to remember what I knew about the beach that separated the North from us. I'd been a child when I last saw it because like the rest of the border line, it was a no man's land with mines.

If my memory served me right, there was a fence that continued into the sea.

But only a little.

Getting up from my chair, I dropped my pen on the pad, grabbed an apple from the bowl on the table, and walked over to look out the window. It was dark outside making the window show my reflection with all the sadness and concern on my face. I let my eyes glaze over as I envisioned the eternal gratitude of Wilma when she reached safety on this side of the border.

If she's scared of water, maybe I could swim over and guide her back here. I'm a good swimmer and it's July; the water will be cold but not freezing.

With a sinking feeling in my chest, the one thing that I'd refused to accept all night stood out clear to me. I would have to cross the border one way or the other.

There's no other way!

I can't tell her of my plans since her brother reads our letters. If he's like the rest of the Nmen, he's one of her tormentors and he'll stop her from escaping.

I bit my lip and met my own reflection again. It'd been a long time since I'd liked what I saw. Not even my long soft hair or large brown eyes could take away from the dark circles under my eyes or the way my shoulders drooped. Before Triple D destroyed my life, I never understood why people would say that grief was heavy or that worries weighed you down. It's not like there's an actual weight to emotions, and yet, my reflection in the window showed me, a twenty-eight-year-old woman, looking like I was sixty.

I tried straightening up, but it took energy that I didn't have so instead I went to sit down again. Patting the sofa next to me, I gestured for Nellie to join me. She complied and placed her head in my lap.

Scratching her behind her ears, I pondered out loud, "We would have the element of surprise on our side, wouldn't we? No one has ever done something this crazy before and the Nmen wouldn't see it coming. We know Wilma lives close to the border, so really, if we can find a way to get to her while it's still night and everyone is sleeping, we could pull it off. Nellie, I know it sounds dangerous, but Wilma and I could be back here within a few hours."

How would I find her house?

An idea took form in my head. *This could work.*

Nellie gave an unsatisfied grunt when I pushed her head away to get up and write another letter.

CHAPTER 6
Getting Intel

Tyton

"She's going to write a book about me."

I was in the doorway to my sister's room, leaning against the doorframe with my arms crossed. "What are you talking about?"

"You heard me." Wilma was on her bed, her young face beaming with pride as she sat against a large pillow with her right ankle resting on top of her left knee and her foot dangling in the air. "My Motlander friend is a writer and she thinks I'm *fascinating*."

Arching a brow, I moved closer and reached out a hand. "Let me see her letter."

With a self-satisfied smile, Wilma handed over the letter and I read it.

Dear Wilma,

Thank you for explaining about the tournaments. Your culture sounds very different from ours, but I'm fascinated and want to learn more about your life.

Did I tell you that I'm a writer? I've written three books, and if you don't mind, I would love to write a book about you.

Anything you can tell me to make it as factual as possible would help. Any pictures so I can get an impression of where you live would be nice. I'd love to see a picture of you, what your room looks like, a map of the area around you. A map of your house so I can see how big it is. And, of course, anything you want to share about growing up in the Northlands will be fascinating to readers on this side of the border. You mentioned your sisters Marni and Claire, but what about the brother you briefly explained about. The one who was strong enough to throw your bottle across the wall? Is he the one called Tyton and does he treat you well?

I too had siblings. Three sisters and a brother. But then, about two months ago we had an epidemic outbreak in this region. Unfortunately, I lost my entire family unit. Now, it's just me and Nellie. She's our old family dog.

I hope you'll write me back soon with as many details as you can think of for my book.

May no harm ever come to you,

Devina

"She lost her entire family!" My eyes lifted from the letter to Wilma, whose smile faltered.

"Yes, it's tragic."

"Fuck! That's brutal. Can you imagine?"

"No, and I don't want to. Can we focus on the part about her wanting to write a book about me?"

I looked down again. "What are you going to answer about how I treat you?"

"I'm going to tell her the truth of course."

I angled my head. "Which is?"

"That you're a pain."

"Ha." With a low snort, I let the letter fall down on the bed next to Wilma. "Maybe I should write Devina a letter of my own and explain how self-absorbed and annoying you can be."

Narrowing her eyes, Wilma sat up. "You wouldn't."

Men of the North – FORBIDDEN LETTERS

"Why not? I could use a friend too." I kept my face straight, loving how easy it was to rile Wilma up.

"She's *my* friend."

"But soon you'll be gone. Then what?"

"I already thought of that. You'll be our middleman. You'll forward her letters to me by mail and I'll answer. All you have to do is throw my letters across the border and collect her letters for me."

"What's in it for me?"

Wilma burst out in a joyful grin. "Isn't it enough that you'll be mentioned in a book in the Motherlands? You can tell everyone that your sister is famous."

"Why would I care what people in the Motherlands think about you? Because of that stupid wall, I'll never meet any of them in person."

Swinging her hand at me, Wilma gestured for me to leave. "I don't have time to talk with you when there are so many things I have to write Devina about. Do you think I should mention the time I almost drowned?" Not waiting for my answer, she nodded her head. "I should. It was a dramatic moment in my life."

"You didn't almost drown. Dad was right there to save you."

"But I fell in the water and it was deep."

"You jumped because you saw me and Frederick dive in. We were all ready to save you, but Dad got to you first."

My little sister was the youngest of us five siblings by twelve years and not only was she spoiled but she was also overprotected. "Don't tell Devina that you almost died when it's not true. People are going to think we're lousy protectors."

"So what? You just said you didn't care about what people in the Motherlands think of you." Wilma got up from her bed and swung her hand to the door again. "Now get out so I can write."

When I didn't move, she pushed at my chest but being a head taller and much heavier, it wasn't hard to stand my ground. "You're not telling her dramatic lies. Do you hear me?"

"Yeah, yeah, I heard you."

When I left my sister's room, I walked downstairs and out in the garden. My dad was weeding nearby and looked up when he heard me. For a short second, I hesitated in walking over to him. I liked my father, but I hated his obsession with the same endless discussion we'd had ten times already.

"Tyton, come over here for a second." He leaned back on his haunches and watched me as I walked closer. "Did you think about it?"

Oh fuck. Here we go again.

"You'll need to raise the money and find a sparring partner. It was easier the last time because you and Frederick had each other."

My jaw hardened and my eyes darted around the garden seeing projects I could be working on. "We need to trim the apple trees."

"Don't try and change the subject, son. In a few weeks, Wilma will be married and you'll be my only child left without a spouse."

"Yeah, well, it's rare to find a spouse when you're a man in this part of the world."

"Frederick did it."

I cracked my knuckles and tried to change the subject again. "How is Frederick?"

"He's fine and he agrees with me. You should sign up for Tamara's tournament. It's not even a year away."

"I doubt Tamara would pick me."

With a stern expression on his face my dad pushed up from the ground and brushed his hands off. "Just because Starr chose Frederick over you doesn't mean Tamara wouldn't pick you. She's met you before and that can be a

Men of the North – FORBIDDEN LETTERS

huge advantage. Besides, because you were already a champion at Starr's tournament, you'll be fighting in the main arenas. There's money to be made on bets if you win."

"I'll think about it."

"Think faster, will you?" He had only just said it when my friend Cameron came walking around the house.

"So, this is where you're hiding. Why the hell aren't you opening the door?"

"Cam, good to see you." My dad stretched out his hand and pulled Cameron into a manly bear hug. "I'm trying to convince Tyton to sign up for Tamara's tournament."

My friend frowned and moved on to hug me. "Why is that even a question? Of course you're signing up."

"Are *you*?" I asked.

"No." He slammed my arm with a laugh. "I won't have to when I win Wilma in a few weeks, will I?"

"See, one less competitor for Tamara," my dad pointed out but we both knew Cam's chances of winning Wilma were slim. Only one out of fifty thousand men in this country would marry a woman in their lifetime and there were many warriors stronger than Cameron.

"I'm not trying to be a pain here, but I want all my children to be blessed in the same way your mother and I have been. To have a family and children of your own is a fantasy for most men, but we could help you raise the money you need to enter the tournament and you've already proven that you can fight your way to becoming one of the five champions."

I was quiet, so he continued with another argument I'd heard a hundred times before.

"It's been three years since Starr's tournament and by the time we reach Tamara's tournament next year, you'll be thirty. Your time is running out, son."

"I said I'll think about it."

"But why? What is there to think about? Most of the fighters have never met a woman in their lives and that gives you a huge advantage when you stand in front of Tamara. She'll know that you've been raised by a mother and that you have sisters. You're as rare as she is, almost."

"She's a spoiled girl," I muttered low and kicked at some gravel on the ground. I had met Tamara a few months ago when she had just turned fourteen, and from the way she spoke to and about people, I'd found her insufferable."

Cameron leaned in. "What was that?"

"I've met her and she didn't seem very nice."

My father and Cameron exchanged a glance and my dad raised his hand as to gesture, *I've got this.*

"She's young and she'll need a strong man to help her find her role as a good wife. I would have thought someone like you would be up for that challenge."

"That's right. A few good spankings to let her know you're the boss." Cameron was finding this conversation amusing but I didn't.

"Is that what you plan to do to Wilma if you win her?" I took a step closer and narrowed my eyes.

"Relax, son. It's normal for a husband and wife to have to smooth things out between them. I had to demand respect when I won your mother. Women of the North are strong and they don't want weak husbands."

"I know that. It's just that the thought of anyone laying a hand on Wilma bothers me. I don't want her ending up like Marni."

My dad gave a single nod and sighed. "No, we don't want that."

Marni was only eleven months older than me and growing up she'd been charming and cheeky. Now, she was defensive and bitter, and her sense of humor was almost gone.

"It's like for every year she's married to Henry, her spirit breaks a little more."

"I know." My dad's chest rose and fell with another sigh.

"Wait, is Henry beating Marni?" Cameron's eyebrows rose up in surprise. "Why didn't you tell me? We should fucking kill him if he's abusive."

"It's not that kind of abuse," I muttered. "There are no bruises or cuts. If there were, we would have taken care of him long ago."

"Henry is more subtle and refined in his way of controlling Marni," my dad added. "The problem is that we can't get her to talk to us about it. And without any information, we can't help her."

Cameron shifted his balance and groaned. "Argh, it's not fair that men like him should be blessed with a wife. Why the fuck did she pick him anyway?"

I shrugged. "I once asked her that and she said that he had a nice smile."

Cameron scratched his neck. "Maybe it would be better if the brides got a chance to get to know the five champions before they made a choice between them."

"At least they have five to pick from. Did you know that at the first tournaments, there was only one winner and he got the bride?"

Cameron stared at my dad. "She didn't have *any* say in it?"

"None. As a father of three daughters, I'm pleased that those days are in the past."

"It's all because of that stupid wall." I threw my head in the direction of south. "There's millions of women on that side and we're killing each other for the few we have. That's fucked up."

"Yeah, well, would you rather be ruled by women and give up your manhood? They castrate men on that side of the border," my dad reminded me.

"No, of course not! I'm proud to be a free man, but..." I scrunched up my face. "It's been almost two hundred years since that border was established. Why can't we break it down and take back power? Why should the women get all of the world while we only get the North?"

"Yeah." Cameron nodded his head in support and then his eyes grew large when he focused in on something behind me. I spun around to see Wilma watching us with a funny look on her face.

"Are you talking about breaking down the wall?"

Cameron gave a nervous laugh. "It was just a joke."

"That's disappointing." She moved closer to Cameron, who straightened up and pushed his chest out, and then she turned her back on him to face us. "I would love to see what's on the other side."

The way he leaned forward, as if he wanted to get closer and smell her hair, had both my dad and me sending out warning sounds. No one touched a woman except for her family members, protector, or other women. Cam was none of those things to Wilma and we were reminding him to keep his distance.

Wilma twisted her neck to look at him standing behind her. "What did you do?"

Both his hands flew up in the air. "Nothing. I didn't do anything."

I almost did a double take when my sister gave Cameron a flirtatious smile. She wasn't a little girl any longer, but it was hard for me to always remember that when she was still acting like a petulant child around me.

"Cameron, would you do me a favor, please?" Her eyes dropped to the bottle in her hands and I knew that she was going to ask him to throw it over the border for her.

"I'll do it." In two decisive steps, I was close enough to snatch the bottle from her. This was *my* thing. *I* threw it over the wall and *I* got to read the letters from Devina.

"Hang on. I'm always happy to help," Cameron piped up but I was already walking away from them.

"Where is he going? What's in that bottle?" my dad asked behind me.

"It's just some seeds she wants me to plant, but I've got it." I shot her a glance over my shoulder with a silent message to keep her mouth shut. To my relief, she understood.

"That's right." The rest of Wilma's words were lost to me since I was moving fast through the garden to the hole in the hedge that led to the green belt in the back of our property. It was only a five-minute walk before I reached the spot where I always threw from. Opening the bottle, I pulled out Wilma's letter and skimmed it over.

Dear Devina,

I think it's the most amazing idea for you to write a book about me. Promise that you'll throw a copy over the wall so I can read it when it's done. I can't believe people will know my name in the Motherlands.

There are so many things I want to tell you about myself but let me start with the questions you asked. I'm sending you a map of our area, a floor plan of our house, and a picture of my room. The painting above my bed was a gift from my sister Claire, who painted it herself. I love the orange and blue colors of the bird. It's from a children's book that she used to read to me when I was little. The bird is called a phoenix and according to the book it can regenerate by literally bursting into flames and being reborn from the ashes. Isn't that amazing?
Do you have them in the Motherlands? I'm hoping the phoenix isn't extinct like so many other animal species that disappeared after the Toxic War.

To answer your question about Tyton, let me just tell you that I have two brothers. Tyton is the oldest at twenty-nine and then there's Frederick, who is twenty-seven and married. Last month he and his wife Starr told us she's pregnant with their second child. We're all hoping that this time it'll be a girl. Whenever a girl is born here in the Northlands, it's shared on the news. That's how rare it is.

My sister Marni is thirty years old and she has four rowdy boys. Claire is twenty-three but she doesn't have any children yet. I hope I'll be blessed with many daughters when it's my time to become a mother.

I read the rest of the letter, but Wilma hadn't answered Devina's question about how I treated her. Studying her floor plan of our house, I frowned. It wasn't very good. For one, the proportions were all wrong. According to her floor plan, her bathroom and bedroom were the same size, which wasn't right. She had also left out the numbers of floors, but it didn't matter. It wasn't like any of the readers of Devina's book would come by to fact-check the floor plan.

I held the family photo that Wilma had enclosed. I never liked this picture since it was taken after a funeral and we'd all been sad and quiet. I was in the back towering over my mom and Claire, who stood with an arm around each other.

Wilma probably chose this picture because it's the only one with all seven of us in it.

Returning everything to the bottle, I put the lid back on. Throwing the bottle across the wall was like throwing a football. I stepped back and exploded in a few fast steps, getting my arm fully stretched and sending the bottle flying through the air.

There was something satisfying in seeing the arc and knowing that soon Devina would pick up that same bottle and touch the same papers that I'd just touched.

For a few moments, I stood watching the massive wall, wishing that it would crumble to the ground and leave a view to the other side. I imagined a beautiful woman looking back at me.

What would I say to her?

Shaking my head to clear it of my daydreams, I forced myself to back away and finally turn my back on the wall. I was giving too much thought to a woman I would never meet in real life.

CHAPTER 7
Rescue Mission

Devina

The minute my toe touched the cold water, I wanted to give up on my mission.

What was I thinking?

We were only one week away from Wilma's being auctioned off in a tournament and her letters were getting more and more desperate. Yesterday she had written that she had a hard time sleeping because she couldn't stop thinking about the tournament, and that she was scared of picking the wrong husband.

Of course, she was scared. Wilma was a child and she shouldn't have to be forced into this situation.

Goosebumps spread all over my body, but I still took another step out in the cold Pacific Ocean, swallowing my discomfort and fear. If only I could have walked closer to the border wall, but the signs warning of mines made me keep a safe distance.

For a moment I wondered how things had been before the Toxic War. Back then the Northlands had been called Canada and Alaska.

They probably had guards patrolling the area.

It wasn't unlikely since there had been eight billion people in the world before the war. Now we were down to one point five and the numbers didn't seem to grow much.

It was twenty minutes past midnight and the downside was that it was dark with only moonlight shining through the clouds. The upside was that it was low tide, which meant less swimming for me. I had to walk out far to have the water cover my chest.

The sooner you get over there, the sooner you can get back.

My hand cramped around the waterproof bag that was tied to my waist and floated next to me. Sucking in a large breath, I slid into the water and began swimming. My skin was screaming with pain from the cold water, but I forced myself to go on.

Getting to the end of the fence that separated our countries was easy since I was carried by the current drifting away from the shore. But once I swam around the fence and began making my way to the beach, it got a lot harder. The bag was now behind me, tethered to the rope around my waist but showing that the current wanted to take us out to sea. I had to use all my strength to move us in the right direction and when I finally made it to land, I was panting with exhaustion.

With my teeth clattering, I picked up my bag and moved away from the water. My hands were shaking as I found a flashlight in the bag and moved it around to see my surroundings. This side of the border was as empty as the other side had been.

Good!

I put on the black clothing that I'd brought and left the bag on the beach before I jogged in the direction of Wilma's house.

The map she had sent me was in my hands as I moved past several houses trying to make no sound. There were no main roads, which confused me until I'd run for about ten minutes, and a drone flew above me. We had them in the Motherlands, but they were rare, and I'd only seen a few in my lifetime. Crouching down to hide, my heart was pounding in my chest, but the drone flew fast and as soon as it was gone, I stood back up and continued running.

I can do this! I'm saving a young girl from a horrible fate.

After about twenty minutes of running, I finally reached the house on the map with a circle around it.

This is where she lives.

With legs of jelly, I suppressed my fear and snuck closer. I was careful not to shine my flashlight directly at the windows while I assessed which room Wilma was sleeping in.

There!

According to the floor plan she had made for me, her room was in the middle, next to the entrance. I hoped I wouldn't have to break in but that I could wake her up by tapping the window.

Okay, here goes!

Holding my breath, I raised my hand and knocked quietly on the window. Tap, tap, tap.

CHAPTER 8
Intruder

Tyton

Tap, tap, tap.

My eyes opened, and my neck craned as I heard the sound again.

Tap, tap, tap.

What the hell?

A quick glance at the clock told me it was one in the morning. Who the fuck was at our house at this hour?

Getting up from my bed, I walked to my window and looked down at the entrance to the main house. There was no one there. Unlike my parents and Wilma, who lived inside the house, I lived in a converted hayloft in one of the side buildings. It had been one of my demands when I agreed to run the family business with my father. I'd wanted my own space and I loved the cozy feel of this place.

Tap, tap, tap.

Could it be a bird making that sound?

I dismissed the idea since birds weren't active at this hour. And then I saw a shadow move.

Someone was lurking outside my family's home and it made my blood boil with protective rage. Was that person trying to warn an intruder that was already inside? Why else would anyone tap at our living room window?

Not caring to put on clothes, I ran down the stairs in my briefs only and chose the back exit. That way I would have a chance to move around the house and sneak up on the man tapping at the window.

The wet grass dampened my long strides as I ran full speed all the way to the opposite corner of the main building. After that I tiptoed forward with slow deliberate movements.

A dark hoodie concealed the face of the man tapping on the window, but the moonlight showed his outline, and the small size of him made me realize that I was dealing with a young boy rather than a man. That didn't mean I would show mercy.

If this boy was the look-out for a thief inside my family's home, then he would be sorry I caught him.

I was moving closer like a patient feline predator, and then I heard his voice in a low hoarse whisper.

"Wilma... Wilma, wake up."

My body stiffened. Was this some lovesick pup who was dreaming of marrying my sister? Relief filled me as I concluded that if he was calling for her, at least he wasn't trying to warn an intruder.

Not sure if I should admire the bravery of this boy or kill him for his audacity, I watched him a little longer.

"Wilma..."

In a leap, I had my hand over his mouth before he said my sister's name again. The boy screamed into my hands, but he was already dangling above the ground with his back pressed against my chest.

"Stay quiet or I'll fucking break your neck."

My warning made him whimper in fear, but at least he wasn't screaming any longer. There was no reason to wake up the whole house, so I carried him inside the hay barn, using my elbow to turn on the light and my foot to close the door behind me.

"You'd better tell me what the fuck you're doing here!" I pushed him hard toward the stack of hay bales and he fell on top of them with a whooshing sound when all the air was knocked from his lungs.

"What do you have to say for yourself, boy?"

The little shit refused to look at me but crawled away like he could find an exit behind the hay bales.

That set me off. I could have broken his neck when I grabbed him, but I'd given him a chance to explain himself. If this coward couldn't even face me, he deserved a serious beating. "You little fucker." In a fast movement I clamped down on his ankle, pulled him back in a harsh jerk, and got on top of him. My arm pulled back and my fist formed as I aimed for his cheek.

It wasn't a clean blow because he turned his head and the hoodie came between my hand and his face. The boy still screamed and sobbed like he'd never been beaten before.

"Shut the fuck up." Clamping my hand under his chin, I turned his head and pushed away the hoodie and all the damp hair that covered his face. With his eyes squeezed tight and him wailing, his face was so scrunched up that I couldn't figure out how old he was, but there was no sign of a beard

"What's your name?"

"Don't hurt me."

A chill ran down my spine. That voice was very light, even for a boy.

"Look at me, boy."

One eye opened, revealing he had brown eyes.

"Open your fucking eyes when I tell you to." I lifted my fist, threatening to hit him again.

His eyes shone with fear when he opened them up wide. Seeing the boy under me with his face free from hair and hoodie I lowered my arm. He was so feminine with his long lashes and perfectly shaped eyebrows.

"Please don't hurt me," he repeated.

"What's your name?"

He swallowed hard and looked away as if searching for someone to help him.

Pressing one hand down on his chest, I sneered low, "Tell me your name."

It was then that I registered something was wrong. My hand was in the middle of his chest, but something felt odd. Moving my hand to the right, I paled.

This is no fucking boy.

I scrambled to get off her and was hit with immense guilt. I had thrown and jerked a woman around. Shit, I had punched her. In the Northlands, a man's touching a woman without permission was enough to get him killed. I had just signed my own death sentence.

"What the fuck? I didn't know you were a woman. Who are you?"

Now that I was off her, the woman pushed her legs to move back and curled up with her knees to her chest and her arms wrapped around her.

"I'm not going to hurt you," I promised and held up my palms to show that I meant it.

She was staring at me like I was a monster from a horror movie.

"Do you understand what I'm saying?" I spoke slow and clear. "Nod, if you understand."

She gave a single nod.

"What is your name and how do you know my sister?"

There was a spark of recognition in her eyes. "Tyton?"

I jerked my head back in surprise. "You know my name?"

"Yes."

"I haven't met you before. I would have remembered. Who is your husband?" This woman was my age and it confused me since I couldn't remember her having a tournament.

"My name is Devina."

I shook my head; not sure I'd heard her right. "Devina... the Motlander Wilma has been writing with?"

"Yes."

"But how... I mean... the wall..." I was stumbling over all the questions I wanted to ask her at the same time. "How did you get over the wall?"

"I didn't."

"Did you dig a tunnel under the wall?"

"No." It was clear that she was still scared of me and I felt awful.

"Devina, listen. I thought you were an intruder and that my family was in danger. I would never hit a woman... if I'd known who you were."

She lifted a hand to her jaw but didn't speak.

"Why are you here in the middle of the night?"

"I need to talk to Wilma."

"About what?"

"That's between her and me."

"I'm her protector so you can tell me."

With a stubborn expression, she looked away, indicating that she wasn't willing to share anything with me.

"Okay. I guess I can fetch Wilma so you can talk to her, but I hope you can see how weird this all seems to me." I scratched my naked chest and her eyes followed my movement.

"Come with me." I nodded to the stairs leading up the back entrance to my apartment. "It's much nicer upstairs." I was halfway up the stairs when I stopped and looked at her. She still hadn't moved. "How about I make you a cup of tea and then I bring Wilma over to talk to you? Would that work?"

One nod was all the answer I got.

CHAPTER 9
Tea with Wilma

Devina

If that devil thought I was going upstairs with him, he was wrong. For all I knew he might have a cage up there.

My plan had failed, and I'd been caught by one of the brutal and savage Nmen. My jaw still hurt from his violent attack and my heart was beating so fast that I worried it might never calm down again. The sheer size of Tyton was terrifying and when he ordered me to look up at him, I'd seen nothing but crazy eyes, naked skin, and bulging muscles. With his jaw-length tousled hair and short beard, he looked like something out of a historical movie.

What now?

I was still on the bale of hay when he descended the stairs again. This time, he was wearing gray soft pants, a pale blue t-shirt, and shoes.

"The tea will be ready soon. Just stay here while I get Wilma." His calmness felt like a ploy and I suspected that at any time he would turn back into the aggressive attacker I'd faced only ten minutes ago.

For a moment he watched me with deep frown lines on his forehead. "When you talk to her, do you think you could leave out that... ehh... that I hit you?"

"What?"

Scratching his neck, he looked to the side. "It was a misunderstanding. I'd never hit a woman."

My shoulders eased a little with all the remorse oozing from him. He sounded so genuine.

Men of the North – FORBIDDEN LETTERS

I nodded because I had no plans to tell anyone anything. All I wanted was to find a way to free poor Wilma from the tyranny of these awful and violent men.

"Thanks, Devina."

Hearing him say my name in his low baritone voice added to the strangeness of this situation. But then he left and it gave me almost ten minutes to calm my nerves and re-center myself before he returned with the girl I'd gotten to know through her letters. Wilma was easy to recognize from the picture she'd sent me, but I was surprised at how tall she was. I'd always been the tallest of me and my sisters, but Wilma had half a head on me.

"Devina?" She hurried toward me and sat down next to me. Her eyes were the same green color as her brother's, only hers were kind and full of concern. "How did you get here?"

I reached out to hug her and when we met in an embrace, I whispered into her ear. "I'm here to save you."

Wilma let go of me and gave me a puzzled look.

Why doesn't she look relieved?

She should appreciate that I'm risking my life for her.

"Did you climb the wall?" she asked and squeezed my hand.

"No."

With a soft smile on her face, she pushed up from the bale and reached out her hand to me. "Come. We'll talk upstairs. Tyton's apartment is much nicer than this hay barn."

I hadn't imagined us talking much. In my mind, I would have woken her up and she would have been eager to go with me. What I wanted was for her to escape with me, but she was already moving and gesturing for me to follow.

Tyton's apartment was a little messy, with clothes lying around. A large bed stood in one corner and in the middle was a worn couch with throw-overs and pillows. I stared at the couch, feeling unsure if my eyes were betraying me.

Is that leather?

In the Motherlands we were all vegan by law and no one would dream of decorating a piece of furniture with another being's skin.

Wilma seemed oblivious to the cruelty that couch symbolized and took a seat. "Come and join me," she said and patted the seat next to her.

I preferred to stay close to her and so I swallowed my moral scruples, pretended it was imitation leather, and took a seat.

With Tyton in the open kitchen busy making tea, I leaned in and whispered. "Wilma, I can get you out of here. You'll be safe in the Motherlands. We just have to shake off your brother."

"But I can't go anyway right now. My tournament is beginning this Thursday and I'm marrying on Saturday."

With a tone of desperation, I whispered, "I know you're scared of your brother, but if we work together, we can find a way to get away. No one should be auctioned off in an awful tournament. You're still a child, Wilma. You have your whole life ahead of you."

"A child?" She looked a bit offended. "I'm a woman."

"But..." I blinked, feeling confused by her lack of gratitude that I'd come to save her. Twisting my neck, I looked at Tyton to make sure he wasn't sending her threatening glares. He had his back to us.

"Wilma." I focused all my energy on her, looking deep into her eyes. "Are you saying that you *want* to get married?"

Pulling the black shawl that she was wearing closer around her shoulders, Wilma confirmed it in a voice that wasn't shaking the least. "Yes, I want to get married. I've been waiting for this day for as long as I can remember."

I shrunk back in the couch feeling like the biggest fool. "But your letters."

She angled her head, as if silently asking, *What about them?*

"You wrote about being scared."

"Yes, but it's more like excitement."

"But what about your hidden message when you wished me a good hike?"

"What hidden message? It's you who always talks about paths and I thought it was how you finished your letters... you know, wishing each other safe travels or something."

"So, you weren't asking me to come and rescue you?"

Wilma took my hands. "No, but I can't believe you were willing to come all this way for me."

My shoulders hung low and I sat quietly on the sofa as Tyton brought us tea. I took it but feeling suspicious of him, I didn't drink any of it.

Sitting down in a chair across from us, Tyton held his own cup and watched me. "Is it normal in the Motherlands to show up at someone's house after midnight?"

I lowered the cup to my thigh. "No."

"Devina came to save me."

Wilma's statement made Tyton raise his brow. "From what?"

"She thought I didn't want to get married, or what was it you called it?" One side of Wilma's lips rose with amusement. "Auctioned off, was it?

"Ahh... so this was an attempt to save my sister from marriage?"

"Yes." For a moment I suppressed my polite Motlander ways and gave him a challenging stare. "I'm here to offer Wilma a better life in the Motherlands."

A triangle formed between his eyebrows. "Interesting. And what would this so-called better life entail?"

"Freedom."

He leaned forward. "Care to elaborate on that?"

Even though Tyton was now dressed and sipping on a cup of tea, he still looked dangerous and unpredictable. I hadn't forgotten how he'd thrown me around like I weighed nothing, but my anger with him made me meet his eyes when I answered, "In the Motherlands Wilma could live the way she chose to. She could live anywhere in the world and get an education. There would be no men telling her what to do."

"So, no husbands?"

"Nooo."

"You sound like the idea of a husband is offensive to you."

"Because it is."

"Why? Do men and women not fall in love in the Motherlands?"

"It's rare."

Wilma pulled her feet up under her. "What about children then?"

"What about them?"

I was looking at her, but it was Tyton who spoke. "Obviously, you'll need to procreate to keep the world going."

Procreate was a word I'd only met in old books. "If by procreate you mean reproduce, then yes, but we have family units for that."

"Ahh, now I get it. Men and women live together and have children – they just don't marry, is that it?"

Wilma was looking from him to me as I answered, "Sometimes a family unit has a father, but it's rare. For every twenty women we have only one man. Many of them prefer to live together in groups.

Tyton held up a hand. "Slow down, pixie. Are you saying that Motlander men could live with several women and have sex with all of them, but they choose not to?"

"Sex? Who said anything about sex?"

Tyton looked accusatory when he pointed his hand at me. "So, it's true then, you *do* castrate men."

"Nooo," I sputtered. "That's grotesque."

"If you're claiming that men on that other side of the border have access to twenty women per man but they don't pursue any of them, then I have to question their manhood. What the fuck did you do to them?"

"Me?" My hand flew to my chest. "I didn't do anything to them. My father and brother were gentle and kind men who would have never treated a woman the way you treated me." My voice shook with emotions. "Just because we Motlanders don't engage in wild orgies doesn't mean there's something wrong with us."

Tyton snorted and rolled his eyes. "A whole fucking country of lesbians."

"Whoa, whoa, can we take this down a notch?" Wilma faced Tyton. "I know this is upsetting to you, but Devina isn't the enemy."

Crossing his arms, he looked like he disagreed.

"She is our guest, Tyton." Wilma gave him a pleading look, but it was clear that her words meant little because he kept going.

"She's no guest if she came to kidnap you." He pushed his chair back and got up to pace the floor in front of the couch. "Everyone knows that if we cross that border and bring someone back here, we'll pay with our life. Kidnapping should be illegal on both sides."

I moved to the edge of my seat. "I was never going to *kidnap* Wilma."

"No? Then how did you plan to get her back to lesbo land? Did you think she'd go willingly knowing that she can never have a full life there?"

I gasped with indignation. "Take that back. We have full lives in the Motherlands."

"Doesn't sound like it to me. I predict that within a year my sister will give life to someone from the next generation. What can be more fulfilling than that? Humanity was almost wiped out and every life is precious."

"She can have children in the Motherlands too. How do you think you Nmen get your boys every year? We have children." With angry tears forming in my eyes, I placed my hand on my chest. "I'm planning to have a child and start my own family."

"How?" Tyton stopped to glare at me. "How do you plan to have a child if you're not planning on marrying?"

I pushed the words out in the fieriest argument of my life. "That's what insemination clinics are for."

Tyton looked like I'd hammered a bat against his forehead. He opened his mouth to speak but then he closed it and swallowed hard.

"That's how I was conceived and everyone else I know."

"You were made in a clinic?" Wilma's tone carried pity in it.

"Yes. Everyone is made in a clinic. Nmen included."

"Not Tyton and me. We were born here and came from our parents' lovemaking."

I stroked my hair back, unsure what to say to that.

Sitting back down again, Tyton gave me a hard stare. "Tell us about the boys that are sent here. How are they made?"

Taking a deep breath, I calmed myself and spoke in a matter-of-fact tone. "All I know is that the women who carry the Nboys are called peacekeepers."

"So, the boys grow inside women then?"

I frowned. "Yes, of course they do."

"Well, what the fuck do I know?" Tyton's hands swung in the air. "Maybe you people developed some sort of cocoon for them or something."

I ignored that comment. "The peacekeepers give birth to the Nboys, but they don't always raise them. It takes someone special to pour all their love into a child knowing that when he turns three years old, he'll be sent to live in the Northlands."

"Why are they called peacekeepers?" Wilma asked.

"Because supplying the Northlands with boys is part of the peace treaty between our countries. Before that, Nmen would kidnap women from our side of the border to have breeders."

The two siblings exchanged a disturbed look. "Did you know that?" Wilma asked her brother.

Tyton groaned. "No, but it was different times back then. Maybe the men were looking for love and went about it in a wrong way."

"They stole women. That's why we have the border to protect us from you."

"Ha! That wall is a joke. Do you really think it would keep us out if we wanted in? I could climb that wall in thirty seconds if I wanted to. If it wasn't because of that peace treaty and the death penalty for breaking it, I would have done it already."

Wilma's young face lit up. "I want to see what's on the other side."

"Then come with me, Wilma. I'm sure that if you came to the Motherlands and experienced freedom, you'd realize that you never knew what you missed out on."

Again, Wilma squeezed my hand. "Do you have big parties and dancing?"

"We do. There are festivals during the summer and everyone is kind and caring."

"Maybe I could just go for a few days." Wilma looked to Tyton, who ran his hands through his hair.

"You're not going anywhere. Not when you're a few days away from your tournament. That's insane."

"Yeah, you're right." She turned back to me. "No matter how curious I am to see the Motherlands, now isn't the right time."

I opened my mouth to tell her that any time before being auctioned off was the right time, but Tyton asked me a question first.

"Going back to the peacekeepers. Why do they only send us boys and never girls?"

"So your numbers can never grow."

"For real?"

"Yes. You're a threat and we don't want the ten million of you to grow in numbers. Everyone knows that."

He leaned forward and narrowed his eyes at me, giving him a menacing look of danger. "Let me get this straight. Are you saying that the clinics can control whether they impregnate the mother with a boy or a girl?"

"That's right."

"Then why the fuck do you still have twenty women to every man? If you're all created in clinics it should only take one generation to even out the numbers."

Knowing that he wouldn't like my answer, I tucked my hands under my thighs and tried to sound casual about it. "It was male aggression and hunger for power that led to the Toxic War. All their warmongering had to stop and with the loss of eighty-five percent of the world's population, only one man was left per twenty-six women. It was natural that women stepped up and formed a new way of living based on nurturing the planet back to life."

"You're not answering my question."

"The reason we haven't evened out the numbers between men and women is that the council fear a repeat of the past. It's safer for everyone if women remain superior in numbers."

Tyton's nostrils were flaring, so I hurried to add:

"Although you have to admit there's been an improvement since the imbalance has gone down from twenty-six women per man to twenty women per man."

"It's been one hundred and seventy-six years since the war ended. How long are you going to blame men for what happened?" Tyton leaned his head back and groaned. "For fuck's sake, this is brutal."

"All right, then let me ask you this." I blushed red because my question was confrontational and impolite. "On our side of the border we've had peace for those one hundred and seventy-six years. Can you say the same?"

His answer was redundant since I already knew that the Northlands had been consumed in war on and off for all that time.

Tyton pulled back and stuffed his hands under his armpits. "We've had changing rulers. I'll admit to that."

"And have the transitions been peaceful, democratic elections or...?"

A snort was followed by an eye roll. "We are men and we do things differently from you."

You mean that you fight, kill, and start wars for power. I didn't say it out loud but turned back to Wilma. "I have to get back. Are you sure that you don't want to come with me?"

She pulled me into a hug. "Yes, I'm sure. But I love you for offering to bring me with you."

Disappointment weighed down on my chest when I stood up. "All right. Then I'll let you get back to sleep."

Tyton got up too. "I'd offer that you stay with us, but the Motherlands would probably accuse us of kidnapping you and I'd prefer to stay alive."

Wilma laughed at his joke while I sighed with relief since part of me had been terrified that he wouldn't let me go again.

Swinging a hand to the staircase, he gestured for me to go first. "Come on, pixie, I'll take you to the wall."

"I didn't climb the wall."

"All right. But I'll escort you to wherever you crossed the border then." He took a step toward the exit, but stopped when I said:

"I would rather you didn't know."

First his back stiffened and then he turned to me and walked over to stand in front of me.

I wanted to step back but the couch was behind me.

Stand your ground. Don't show fear.

Tyton and I stood watching each other in a silent power struggle. My head was leaning back to meet his eyes, which were shining with stubborn resolve. I was a strong person, but this man exuded confidence, power, and danger in a way that I hadn't encountered before. He wouldn't take no for an answer, but neither would I.

CHAPTER 10
Don't come

Tyton

"You might as well tell me since there's no way in hell that I'm letting you out of my sight until I know you're back on your side of the border."

For someone like me who was raised to protect women it was annoying as fuck that Devina refused my protection.

She tried to keep her face impassive as to not reveal anything, but it wasn't that hard to guess.

"Look, there aren't that many options and since you insist that you didn't climb the wall, I assume that you swam around it.

The subtle widening of her eyes told me I was right.

"Fine. I'll take you to the beach then."

Raising her chin up, she crossed her arms. "Maybe, I crawled under the wall."

"You're too clean for that and the edges of your hair are still damp, so I'm gonna go with the swimming."

"I got myself here and I can get back without your help."

Leaning closer, I used a low firm tone. "I'm not asking you, Devina. I'm telling you."

This would have been enough to make Wilma or any Nwoman give in, but Devina just turned on her heels and walked down the stairs and outside.

Wilma rushed after her and I took the stairs in three long steps.

"Devina, don't worry, you'll be safe with my brother," my sister insisted.

The way Devina arched her left eyebrow, giving Wilma an incredulous look, made my throat feel dry as fuck. Anytime now she would tell my sister how I'd manhandled her when I found her snooping around outside our house.

But Devina didn't rat me out.

Instead she walked over and took Wilma's hands. "I have to go now, but if any man ever mistreats you..." Devina didn't finish the sentence but Wilma still nodded in understanding.

When she turned and began walking away from us, it sunk in that she was serious about leaving without my protection.

No sane Nwoman would take a risk like that and there was no way I could stand by and watch her leave unprotected.

"Hey, wait up." I ran over to my hoverbike and got on it. Wilma had caught up to Devina when I got there and the two women stood in the light from my bike. "Hop on. I'll take you to the beach."

Devina took a step back and stared at my bike.

"What's wrong, haven't you ever seen a hoverbike?"

"Yes, in movies. It looks like something from before the Toxic War."

"Sorry to disappoint you but this bike is only a few years old. You really don't have hoverbikes in the Motherlands?"

"No, at least not where I live. For the most part, technology is frowned upon in the Motherlands."

"Why?"

Devina shrugged. "Because of all the damage it caused in the olden days."

"You can't blame that on technology. It was the people who mis-used it," I argued.

Wilma tilted her head. "Are you saying that you don't use *any* technology?"

"No, we do. But mostly when it comes to cleaning up the earth or fighting disease."

"Or making babies in clinics. I mean that's pretty sophisticated technology," I pointed out.

"I suppose, but with most other things there's a real skepticism toward technology. We prefer things that are natural and basic and that's why a lot of knowledge has been lost."

"Well, I'm not saying that we Nmen are anywhere close to being as technologically advanced as they were before the war, but if you need our help with hoverbikes, let us know."

Devina gave me a nod and turned to Wilma, who was talking to her.

"Promise that you'll keep writing me."

"I will, Wilma, but about the book... the thing is that..." Devina trailed off and looked down.

"It's okay. I already figured out that you just said it to get information for your rescue mission."

"Yeah."

Wilma gave a smile. "You should still write a story about the Northlands though."

"Maybe I will."

The two women hugged each other like they were old friends and then Devina raised a hand to me and gave a single wave as a goodbye before she took off.

"Stubborn fool," I mumbled.

Wilma gave me a sideways glance. "You're going to make sure she's safe, right?"

"Of course." I threw a nod to the house. "Sis, get inside. I'm waiting here until you lock the door after you."

Wilma didn't argue, and ran to the house and closed the door behind her.

When I caught up to Devina she was jogging at a nice steady pace.

"You would get to the beach faster if you got onto my bike."

"Thank you for offering your help, but I don't want it."

"Fine, then I'll just follow you to make sure you're safe."

She kept her eyes ahead and ignored me.

"Doesn't it seem silly to you that you're running while I'm right here with a bike?"

"I like running."

"Me too. But not in the middle of the night. You could trip and fall."

"I wish you had roads."

"Roads? What would we need roads for? We fly everywhere on hoverbikes or in drones."

"Don't you ever just go out for a run?"

"Sure, but I prefer to run in the forest. We made a trail that loops back to our house."

She ran another five minutes without us talking and then we passed a house and it made me furrow my brow.

"Is this the way you came?"

"Yes."

"Why would you get this close to houses? You could have been seen."

"Everyone is sleeping."

"You can't know that for sure. The men in that house are old grumpy assholes."

She didn't answer me, so I pushed harder. "Just promise that if you ever decide to come and visit us again..."

"I didn't come to visit *you*. Only Wilma."

"Yeah, well, still. If you ever decide to come visit again, let me know and I'll pick you up. It's too dangerous for you to run around by yourself."

"Is that why you told Wilma to run inside and lock her door? Is she in danger here?"

Men of the North – FORBIDDEN LETTERS

"Ah, so you heard that." Turning my head to look at Devina, I considered my words. "We have two women in the house and that makes us a target for crazy people."

"What crazy people?"

"There will always be people with a disregard for rules and laws. About thirty-five years ago a family was killed when a sick man believed himself in love with the unmarried daughter."

"That's horrible."

"Which is why we lock our doors and react strongly when we see anyone lurking outside our house."

She was so slow to answer that at first, I didn't think she would respond, but then she said. "Don't worry. I have no plans of coming back."

"That's probably for the best. We don't want your people to accuse us of kidnapping you."

By the time we reached the beach, Devina was panting hard and raising her hands above her head. It made me suspect that she had run faster than she would have if I hadn't been there.

When I wanted to get off my bike, she held out a hand to stop me, her voice still out of breath. "You can go back now."

"But..."

"I don't want you to watch me swim back."

"And what if you get tired out there? You just ran four miles."

"I'll be fine. Now will you please go?"

"It's not in my nature to leave until I know you're on the other side. I would prefer to swim out with you, so I can see you getting back safely."

"That's not happening!" She stepped back and shook her head vehemently. "Don't get off that bike."

I wanted to ask her why she was so scared of me, but with the way we'd met, it wasn't hard to guess that she thought me violent and dangerous.

"All right. I'll stay here. But you've got to promise me that as soon as you wake tomorrow, you'll throw a letter over the wall, so I know you made it back to safety."

Confusion ran over her face as if she wondered why I cared so much. "I can do that."

"Good. Can I at least stay here just in case you need me?"

"No, I want you to leave."

"Why?"

"Because I don't want to undress with you still here."

"Oh, right." My chest felt like a drummer had taken up residency and I put my hands back on the handles of the bike to hide how they were shaking. The images of Devina stripping out of her clothes had my pants tightening. To hide it, I turned the bike around, so I had my back to her. "Goodbye then."

"Goodbye."

It was so unnatural for me to leave a woman standing by herself. "You sure?"

"Yes, I'm sure. In fact, I'm not giving you a choice. Either you leave, or I'll write Wilma that you hit me."

I narrowed my eyes to indicate that I didn't like her threatening me.

Her finger lifted to point in the direction we'd come, and I could tell she was getting impatient. "What are you waiting for? Just go!"

"Here's a thing you need to know about us Nmen. We don't take orders from women."

"Then consider it a request. I would like for you to leave me alone."

"All right, but before I go though…" I was dragging out the moment, unwilling to part from her. "I just wanted to say that… I shouldn't have hit you."

"No, you shouldn't."

"I get extremely protective of my family."

"I've noticed."

"Does it hurt? Your face."

Shaking her head, Devina put a hand to her cheek. "I think the hoodie protected me a bit and with all my fear, the adrenaline made me not register the pain much. "

"That's one hell of a first impression to make." Attempting to ease up the atmosphere, I joked. "I'll bet you'll never forget me now."

Devina studied me for a short moment. "No, I don't think I'll ever forget you... or Wilma."

"She wants to continue writing with you when she moves away."

"That's nice."

"I promised her that I would pass on your messages and deliver hers to you."

"Thank you." She waited for me to leave but there was one last thing I needed to say.

"I'm truly sorry about your loss."

Her eyebrows drew close as if she wasn't sure what I was talking about.

"When I read in your letter that your entire family died, it touched me deeply. I can't even imagine what you must be going through."

Her head turned down and she muttered a low "Thank you."

"I hope you will one day have a large family again, because family is everything."

Devina raised her gaze and stared at me with the strangest look before she turned around and walked into the darkness of the beach with only her flashlight to guide her.

"Remember to throw over a letter tomorrow morning," I shouted after her.

"Okay."

Leaving a defenseless woman on the dark beach was one of the hardest things I ever had to do.

CHAPTER 11
The Beginning

Devina

All the way home to my house, Tyton's words kept repeating in my head: family is everything.

It had been my nana's last words and now I couldn't stop wondering if his saying it was a sign.

I have to stop overanalyzing everything. Look where it got me with Wilma's letters.

After taking a hot shower, I crawled into bed only to toss and turn unable to fall asleep. *I've been to the other side of the border. I've spoken to a real Nman and I've met one of the rarest women in the world. A woman of the North.*

No one would believe me if I told them, and still I felt like shouting it to the world.

Lying in my bed, a story began taking form in my head about a curious woman who began corresponding with an Nman as big and dangerous as Tyton.

She would ask him all the questions that I would never dare ask and she would venture out in the Northlands and explore their culture.

Exciting scenes of being a spectator at a bridal tournament played out in my imagination. My main character would be witty, fierce, and twice as brave as me.

Eventually, I dozed off and when I woke around ten the next day, the story was the first thing on my mind.

I didn't worry about packing stuff into boxes. All I could think about was getting all my thoughts and plot ideas down on paper.

Getting out my mother's electric typewriter, I sat down and poured the words from my head onto the paper.

Men of the North – FORBIDDEN LETTERS

It was a forbidden letter from the North. Deidra knew it the moment she picked it up. She should have left it there among the leaves and dirt on the ground, but the sad truth was that an unexpected letter was the only interesting thing that had happened to her in months.

Not many people lived in this rural border town and as far as she knew, she was the only one who ever came this close to the protective wall.

At least ten of the locals had warned her not to get close to the border wall and told her horrible stories of the savage men who lived on the other side. And yet, the wall had become the only place Deidra felt young, reckless, and fully alive.

When Deidra first took the assigned position as a caregiver at the local community home, no one had told her she would be the youngest person in a twenty-mile range.

It wasn't that Deidra disliked her job. But she was twenty-five and if she lived the rest of her life without another game night, she wouldn't complain.

Opening the letter in her hand she began to read but after no more than a single line, her head was exploding with questions about who the sender was. Turning the paper around, she saw a name: Mark.

An Nman. The letter had been written by a real Nman. With her pulse speeding up, she turned the letter again and read his message from the beginning.

It wasn't until Nellie pushed at my arm and gave me a blameful look that I came out of my writer's bubble.

"You want to go out? What time is it?" A quick glance at the clock made me gasp. "It's almost two o'clock. Nellie, I'm so sorry." Nellie had a dog door and could get out whenever she wanted but our daily walk in the forest was one of her favorite things.

I checked her food bowl, but there was still something left from last night. Over the years she had grown picky and preferred human food to her own dry food.

"Here you go." I shared a banana with her and then I remembered that I'd promised to write Wilma and Tyton to let them know I was safe.

After scribbling a quick note, I trotted through the forest to deliver my message.

When I got to the place where I'd first found Wilma's letter, there was a bottle with a one-sentence letter waiting for me.

You promised to write.

This had to be from Tyton. Wilma would have never written something this short and the handwriting was more masculine.

A shiver ran down my spine because all morning I'd written about letters from an Nman and here I was holding the real deal in my hand.

Admittedly, this one was much shorter and not as exciting as the letters Deidra was getting from Mark in my book, but never the less, the message was written to me by a real Nman.

Don't smile, I scolded myself, but the thought that someone cared about my safety warmed me from inside. Even if the one caring was a brute of an Nman.

Using the catapult, I delivered my letter and went straight back to my house to continue writing. It was so much fun to allow Deidra to do all the things I could never do in real life. Tyton's one-line letter was next to me on the table and at least ten times my eyes strayed to the paper.

What if there's an answer for me?

I didn't want to be running back and forth between my house and the border, but my foot was tapping like it was just waiting for the rest of my body to come along.

"Nellie, what do you say? Do you want to see if there's another letter?"

It was a rhetorical question since she always welcomed the chance to be outside.

There *was* a letter!

Sitting down on a fallen tree log, I opened the bottle and pulled out the paper.

Dear Devina,

I'm so happy to hear you made it back without any problems. We worried about you.
To be honest, I'm still in shock that you came to rescue me. It's the sweetest thing anyone has ever done for me, except for the time my sisters threw me a surprise party when I turned thirteen.

I'm not going to lie. Of course, I'm disappointed that you're not really writing a book about me, but it's good to hear that your visit here has inspired you to write another book about the Northlands. If you need help with your research let me know.

Peace and Love,
Wilma

Turning the letter over, I found an added message in Tyton's writing.

Hey D,
Mind if I read what you've written? I'm curious.
T

Lowering the letter, I leaned my head back and looked up through the tree crowns to the clouds drifting by.

Should I let Tyton read my story?

I was torn. My vanity as a writer feared that he might hate it, but at the same time, who better to critique a story about an Nman than an actual Nman?

Taking a deep breath, I decided to be brave and let Wilma and Tyton read it.

"We'd better fetch it before I lose my courage," I told Nellie and hurried home. The electronic typewriter had memory like a small computer and was also able to print the fifteen pages I had written so far. Rolling them tight, I tied a band around the papers but they still didn't fit inside the bottle. My solution was to roll the papers around the bottle and put it all inside a biodegradable see-through bag in case it started raining before they picked it up.

This will have to do.

When fifteen minutes later I watched the first chapters of my story fly across the wall, my initial relief that it had worked was followed by complete dread that Tyton was going to read my story about an Nman who looked a lot like him.

CHAPTER 12
Best Idea Ever

Tyton

I swallowed the fifteen pages of the story that Devina had allowed me to read. Wilma and I had fought about who got to read them first until I came up with the idea to make a copy so we each had our own version. "That way we can both make notes if we give her feedback."

Wilma had found a place to read inside, while I had retreated to the hammock in the back part of our property.

Twice, I read the chapters that she had sent us before I began making notes. It didn't escape me that the Nman, Mark, was described as a copy of me, but then I couldn't blame her since I was the only Nman she'd ever seen.

What fascinated me was Deidra's reaction to the picture he sent her of himself. For a third time I read that part of her story.

She studied the picture and was disturbed by the size of his neck and shoulders. Never had she seen a man with that much muscle except in historical pictures. Studying his stubble, she wondered why he hadn't cut his facial hair into a cute pattern like men here did. It gave the impression that it was there for convenience rather than fashion. The same could be said about his brown hair, which fell to his chin and looked tousled, as if he often ran his hands through it.

The men she knew cared about their appearance and spent a lot of time grooming themselves. Mark didn't even appear to color or pluck his eyebrows. Although she couldn't see his nails, she suspected he didn't paint them either.

Still, there was something about his eyes that drew her in.

Placing her hand on the picture, she covered the bearded part of his face and zoomed in on the green color. Maybe it was the confidence radiating from him or maybe there was a hint of humor there. Angling her head, Deidra couldn't decide what it was about Mark's eyes that she liked so much, but something about him had the same effect on her as the border wall did. He had an intensity and unpredictability about him that spoke to her. Like a sense of danger that made her feel wildly alive.

I thought about my first reaction to Devina and how I had mistaken her for a boy at first. I groaned when I remembered that I'd kept her pinned down with a hand to her chest. I had fucking felt her breast before I realized she was a woman.

Looking back, it was strange that I hadn't caught onto that sooner, but in my defense the idea of a woman lurking around by herself was so ludicrous that it never entered my mind.

As I scribbled my notes, I felt inspired to add to Devina's story. If it was to be authentic, she would have to inject some more curse words into Mark's vocabulary. No real Nman spoke in such a polished way.

After making notes all over her script, I rolled it up around the bottle and put it back in the bag. I didn't want Wilma to see my notes as I was a hundred percent sure that she would object to some of them. It would have been so much easier if I could sit down with Devina and talk to her about my ideas, but this would have to do.

Wilma took her time going over the script and unlike me she didn't have any notes, except for a heart below and the words "I love it."

"You love it?"

Tilting her head, she looked up at me. "Don't you?"

"Ehh... don't get me wrong. Devina is a great writer but are you okay with the way she portrays us Nmen?"

"What do you mean?"

"She called us primitive brutes."

"Maybe you are." Wilma turned her upper body from side to side, a sure sign that sitting still to read the fifteen pages had left her with restless energy. "I mean compared to the men she knows."

"Fair enough, but anyone reading this book is going to think we're illiterate monkeys."

"Now you're just exaggerating."

"Am I?"

"These are just the first chapters."

"But what is it that you love about it?"

"That Deidra is curious about our culture and that she's asking to see a tournament." Wilma gasped out loud and clasped her hands to her face.

"What?"

"I just had the best idea! We should have Devina come to my tournament. That way she can see it in real life and describe it in her book."

"Are you crazy?"

"No, it's perfect. She already knows how to get here." Wilma's voice rose to a small shriek. "I would looove for Devina to be at my wedding."

"That's impossible! Everyone would demand to know where she came from and the moment they find out she's a Motlander all hell will break loose."

"They won't find out because we're going to disguise her as a boy, of course."

I crossed my arms. "It must be nice to live in a fantasy world, but out here in the real world, shit like that doesn't work. She's too pretty to be a boy and her voice is that of a woman."

"Then she'll pretend to be mute."

"Ha! I've never known a female who could go a whole day without speaking. And how would you even explain the sudden appearance of a boy in our inner circle? Don't you think our family and friends would wonder about that?"

"Agrh, I'll think of something. It'll be fun!"

"No, Wilma. It won't be fun because it's not happening. You need to forget about the idea, right now!"

My sister gave me one of those cheeky smiles and I knew she had made up her mind, so I cursed loud, "Lucifer's ass."

"No, Tyton, don't leave yet. You need to return the script to Devina for me."

I groaned and reached my hand out for the papers.

"Let me just add something."

I waited and wasn't surprised when my sister shared her horrible idea of Devina coming over to see the tournament for herself. At least I had zero doubt that Devina would hate the idea as much as I did. I could count on her to say no.

CHAPTER 13
Criticism

Devina

A number of times now, I'd sat down and stood back up again. The way Tyton had smeared his comments all over my script was shocking. To criticize another's work should be done with gentle consideration for the person's feelings, but Tyton didn't seem to think I had any feelings to hurt at all.

The only positive thing he had mentioned was a line that he found funny. Problem was that it wasn't meant to be funny. And then there was the name of the Nman. I read Tyton's comment in the margin next to where Mark's name was mentioned the first time.

You should change his name to Tyton since we both know you're writing about you and me. Deidra is so close to Devina that you gave that away. Also, may I suggest you shorten Deidra to Dea; it means goddess.

I turned a few pages and found his remarks next to a passage describing Deidra looking at a picture of Mark. In big red letters, Tyton had written:

So, you think I have nice eyes. Thank you, I'll take the compliment.

If I had known Tyton would misunderstand and think that I was Deidra and he was Mark, I would have never shared my story with him. This was both infuriating and humiliating at the same time.

But he has a point. Mark does look like him.

I got up from my chair again and paced the room. *Just because Mark looks like Tyton doesn't mean that he is based on Tyton.* I snorted as I thought about his comment that Mark was too polished to be an authentic Nman.

You did the research, now use it had been his exact words.

What he failed to understand was that I couldn't curse in a book or readers would have a heart attack. Sure, there were antique books with awful language in them, but few people read them and by now most of the sayings and slang used from back then were so outdated that they didn't offend anyone. The last book I'd read had used the strangest expressions. Chillax I figured was slang for chill and relax, but others I'd had to look up on Wise-Share. Unfortunately, Wise-Share didn't offer an explanation for weird words like wankface and douche canoe.

I put down the pages with Tyton's notes and picked up the other set of papers with Wilma's comments on them. The fact that they had made a copy of my writing was both flattering and surprising.

Wilma had drawn a heart and written that she loved it. As always with that type of general feedback, it left me unsatisfied. Tyton was ruthless but at least he was concrete. I wished Wilma had told me what it was that she liked specifically. Her last words looked like a hurried message.

If you're writing about a tournament, you really need to come and see mine. We'll disguise you as a boy. Think of it as research and come to the beach at six a.m. on Saturday. Tyton will pick you up. It'll be a great adventure and you'll get to see what husband I pick.

I can't wait!

Wilma

The first time I'd read her words, I'd laughed at the absurdity, but it had been more than an hour since I picked up the letters and the idea had taken root in my mind.

I'd always been drawn to fantasy novels and the idea of getting to experience a world different from mine spoke to me.

This isn't a book. She's asking you to go to a real tournament and see fighting.

I'd never seen a fight in real life. There were movies of course, but no good parents would allow their children to see them. Growing up it had been ingrained in me that violence was primitive and toxic. Hundreds of years ago it had poisoned the minds of people and caused the Toxic War, which almost annihilated the entire human race and most other species on the planet.

No part of me thought that I'd enjoy seeing large warriors fight for Wilma. Except that she was right when she said that it would be an adventure. If I could sneak in like I did the last time and be a silent observer to the strange culture of the Northlands, I would be able to describe it in detail to my readers.

I wouldn't just see fighting, I would see hundreds of Nmen and hear them talk. I would see what they eat, wear, and how they interact.

My hands were shaking a little when I found a pen and wrote my answer.

My dearest Wilma,

How could I say no to being at your wedding? I'm terrified and yet I don't want to miss it. If you're sure that I'll be safe, I'll come.

May you experience only love and tranquility in your life,
Devina

I put my letter in one bottle and found another one to answer Tyton's letter.

Dear Tyton,

I scratched out dear and crumbled the paper up.

Hello Tyton,

No, that sounded too informal.

Hi Tyton,

Thank you for your feedback but let me make it perfectly clear that Mark is not you and Deidra is not me!
I might be able to spice up Mark's vocabulary but having him say fuck is not an option. If I used curse words, the book would never get published.
Also, I wasn't talking about your green eyes, but his. And the fact that Deidra likes them doesn't mean I would like them because as I already said, I am not Deidra!

If you think I should change so much of my story, then why don't you write your own book and let me critique it? It would be interesting to see if you take criticism as well as you like to give it.

Devina

CHAPTER 14
A Few Ideas

Tyton

"Why don't you look happy?"

My sister was staring at me after she had just pulled me into her room to show me Devina's last letter.

"Happy? Why would I be happy about you putting Devina in danger? What part don't you understand? It's one thing for her to sneak in and out in the middle of the night, but you're suggesting that she go with us to the biggest event in the Northlands, where thousands of people will see her."

"But I'm so proud to have a Motlander friend. No one else does."

"This isn't about you!" My tone got hard and Wilma pouted a little.

"It kinda *is* since it's *my* wedding."

Closing my eyes, I rubbed my forehead. "Sometimes you can be the most selfish person in the world."

"I want Devina to come and I've already come up with a good way to disguise her as a boy. No one will know she's female. I promise!"

"Fine!" Holding up my hands, I drew in a deep breath. "But my condition is that we tell Mom and Dad. We'll need their help if we're going to pull this off."

"Done!" Wilma reached out her hand to seal the deal and as soon as I took it, she grinned. "That was easy since I planned to tell Mom and Dad anyway."

I swung my hand toward her door with an expression saying, *Be my guest*. Following her to the kitchen, I muttered, "I hope you find a husband who likes to hear the words *I want*, because you say it a lot. Do you know that?"

Wilma turned her head and stuck her tongue out.

"Oh, that's very mature. Are you sure Devina wasn't right when she said that you're more girl than woman?"

"Argh, that's offensive."

I shook my head when Wilma ran ahead. I had always found it a major fail in our system that brides were so young. It took time for us men to save up enough money to take part in a tournament and even if by some miracle a young man could raise the money, it still required years of fight training to stand a chance. It was rare to see a contestant under twenty-five and it wasn't uncommon for the bride to end up marrying someone twice her age.

Most men didn't consider it a problem because they had no experience with women, but I had three sisters and had seen first-hand how much they changed between the age of fifteen and twenty. Wilma might think she was all woman, but I wished she had been given another five years to mature and find herself before she married. Not only for her, but for her future husband as well.

When I got into the kitchen, Wilma was already explaining about her plan to our parents.

"Is it true?" our father asked me. "Was this Devina really here?"

"Yes, she was here."

"Why didn't you tell us?"

"We're telling you now, aren't we?" Wilma pointed out.

"A Motlander." My mother blinked her eyes in confusion.

"Yes. A woman who lives on the other side of the border." I said it slow to help my parents catch up.

"She's my friend and she wants to come to my wedding."

My mother opened her arms to Wilma. "Oh, how exciting. This will make your wedding even more special."

"That's what I told Tyton, but you know how negative he is."

"You keep confusing the word negative with the word realistic. There's a difference."

"Are you sure no one will notice that she's gone?" My father at least seemed to understand the danger of Wilma's plan. "If they think we kidnapped her you could be starting a war."

"Tsk. Now you sound just like Tyton, but it's not like anyone is going to notice if Devina is gone for a few days when her whole family is dead."

"What do you mean, her whole family is dead?" When my dad looked to me for confirmation, I nodded.

"It was an epidemic. There were eight members in her family and she lost them all."

My dad frowned and my mom raised both hands to her face. "Poor girl!"

A moment of quiet filled the kitchen before Wilma broke the silence. "Yeah, so you see: she can stay away for a day or two without anyone worrying about her."

Shaking her head as if she wanted everything to fall into place and make sense, my mother put on a brave smile. "Well, in that case, why don't we just keep her here as a bride for Tyton and make her part of our family?"

"No, Mom, she doesn't like me."

Placing an arm on my shoulder, my dad leaned in. "You shouldn't take that personally. Everyone knows that Motlanders don't like men."

"It's not her fault. She doesn't know any better," Wilma defended Devina.

"Don't you worry, we'll be nice to her," our father assured Wilma while our mother wanted to hear more about Wilma's plan to disguise Devina as a boy.

"Well, she's little so we can't dress her up like a man or people will wonder. I'm thinking a boy around twelve or thirteen."

"Oh, why don't we say that she's – I mean he's – a new worker on our lands." My mother pointed to my dad. "If anyone asks, we could tell people he's one of those troubled kids who benefits from a bit of practical work experience before they go back to school."

Our dad thought about it. "But would we bring a worker to the tournament?"

"Just because we haven't done it before doesn't mean we can't do it now. It's our daughter getting married and we're proud parents."

"A troubled boy it is!" Wilma declared and that seemed to be it.

Not happy with the situation, I made a last instruction. "Just make sure that she wears a hoodie or a hat to cover her face."

"We could try finding a fake beard."

My mom rolled her eyes. "Don't be a waffle, Wilma. When did you last see a twelve-year-old boy with a beard?"

"Okay, okay, but I'll need to make her eyebrows bigger and bushier. Mom, you'll help, won't you?"

"Of course I will. I'm so excited to meet a real Motlander."

With that settled, I walked over to my loft with the bottle in my hand that contained Devina's letter to me. I'd already read her answer when Wilma first gave it to me, but I still pulled it out again and re-read it. It was almost amusing how adamant Devina was about Mark and Deidra not being based on us. If anything, it just told me that they were.

Her idea that I should write my own book seemed like a perfect opportunity to rile her up a little. I didn't start my own book from scratch but built on what she had already created. My version of the story, however, was way more colorful and fun.

When I had written five pages, I read them through, corrected a few typos, and grinned. Yup, if she couldn't put curse words into her book maybe she could make it steamy at least.

How I wished I could be there when she read it.

CHAPTER 15
Kama Sutra

Devina

My professor's words from years ago kept resounding in my head. *Good writing makes your blood boil, your head spin, or your pulse speed up. You may hate what you read, but if words can affect you that much, the author did well.*

Tyton's five pages did all of those things for me and yet it wasn't great writing. He had run-on sentences, a loose relationship with commas, and he repeated the same word three times in a sentence.

But my heart was racing, my head was spinning, and my blood was boiling with anger that he thought he could hijack my story and take it to a place it was never meant to go. My eyes fell to a random page of his writing and again, I read the words.

"I'm not judging you for having no experience. I'm just saying that I'm willing to teach you."

Dea looked down at the book which Mark had just given her. "Kama Sutra," she read aloud. "What is this?" As she spoke, her fingers caressed the old book with the beautiful wrapping and a soft smile spread on her pretty face. "How old is this? I can't accept a gift this precious."

"But I thought you loved books."

"I do! But..."

"Open it." Mark studied her with anticipation and broke into a laugh at the expression on Dea's face when she flipped the book open to a random page and saw images of a couple having sex.

"Is this a joke?" She turned a few more pages but each side showed a picture of the couple in a sexual position with a title and a description.

"No, it's not a joke. Kama Sutra *is an ancient book from when sex between men and women was considered beautiful and sacred. It teaches about making love in a multitude of positions."*

To his surprise, Dea kept flicking the pages, taking in the variations of sex.

"Whoa."

He was amused by her reaction to one of the illustrations of a woman under a man. "Yeah, she's pretty flexible."

"It looks painful with the way he forces her legs up to her ears."

"What makes you think he forces her? Maybe she likes it that way."

Meeting his eyes, Dea arched an eyebrow. "Tell you what, why don't you get down on the floor and try seeing how being in that position feels to you."

"Nah, everyone knows women are softer and more flexible than men. Look, his role is to be on top of her."

"Tsk." She smacked her tongue. "What you're saying is that you couldn't do it."

"I doubt you could either. Women back then were used to having sex, but if you're right that women gave up on sex after the Toxic War then it probably wouldn't be fair to compare you to them." He shrugged with a smile. "That's the thing about evolution, it gets rid of redundant things so I bet you modern women are left with dried-out and inflexible bodies."

His words provoked Dea. "Are you saying I'm dried-out and stiff?"

"I don't know. Are you?" The prolonged eye contact between them made her heart race and she refused to look away.

"You want to see if you could do what she does?" Angling his head, Mark added, "With your clothes on, of course."

"Nice try, but I'm not going to get into acrobatic sexual positions to prove that I'm as much woman as my ancestors were."

"All right. It was just an offer." Reaching in and turning the pages, Mark settled on another one. "Maybe this one is more to your skill level."

In the illustration the woman was on her back with her legs spread while the man had his head buried between her legs.

With a loud sound, Dea closed the book and handed it back to Mark. "Thank you for your gift, but I can't accept it."

His eyebrows drew close together. "Don't be silly. The book is only part of my gift." Pressing the book back against her chest, he lowered his voice. "The real gift is that I'll let you pick out any of the one hundred and one positions in that book and let you try them on me."

She opened her mouth to protest and tell him he was out of his mind, but her curiosity created a funny tingling sensation that ran down between her thighs and made her close her mouth again.

"Any position you'd like!" he repeated with a wicked gleam in his eyes.

Just like Deidra in the story, my heart was racing fast too. Why would Tyton write me sensual stuff like this unless... Was this his way of making me an offer himself?

I had written and torn apart several responses to him, but with my hands shaking and my foot tapping it was hard to get it right.

Sleep on it!

It was almost like my nana stood next to me and offered the same advice that she'd given me so many times in the past.

But sleep didn't bring me peace. Instead I woke up from an erotic dream with a deep longing inside of me. Groaning, I rolled onto my stomach and tried going back to sleep, but the scenario from my dream wouldn't go away.

I'm not crazy. It's just because I've been inside my characters' heads all day. It's just my imagination playing tricks on me.

Still, recalling my dream of being pressed into the mattress by a large, strong, and very aroused Nman made everything from below my navel feel molten with lust.

Mark, it was Mark... I told myself because admitting that my dream had been a sexual version of what happened in the hay barn between Tyton and me would be mortifying.

I'm not interested in sex with a man and I'm not turned on by male dominance in any way. That would just be ridiculous for a modern woman like myself.

Ridiculous and sad!

Turning over on my back again, I covered my face with my hands and groaned.

The idea to include some of Tyton's writing in my book came sneaking. If it could affect me the way it had, maybe readers would feel the same way. What better way to write a book about the Northlands than to have the perspective of an Nman?

It would have to be a romance then.

Few wrote romance novels nowadays, and none that were steamy, but there was still an audience for the antique books in that genre, so why not?

Sitting up with the energy of someone who had slept twelve hours, I pushed my comforter away, grabbed Tyton's pages, and raced down to the typewriter.

CHAPTER 16
Bloody Hell

Tyton

There was still dew on the grass when I walked to the border wall. The morning sun had only peeked over the horizon and was bringing the promise of a warm August day.

Yesterday I'd given Devina five pages with strong sexual undertones and at that moment it had seemed like a good idea.

Now, I was worried that she'd be offended or worse: scared. What if she changed her mind and stopped writing us because of my attempt to be funny? If Devina changed her mind and decided not to come for Wilma's wedding after all, my sister would be so disappointed.

And so would I.

The truth was that I'd gone from hating the idea to looking forward to picking her up on the beach.

My interactions with unmarried women outside my family were almost nonexistent, and Devina had become the biggest puzzle in my life since she showed up at our doorstep. For a woman to be that brave and independent blew my mind, like the way she had refused my help and run to the beach rather than getting a ride from me!

She was different from Northlander brides and it intrigued me. Not only was she close to my age, she was calm, mature, and possessed natural beauty that she didn't cover up with heavy make-up.

My only chance of getting married and starting my own family in this lifetime was to enter Tamara's tournament and fight for her. Unless...

My heart almost skipped a beat when the hunter inside me rose up to his full height.

Unless I can seduce Devina and make her mine.

Reaching the border wall, I spotted the bottle in the grass and jogged to it, while my eyes searched for the other bottle. Disappointment made my lungs feel too small. There was only one bottle and that meant she hadn't answered me in a separate message like I'd hoped for.

Fuck! I shouldn't have sent those pages.

Squatting down, I picked up the bottle and opened it. Expecting to see a letter for Wilma, I was excited to see my name on top of the paper.

I hope this letter finds you well, Tyton.

Thank you for your contribution to my book. I found your unexpected angle to the storyline intriguing. I've included most of it in my book with a few edits for a smoother flow.

After searching on WiseShare, I found an article that talks about Kama Sutra. *I assumed it was a fictional book, but since it's real I'm hoping – do you have a copy of it? If so, I would like to see it when I come for Wilma's wedding on Saturday.*
You mentioned that it demonstrates one hundred and one positions. That's more than my imagination can fathom so I have to ask: is that number made up or real?

Also, since you know people who have sex would you mind asking them if they practice those extreme acrobatic positions that you described? If not, there's no need to include it in my novel.

I'll meet you on the beach at six a.m. Saturday morning. May your day be full of happiness,

Devina

PS: I noticed that you changed Deidra's name to Dea. I can agree to making Dea her nickname, but her real name will still be Deidra.

A feeling of pure relief and elation made me lean back my head and smile at the sky. Not only was she not offended by what I'd written, she was also still coming for Wilma's wedding.
It seems the little Motlander is full of surprises.
I ran back to my apartment, and almost slid on the wet grass as I rounded the building and stormed up the stairs to find pen and paper.

Devina,

Bloody hell, I never thought you'd actually include any of my writing in your book. Let me just say that I'm honored.
Yes, Kama Sutra *is a real book, but I don't have a copy. I can show you all the positions from the book when you get here. It's on the Internet. Unlike you, we didn't scratch the Internet but still use it.*

I think there are more than one hundred and one positions in the book, but the number sounded good, so I went with it; artistic license and all.

Okay, so here's what I know about having a sex life: every couple is different.
Some may like to try as many positions as possible, but for most I think they find a few that they prefer. Personally, I know exactly which ones I'd like to try first. Do you?

Anyway, we're leaving for the first day of Wilma's tournament tomorrow morning. It's only about an hour from here, so we'll be back for the night. I'm sure Wilma will check for your messages several times today and before we leave tomorrow. She usually checks at least three times a day.

Tyton

There was no need to tell Devina that with Wilma being occupied by wedding preparations, I was the one who checked three times a day.

At noon, two bottles came back.

The letter to Wilma was short and just reassured her that Devina looked forward to being at her wedding.

But the letter to me was longer and a childish part of me took pleasure in getting more from Devina. I read it again.

May peace surround you, Tyton.

Thank you for your answers.
If Mark and Deidra end up having sex in the book, it will be useful for me to see the illustrations that you talked about. I don't have any experience with sex, but there are cities here in the Motherlands where they have sex-bots based on technology from before the Toxic War.

I don't believe they are very popular because for most of us our physical need for touch is taken care of by having weekly or bi-weekly massages. We're not unaware that there are benefits to orgasms in terms of stress relief, but that can be taken care of by a simple in-and-out massage that includes finger penetration and stimulation of the clitoris.

My eye-bulbs just about popped out of my sockets as I reread the last paragraph.

"Holy fuck!"

Either she was messing with me to get back at me for the pages I had sent her or I was corresponding with a real woman and discussing her sexuality.

This was by far the most interesting thing that had ever happened to me. Refocusing, I read the last part of her letter.

In regard to a preferred position, I hope you don't mind my asking if you Nmen have sex-bots too, and if so, how accessible are they? Have you been with one?

Again, thank you for all your assistance in making my book as authentic as possible. I appreciate your willingness to help with my research about the lives of Nmen.

May you experience only good things today,

Devina

She hadn't commented on what position she'd prefer, but it didn't matter. She was still talking to me and asking more intimate questions now and it felt like a huge victory.

Rising back up, I looked at the wall. On the other side was a woman who knew my name and thought about me.

I was whistling when I walked back to the house with Devina's letter for Wilma.

"Did she write you?" my sister asked when I handed her the bottle.

"No," I lied and felt like a hypocrite, because my correspondence with Devina felt private.

Wilma read Devina's short message and smiled. "She's still coming."

"I know."

"Oh, I can't wait to see her. It's going to be so much fun."

"Uh-huh," I said in a nonchalant manner and turned around, so she wouldn't see my wide grin of excitement.

CHAPTER 17
Breakfast and Plans

Devina

Not only was Tyton on the beach Saturday morning when I walked up from the water half an hour early, he had also brought a large towel for me.

"Thank you."

"You're welcome."

It wasn't even six in the morning, but the sun was coming up. Using the towel to dry my hair, I noticed he too had damp hair and concluded that he'd just showered. "How is the tournament going?"

"Didn't you read Wilma's letter from last night?"

"No, I checked at eight and there wasn't anything."

"We came home at ten and I threw over a message from her, but since you didn't get it…" He stopped talking when I gestured for him to hold the towel while I searched for dry clothes in my bag.

"Since I didn't get it…?" I said to get him back on track and turned my face to see what was wrong.

I had swum in my black underwear and caught Tyton staring at my behind before he diverted his eyes with a flash of guilt on his face.

"Stop staring at my behind."

His eyes blinked and then he seemed to recover. "I'm sorry, but I'm only human and when you're wearing only a top and your panties, it's a little difficult to concentrate."

I had fished out my clean clothes and stood back up. "If it's so hard for you, turn around. I have to change out of my wet clothes."

A deep groan sounded from Tyton, who turned around and covered his eyes with the towel. "It doesn't help. I can still see you."

I smiled. "Liar. I don't see eyes in the back of your head."

"I don't need to *see* you with my eyes. My imagination is showing me everything."

No man had ever flirted with me and I had no experience with anyone showing a sexual interest in me. "Do you see the large mole on my hip too?"

"You have a mole?"

"Not one, but seventeen and they're all brown and hairy. And then there's the angry-looking scar from the time I had surgery. It goes all the way from my hip to my collarbone."

"What surgery?"

"Ehh... it was an, eehhh... heart surgery."

"Who's the liar now?"

"You don't believe me?"

"Your top revealed enough skin for me to see your collarbone and there were no scars or moles."

"All right." I wasn't sure what to do with my wet panties and top and looked around. In a few hours there would be sun on this beach, so I left my underwear to dry on a large rock and then I closed my bag. "I'm ready to go now."

Tyton watched me as I walked to his bike and took in the large machine. "How do I get on this thing?"

"I just swing my leg over, but I guess you're too short to do that."

"Can I step on that thing?" I pointed to a pipe of some kind.

"I'd rather you didn't." He got onto the bike and scooted back to make room for me. "If you come over here, I'll pull you up."

"Nuh-uh, I'm not sitting in front of you."

"I always have Wilma up front. How else can I make sure you're safe?"

The thought of being surrounded by his strong body made my stomach act up like the first time I had to read from my debut novel in public. I hated when nervous energy filled me like that, but I wouldn't let him see it.

"I'm either sitting behind you or I'm running."

"Why? Are you afraid I'm going to hurt you?"

"No, but I don't want a large Nman pressed up against me."

His brow shot up. "What's the difference between me pressing up against you and you pressing up against me?"

"The difference is that I won't press up against you."

For a long moment we locked eyes in a battle of wills.

"Okay, then you sit behind me... for now."

He gave me a hand and pulled me up on the large bike. "Hold on to me."

"No thank you."

"All right..." He said it drawn out with annoyance. "Then I'll just go extra slow, so you won't fall off." It was clear that his snail's pace was a deliberate provocation.

"I could walk faster than this."

"Then hold on to my waist."

With a sigh of resignation, I snaked my arms around him, but I still wasn't holding on.

Speeding up a little, he suddenly hit the brakes. It was enough for me to feel the momentum force me forward. In reflex from the unpleasant feeling of losing control, I tightened my grip on him, and complained, "You did that on purpose."

"Uh-huh. I'm not joking. I can't protect you back there so either you hold on tight or you come up front."

I could feel the satisfaction spreading from him when I locked my arms around his waist.

We rode through the early morning darkness with me pressed up against him and when he raised my folded hands a little higher, it hit me that I might have been holding my hands too close to his crotch.

"Have you ever done this with anyone but Wilma?" I asked him. "I mean anyone but your family."

"No. For me to be this close to an unmarried woman would be unheard of. Her protector would kill me for it."

"Then it's a good thing that I belong to no one but myself."

He nodded and kept going.

There was nothing much to see because of the darkness, but five minutes into the ride, I began relaxing against his broad back.

Obviously, my parents had protected me as a child, but as the oldest sibling in the family, I'd often been the sensible one keeping the younger ones safe. Never in my adult life had I experienced someone so concerned with my safety as Tyton.

"Let me help you off the bike," he offered when we got to their house. I chose to slide down by myself and would have tripped if Tyton hadn't reached out to steady me.

Heat crept into my cheeks. "Thank you. It was a bigger step down than I thought."

"It's fine. Just let me help you next time."

I looked away.

"Devina."

"Yes?"

"You really don't like being helped, do you?"

"It's not that."

"Is it because of what happened between us the last time?"

There was no need to bring up our unfortunate first meeting again, so I turned to the house. "I don't see any lights…"

"We got here early, which gives you time to answer my question."

This was so typical of Tyton. Always direct and to the point. With a sigh, I admitted, "I don't have a problem with people helping me in general."

"So, it's me then?"

"Can you blame me for not trusting you?"

"I told you... I didn't know you were a female when I grabbed you."

Just then a light turned on inside the house and the entrance door swung open. Wilma came running out still in her nightwear. "You're here!"

I almost got knocked back by Wilma's fierce hug. "Can you believe I'm getting married today?"

"I know."

"What did you think of Emmerson making it to the finals?"

Tyton cleared his throat. "Actually, Devina didn't get your letter from last night. She doesn't know anything about it."

"You didn't?" Wilma sucked in a breath. "Then I have so much to tell you. Come on."

We didn't wait for Tyton to park his bike before we went into the house.

"My parents can't wait to meet you." Holding my hand and leading me into a kitchen, Wilma talked over her shoulder. "My mom and I found the best disguise for you. We've decided that your name is Devin. That way it will be natural for you to react if we talk to you and oh, you're fourteen years old."

"Fourteen?"

"Yes. If anyone asks about your small frame, we'll just say that you're a late bloomer. Sit here while I make us some breakfast."

Tyton came through the door and rolled his eyes with a chuckle. "What are you doing?"

"Making breakfast."

"Did you forget that your friend doesn't eat animal products." He nodded to Wilma's hands that were holding eggs and bacon from the fridge.

Wilma frowned. "I was going to make her some fruit and pancakes, but the rest of us can still have our breakfast, can't we?"

"Yes, of course." I didn't feel it was my place to challenge their food habits. My purpose here was to research the culture of the Northlands, not to preach.

"How were you going to make pancakes when she can't have eggs and milk? How about you leave the cooking to me while you make sure Mom and Dad are up."

"Okay. I want my egg with the sunny side up."

Tyton washed his hands and looked back at her. "You forgot to say please." But Wilma was already gone.

"Do you like to cook?" I asked when it was just him and me.

"I wouldn't say that I like it, but it comes with being an adult, doesn't it?"

"Someone should have told my parents that. When I moved to the city to study, I'd never learned how to cook for myself. Here I was, ready to conquer the world and too proud to call home and admit that I was sick of living off salad, pancakes, and store-bought soup."

Tyton was cracking eggs on a hot pan but looked up. "So, what did you do?"

"The only thing I could do. I signed up for cooking classes. They offer them at all universities, I think."

"And did it help?"

"I'm no master chef, but I learned how to bake, and I make a wicked spinach lasagna."

His lips pursed up. "According to whom?"

"According to me." I was sitting on a bar stool at the kitchen counter and rose up in my chair.

"How about you make me your lasagna one day and let me judge for myself." Tyton didn't look at me when he said it. In fact, he made it sound so casual, as if it was a given that I'd be back to visit his family in the future. No, not his family, since he had only referred to himself.

Woosh, another rush of nervous energy made my stomach bubble up in that tickling feeling that I got from sudden drops in airplanes or roller coasters.

Why does he make me so nervous?

"Or are you too scared to let me judge for myself?"

"What?" For a moment I was lost.

"You said that you make a wicked lasagna and I challenged you to a test, so I can see if you're right."

"Do you even like spinach lasagna?"

"I've never had it. We make lasagna with meat."

"With meat?" I wrinkled my nose up. "Why would you ruin lasagna with meat? In the Motherlands we're all vegans."

Tyton looked confident in a kitchen and was doing a lot of things at the same time.

"I'm pretty sure that the original recipe had meat in it and that..." He was interrupted by his parents and Wilma, who came barging into the kitchen.

Getting up from my chair I reached out my hands to greet their mother, who looked eager to meet me.

"Ah, so this is the mysterious Motlander that we've heard so much about."

I smiled. "May peace surround you. I'm Devina."

"I know and I'm Joan, like Joan of Arc and this is my husband, William. We're so happy to meet you."

Letting go of her hands, I turned with a large smile and reached out both my hands to her husband but instead of taking my hands in a formal greeting he held his palms in the air and stepped back.

"Whoa, careful there."

"It's okay, Dad, Devina isn't a Northlander. You can touch her," Wilma assured him.

William was an older version of Tyton with the same muscular build. "I'd better not. In case this stunt goes to hell and we get caught with a Motlander woman. I don't want to have touched her."

Tyton stiffened and his eyes swung to me with a worried expression.

"Relax, we won't get caught! Mom and I are going to change Devina into Devin and you won't be able to recognize her."

Their mom began setting the table while their dad listed all his worries.

"It's important that you say as little as possible – in fact, I'd prefer if you pretend to be mute. That way no one hears your girly voice. Also, you need to stay close to Tyton at all times. No sudden impulses to investigate on your own."

Again, Tyton and I exchanged a glance and it was a little longer than it needed to be. The weirdest sensation, of my neck heating up and my heart hammering extra fast, made me wonder what was wrong with me.

"I won't take my eye off her," Tyton promised his dad.

"Good." William nodded and sat down at the table. "You should know that we've told Frederick but that's it. The fewer who know, the better."

"Frederick is my other brother," Wilma reminded me.

"Let's get some breakfast and then we'll prepare." William looked up at a digital clock on the wall. "We're leaving here at 7:45 sharp. The first fights start at nine and I want to be there.

"That doesn't give us long to get ready," Joan complained.

"Then we'd better get this breakfast going."

Turning to Tyton I asked, "Can I help with anything?"

William pulled out a chair at the table. "No, you just sit here and think about how a boy around fourteen moves and behaves."

Tyton snorted. "How would she know when she's only seen boys in the Motherlands? I don't think they're the same as our boys."

"Well, how did you two look and move when you were fourteen?" I asked Tyton and William.

"I have no idea. It's been more than forty years since I was that young."

Joan broke into a laugh and pointed to Tyton. "I remember you had that phase when you walked around funny."

"Funny how?" I asked.

Joan demonstrated. "Oh, he would walk around like this, pushing his chest out to make himself look bigger and stronger."

"Yeah, do that!" Wilma nodded to me. "You'll look like an idiot, but that's okay."

"No, don't walk like that. I got into fights all the time. Nobody likes a cocky kid. It's like wearing a stamp on your forehead asking to be taken down a notch."

"Then how should I walk?"

"Well, how do you normally walk?" Tyton took a seat at the table that was now bursting with food. "Show us."

I had never thought about how I walked and now everything I did seemed weird.

"Is that how you walk?" Joan frowned.

"I think so. No, maybe more like this." I took another turn back and forth on the kitchen floor.

"Hmm... no, that won't work. You swing your arms too much."

I stopped at Wilma's chair. "What about at your school; how do the boys walk around there?"

They all looked at me like I'd asked her if she'd seen aliens.

"I don't go to school. My mom teaches me at home."

"Oh." I jerked back. "Is it just you or is that the case for all girls?"

"There aren't that many of us, but yes, we all do home schooling."

"It's safer that way," William explained.

Taking a big bite of a bun with cheese, Tyton got up from his chair. He chewed fast and swallowed. "How about you walk like this?" Stuffing his hands in his pockets, he let his shoulders and head fall a bit and walked like he wanted to avoid being seen. "You could be shy and socially awkward. That way most people would leave you alone."

"Yeah that's a good idea, and make sure you keep the hoodie up the whole time," William instructed. "Even pretty boys can get the wrong kind of interest and we don't want to fight off drunken men who want to seduce you."

"Is homosexuality a big thing here?"

"What do you think?" Tyton sat down again and nodded to my chair for me to do the same. I got the feeling he didn't want to talk about it.

"It's considered a taboo," Joan whispered to me.

"Why? There's nothing wrong with homosexuality."

"What would you know about it? Didn't you say Motlanders are all asexual?" Tyton's words sounded like an accusation.

"Asexual – does that mean you don't like sex at all?" Joan looked at me with pity.

I gave a curt nod and an awkward silence filled the room. All I could do was focus on eating my breakfast. The strawberries, and the piece of oatbread with orange jam that I ate tasted amazing. I didn't ask if there was milk or eggs in the bread. I needed something to eat and with everything else on the table being animal-based products, I chose to pretend the bread was vegan.

In the meanwhile, Wilma and her parents discussed the champions and how they all hoped that a man called Emmerson would make it to be one of the five champions for her to pick from.

William chugged down a large glass of milk. "It's a shame that Cameron got knocked out."

"Mmm." Tyton made a sound of agreement. "I hated that fight."

"I know, son. It's always hard to see a good friend get beaten unconscious and not be able to help."

Tyton nodded. "He survived and that's what matters."

"I wouldn't have minded Cameron as a son-in-law. He's a good fighter," his mom chimed in. "But now he and you can train together for Tamara's tournament next year."

Tyton didn't respond to that and Joan turned her attention back on Wilma. "By this time tomorrow, you'll be a married woman."

"I know." Wilma was grinning from ear to ear and leaned her face against her mother's hand when Joan caressed her cheek.

"I can't believe my little girl is a bride." Joan teared up.

"Well, she won't be if we don't get moving." William pushed his chair back. "Tyton and I will clear the table while you three get ready. We're leaving in an hour."

CHAPTER 18
Woman in Disguise

Tyton

When I saw Devina next, she had been transformed from a twenty-eight-year-old woman into a teenage boy. Her eyebrows were bigger, and she was wearing glasses and baggy clothes.

"Not bad." My dad crossed his arms. "Devin, was it?"

"Yeah, my name is Devin." Devina's voice sounded different because she made it deeper and darker.

Turning his body to me, my dad shrugged. "I think it could work. What do you say?"

I was impressed with the disguise but still wary about everything that could go wrong. "Yeah, it'll have to do."

We flew to the tournament in my drone. They were expensive and not many could afford them. When my brother and I had entered Starr's tournament three years ago, we had made a promise to each other. If one of us got chosen by Starr, we would buy the other a drone as consolation for not being picked.

Frederick got the bride and the fortune. I got the drone as promised.

"Wow, this is so nice." Devina kept her hands folded in her lap while her eyes took in the interior.

Wilma on the other hand was used to it and made herself comfortable by pulling her legs up under her and turning to Devina. "Is it true that you don't have drones in the Motherlands?"

"We do, but not for ordinary people. We use carbon-neutral cars and buses to get around, and of course bikes."

"But what about when you have to go long distances?"

"Well, for us regular people there are boats, high-speed trains, and planes. But to do long-distance travel would require a lot of energy points."

"What are energy points?"

"It's sort of a reward system that starts from early childhood. For instance, when I was in school, we had three stationary energy bikes in each classroom. The school was powered by the electricity that we students generated, and excess power was shared with the community home next door."

"Kids bike while in class?" I wrinkled my forehead.

"Not everyone at the same time, but some kids found it hard to sit still for long, so they were encouraged to bike while listening or reading a book. Others did it while taking part in a discussion group. We didn't have to bike fast, just keep the bike going; and with more than ten classrooms and three bikes in each, creating enough power was never a problem. But anyway, the energy points are given to each person that contributes to creating natural power. It's also a motivating factor to go to the energy centers. We can create power by running, biking, rowing, dancing, and other forms of movement."

"What if you can't move? Or don't want to?" my mom asked.

"In that case you can buy energy points. It's rare for someone not to have a job that gives them that option."

My dad wrinkled his forehead. "Sounds like forced labor to me."

Devina looked so different with her bigger eyebrows and glasses. "I like it. It's a great way to access clean energy and at the same time make people feel that they're helping. I'm sure you agree that there can be no further pollution of the planet."

With a low chuckle, my dad leaned in and whispered to me. "Sounds like you can't even take a dump over there."

Men of the North – FORBIDDEN LETTERS

Devina heard him and didn't look the least bit offended. "You can, of course... but only on your assigned deposit days. All feces are collected for fertilizing purposes."

"What?!!" My dad jerked his head back. "You're not allowed to shit whenever you want to?"

The smallest smile made her lips purse upward.

"Dancing devils." My dad laughed and shook his head. "And here I thought Motlanders didn't have a sense of humor." Looking to the rest of us he admitted, "Devina got me good on that one."

"Devin," Wilma corrected him. "It's better if we stick to Devin so we all get used to it."

"Fine." William raised up a hand to signal he understood.

My mom wrinkled her forehead. "I still don't understand what Motlanders have against drones? Why would you use cars and bikes when you can fly around?"

"Mom, it's something about them rejecting technology." Wilma spoke over the rim of her tea. "They're afraid after what happened during the Toxic War. That's why they prefer everything as natural as possible."

Devina gave Wilma a nod. "That's right. We don't strive toward technological breakthroughs. What matters to us is a life full of purpose."

"Purpose... like how?" my mom asked.

"We care about each other and it's our goal that each generation leave the planet cleaner than we got it. So much of the world is still uninhabitable because of pollution and radiation, but we're cleaning up oceans and streams one at a time. One of our Council members compared it to spending your life cleaning up after a party you didn't attend."

My parents had a ton of questions for Devina but I had a hard time concentrating because the responsibility of her safety lay on my shoulders like two heavy blocks of lead. I'd been a protector for as long as I could remember, but this was different. Devina didn't know our customs and expectations. She wouldn't know how to read a situation and had already proven by coming here the first time that she was a curious risk taker.

When we arrived at the large fields that had been transformed into a marketplace with ten arenas for fighting, we flew over the area very slowly.

"I love that we're allowed to park inside the VIP area," my mom mumbled low with her nose pressed against the window.

"That's because it's *my* tournament." Wilma sat up taller. "I'm the only one who gets to do it. Well, except for the King of course."

"About him." I lowered my voice and spoke directly to my sister. "Keep your distance. Just nod and smile but do not under any circumstance go with him anywhere."

Wrinkling her nose up, she snorted. "Eww, why would I? He's so vile."

I could feel Devina's eyes on me but explaining how crazy and unpredictable our king was would have to wait.

My dad and I were the first to exit and we helped our mother and Wilma out.

"Devina." I held on to her arm as she exited last. "Promise that you won't do anything stupid."

A triangle formed between her eyebrows. "Like what?"

"Like getting me killed."

Inhaling deeply, she shook her head. "I promise to follow your lead."

"Good." I should let go of her arm, but the connection between us with my touching her and both of us looking deep into each other's eyes made my body tingle with excitement.

"I..."

She waited for me to finish my sentence.

Men of the North – FORBIDDEN LETTERS

"I'm sorry, but I like touching you." To soften my rude words, I laughed a little.

Devina smiled a little. "It's just because it's new and otherwise forbidden to you, don't you think?"

"Are you coming?" My sister was shouting for us and after locking up the drone, we hurried after her as I thought about Devina's question.

Is my attraction to her only because I can't touch other women?

No! The answer rose up from within. Even now that Devina was dressed as a moody teenage boy, my body reacted to her. There was something about her personality and the old soul looking back at me every time our eyes met. Devina wasn't a girl bride. She was a woman with about the same amount of life experience as me. She had known joy and suffered devastating loss. She was complex and flawed, but at the same time fascinating and beautiful. If I was honest with myself, she'd been on my mind morning, noon, and night since before I met her in person.

My dad stopped and hurried us along. "The fight is about to begin."

Devina and I jogged to keep up with my parents and Wilma but as we were about to enter the VIP area up front, I stopped them. "Wait. Everyone will be looking at Wilma and her entourage. It's better if Devina and I blend in with the crowd."

"It's Devin," my dad reminded me while my sister begged in a loud whisper:

"No, I want Devina with me. We're shielded off from the masses, so she'll be safer in the VIP area."

"Except everyone will be talking about who the boy is and you can't be seen whispering to a young male as if you're best friends. Think about it; if Devina's identity is a troubled boy, that would look suspicious."

With a pout, Wilma gave in and squeezed Devina's hands. "I'll see you later then."

"Okay." Devina looked to me for instruction and I assured her that we would meet up with the others later.

As the others walked ahead, I threw a nod. "Come on. Let's find some seats up back."

I stopped talking when we were swept up into a large group of Nmen all trying to get as close to the fight as possible. Devina looked small but kept her head down just like we had instructed her. With the hoodie covering parts of her face, no one would get a clear look. I thought I saw her pinch her nose and I didn't blame her. The reek of unwashed bodies was overpowering until we got up to the back row of the bleachers.

Devina sat down next to me and muttered a question, "Is hygiene not a thing here?"

We were at a distance from other spectators, but I still leaned forward and kept my head straight ahead, speaking almost without moving my lips. "Most of these men are camping in tents. You saw the large areas when we flew in."

"Uh-huh."

"Most of them arrived on Wednesday and they've filled their days watching fights and drinking beer. There's a lake about ten minutes from here where people go to bathe, but some don't bother and with the heat wave we've had, it makes little difference since we're all sweating like pigs anyway.

"You don't smell bad."

That comment made me turn my head and look at her. "You think I smell good?"

"Compared to this bunch, you smell lovely."

It was hard to keep a disinterested façade. "That's a first."

"What is?"

"No one has ever used the word lovely while describing anything related to me."

She was quiet for a few minutes as more people filled up the rows in front of us.

Using a deep voice to imitate a boy, Devina whispered, "I didn't realize that you'd have to give up good seats in order for me to come. I'm sorry about that."

I shrugged because I couldn't tell her that I was excited to be alone with her.

"Are you mad at me?"

"No. I'm doing this for my sister. It's not your fault."

When the two fighters entered the ring, they made a spectacle out of flexing their muscles and scowling at each other. This part was for the audience and I'd always felt stupid for doing it when I'd fought.

"What are they doing?"

"Pumping up the audience and trying to intimidate their opponent."

Devina's eyes widened. "Did he really just smack his chest like a caveman?"

"Wayne is a show-man, but he's got the skills to back it up. He's a great fighter and one of Wilma's favorites because he's only twenty-eight and charming."

She crossed her arms. "But look at the way he prances around."

I had seen more than thirty fights these past few days and even though this was one of the finals and I had bet money on Wayne, I was more focused on Devina's reaction to the fight than the actual fight itself.

When the two men began throwing punches through the air, the audience cheered, while she squeezed her eyes closed. It didn't take long before she was pushing herself back against the barrier behind us as if it could swallow her whole and take her away from the violence in front of her. Both her hands were formed into fists and pressed against the lower part of her face.

"You okay?"

"No."

"Just remember they pay to be here. The contestants and the audience members. We all love this."

Shaking her head in a slow movement, she looked at me. "How can you enjoy another's pain?"

I gave a grimace. "I wouldn't say that I enjoy their pain, but for someone to win there has to be a loser and I want my sister to marry the strongest protector. You get that, right?"

"Even if it means that he's a violent lunatic?"

I frowned. "He won't be violent toward her."

"How do you know for sure?"

"Because if he is, she can divorce him and that would be the most humiliating thing a man could ever experience."

"To get divorced?"

"Yes. The prestige of winning a wife is enormous and for someone to screw it up and mistreat a woman is unthinkable. A husband is expected to protect and care for his woman. We have so few women that they are considered the most rare and precious thing in our country."

"Women aren't things."

"You know what I mean."

For two rounds of fighting, we didn't talk. Devina looked sick but stayed in her seat.

When Wayne jumped up into the air and planted his foot in the other man's face, blood spurted out and a loud roar of excitement was heard from the audience, who rose to their feet just as Wayne's opponent fell backward.

We were sitting high up and with no one blocking our view, we could see it all.

"Oh, Mother Nature." Devina gasped, her eyes fixed on the fight ring where Wayne was waltzing around with a cocky attitude, riling up the audience.

Men of the North – FORBIDDEN LETTERS

"He's taunting him." Devina tucked her sleeves over her hands and pulled the hoodie closer as if she could shield herself from what was happening in the fight ring.

"The audience loves a show and Wayne is popular because he always delivers." My words were unnecessary since the wild cheers and stamping feet from the audience told that much.

Not far from us a man in a tank top and a leather vest stood cheering with his fist swinging in the air. "Wayne. You're the fucking champion. Kill the loser."

Devina's eyes went from the man to me and in her eyes, I read the question that she didn't ask. She wanted me to assure her that he wasn't serious. I looked straight ahead.

When the man on the ground tried to get up with slow and uncoordinated movements, Devina whispered as if she was speaking to him, "Don't get up."

The man couldn't hear her and kept pushing up from the floor.

"I think he suffered a severe concussion."

"Could be," I agreed.

"Then he should stay down."

It was clear Devina didn't understand the rules of fighting.

The man on the floor made it up on all fours and was trying to lift his knee to find his footing when Wayne planted a solid kick in his ribs that made him groan out in deep pain.

Laughter and boos followed when the man on the floor vomited.

By now Devina's foot was tapping like she wanted to run away. "Why don't they stop it? He clearly needs medical treatment."

Some of the people in our row looked over.

"Stop tapping your foot," I muttered low enough for only her to hear. "It's making the bleachers vibrate and people are looking over. Play it cool and pretend you're either bored or enjoying the show."

"But can't you see the poor man needs help? Why don't they stop the fight?"

"The only one who can stop is himself."

"How? He's throwing up and he's injured."

"Unless he gives up, the fight continues."

Like a true performer, Wayne was showing disgust for his opponent by making faces of revulsion and pulling the man away from the pile of vomit. The fact that he pulled him by his hair made the audience laugh and for the first time in my life I didn't feel amused by any of it.

The empathy and distress that radiated from Devina made me see our culture through her eyes and it wasn't pretty. "All of this happens with consent, you know. We love the adrenaline kick of fighting and every time I walk into a ring, I understand that it comes with a risk. So do the men down there."

"Why doesn't he give up then? He has to understand that he's losing."

"Because giving up a fight means giving up your dignity."

"So?"

I sucked in a deep breath and spoke on my exhalation. "A life without honor and dignity is no life at all."

Devina couldn't fathom what honor meant to us Nmen, and it wasn't something I could explain to her in a few mumbled sentences.

In the ring, the loser was taking another round of beating to his face and from this distance he seemed unconscious.

"Kill, kill, kill," the men around us chanted and sure enough, Wayne lifted his elbow in the air.

"Close your eyes," I warned.

"Why? He's not really going to kill him, is he?"

A sunbeam landed on Wayne as he stood over his opponent. It made the perspiration on his face shimmer. Closing his eyes, he smiled like this was his moment in the spotlight.

"Kill, kill, kill," the audience continued, but instead of crushing the man's throat with his elbow, he spread out both arms and spun in a full circle until he faced Wilma and our parents.

The VIP section where Wilma was sitting was on the right side of the ring and I could see my sister smiling at Wayne. Unlike Devina, who saw only a monster, Wilma saw a strong and powerful warrior and she was pleased he was winning.

"He's giving her the choice."

"What choice?" Devina's fake bushy eyebrows were drawn so close they gave her a unibrow.

"Whether to spare the man's life or kill him."

Wilma rose to her full height and beamed from all the attention. Even from this distance I could see the blood rush in her eyes, but then my mother tugged at her dress and whispered something to her. Wilma turned her head in our direction and her shoulders fell.

Thank you, Mom. My chest eased a little. I had no doubt Wilma would have asked for the kill, but my mother had reminded her that a Motlander was watching and that Devina wouldn't understand that killing the man on the floor was the kind thing to do.

"Let him live," Wilma said and sat down again. My dad shook his head in disappointment and the audience booed.

"As you wish." Wayne bowed his head to her and the referee came to raise his hands in victory.

With the loser lying passed out on the floor, the audience rose up on their feet and applauded the winner.

"Get up." I pulled Devina up with a strong hand to her arm.

"Just so you know, I'm only clapping because he spared his life."

"Wilma only made that choice because of you."

"Then it was a good thing I came today."

I frowned. "You have no idea how much that man is going to hate being spared."

She gave me a skeptical glance, so I continued my low mutter, "It's different in the early rounds, but this was a champion fight and it's always to the death. Being spared by a woman will make him a laughing stock wherever he goes."

"But at least he'll be alive."

"Yes, but it will take years for him to rebuild his pride."

Devina arched a brow and looked deep into my eyes. "And he'll have those years now. Maybe if he uses his time wisely, he'll come to realize that what others think of him is of little importance."

"Wow." I let the audience leave to avoid getting caught up among them again.

"What?"

"Just turn down your Motlander vibe. It makes you sound like a girl."

"I'm hot." She pulled at the blue hoodie and blew down the front. My mom and sister hadn't thought this through. It was August and we were in the middle of a heat wave. Devina would be the only one wearing a sweatshirt and she would be dying before noon if the heat continued to rise.

"Let's keep you hydrated." I got up and counted on her to follow me.

A man waited by the stairs, and as we passed him, he smiled at her. "Hey there."

I put a strong hand on her shoulder and guided her in front of me.

"Oh, I see, I didn't realize that you and the boy were a couple."

To be accused of being gay in public was a first and I scowled at him. "We're not, but he's under my protection, so fuck off."

He was tall but not as well-muscled as most men. "Don't worry, I can keep a secret. Let me know if you want company."

I didn't have time to respond because Devina hurried down the stairs and I followed.

Finding a food stand, I bought her a large bottle of water and pressed it into her hand. "Drink this."

"You have money?"

"Uh-huh. Do you want something else?

"No, I meant that it's surprising to see actual money notes. We got rid of the monetary system more than eighty years ago. Now there's a fair distribution of resources through the point system I talked about. Meaning that people contribute in any way they can and in return everyone is taken care of."

"Wouldn't you rather have money, so you could buy stuff?"

She looked around at the men passing by us. "I've never thought about it."

"Money and prestige are why so many are risking their lives in this tournament."

She took a sip of the water and gave me a piercing look. "I thought they did it to marry Wilma and find love."

I straightened up. "Yeah, that too of course."

Raising her chin, she assessed me. "Which comes first?"

"Love."

"You sure?"

"Marrying means the chance to start your own family and to me that's everything."

"Are you going to marry then?"

I looked down and dried off droplets from my water bottle. "If I'm lucky. There's a tournament next year that I'm considering, but..."

"But what?"

I shook my head. "I don't want to talk about it."

"Why not?"

Shrugging my shoulders, I didn't answer.

"Is it because you worry about getting killed?"

"No. It's just that..." I sighed and shifted my weight. "You wouldn't understand."

Devina pulled at her sweatshirt like she wanted to take it off and then she walked over to sit on a bench that stood in the shade of a tree. "What does it matter if I understand? I'm here for research and you're my source of inspiration. I'm trying to get inside your head."

"Ha!" I laughed and joined her on the bench. "Trust me, you don't want to know my thoughts."

"Maybe I do."

I leaned back on the bench and rested my arms behind me. "You've read the five pages I sent you. You know what's on my mind."

"Ehh... you mean sex?"

I gave her a wicked smile.

"Okay, so would you say that sex crosses your mind sometimes, often, or all the time?"

Leaning forward I placed my elbows on my thighs. "You sure you want the truth?"

"I'm not scared of the truth."

"Well, in that case the truth is that when I'm around you, sex is pretty much all I think about."

"Hmm..." She crossed her legs. "I wondered about that because you never answered the question in my last letter."

"Spread your legs."

"Excuse me?"

"A boy doesn't fucking cross his legs like that. Spread out and look masculine."

She uncrossed and leaned back while spreading her legs. "Better?"

"Yeah." I was scanning the area making sure no one was on to her. "I got your letter. I just haven't had time to answer you."

"You could do it now."

"All right. We do have sex-bots, but they are expensive to use."

"Have you tried one?"

"Uh-huh. But I imagine it's nothing compared to the real thing. What about that in-and-out massage you talked about. How often do you get it?"

She didn't even hesitate before answering me, "I used to do it twice a month but since I came back, I haven't had any." Taking another large gulp of her water she frowned at me. "Why are you grinning like that?"

"Because never in a million years did I think you'd answer me. I can't believe how casual you are about sex."

"Massage isn't sex. It's just a way to satisfy a physical need and release stress."

I moved a little closer and lowered my voice. "If you really feel that way then how about you let *me* massage you?"

"Are you qualified?"

"Very!"

"No, I mean did you have training?"

"Do you need training to finger a woman?" Putting out my hands in front of me I turned them around. "I have strong hands and I guarantee that my fingers are longer and bigger than any of the ones you've tried in the Motherlands."

I expected her to move away or get offended, but Devina's voice danced with humor. "There's a technique to it and since you have no experience with massaging women, I don't consider you qualified."

"Then teach me." There was a raw eagerness to my tone.

My eyes were fixed on her as she moved her body toward me and for a moment we just stared into each other's eyes. We had done it before but always as a sort of power struggle when we disagreed. This time it was different and we both had small smiles on our faces.

"Please, Devina." It came out as a whisper.

"Why would you want to?"

My eyes grew a little. "Why? Look around you. Most of these men will live a whole life without ever touching a woman's soft skin. To massage you would be a dream."

She looked thoughtful. "We're not talking about sex, you understand that, right?"

My throat felt so tight like I was afraid of saying the wrong thing. If there was the slightest possibility that this beautiful woman would let me massage her, then I would die a happy man. "No, I know. Just a massage."

Devina exhaled and looked around at the people passing us. "Maybe one day if we're alone."

"I can arrange for us to be alone any time you want to."

For the first time, she nailed the obstinate teenage look when she crossed her arms and leaned back. "My altruistic nature feels that it's only fair that I let you explore too. After all, you're risking your life to let me research what it's like on this side of the border. Letting you massage me seems like a minor thing, but I worry that you might not be able to control yourself if I'm naked in your hands."

My Adam's apple jumped in my throat. "Did you say naked?"

She looked away when she spoke. "Yeah. I know how strong you are and that if you decide to take it further than I wish to go, I won't have a way to stop you."

"You're messing with me, aren't you? You wouldn't really be naked."

She frowned. "Who gets massages with clothes on?"

"So, you're not messing with me?" My hands ran through my hair. "I'm so confused."

"Where I come from a massage requires that you take off all your clothes. Nudity isn't a big deal to us, but if that makes you uncomfortable..."

"No!" I shook my head. "No, of course not. I mean, I'd probably be a little nervous, but damn... the thought alone."

She sighed. "You're making it sexual. I told you it's not."

Leaning back, I held up a hand. "No, it's not. I promise!"

For a moment she didn't speak, but just looked around us, taking in all the people walking in all directions. I was watching two men pranking their friend by pulling his pants down and laughing. They were young and foolish, but their friend laughed with them and tried to trip one of them up in retaliation. My attention was pulled back to Devina when she spoke again.

"This morning when you said that we Motlanders are asexual, I know you meant it as an insult, but it's true. I mean, there are couples of course, but most of us fill our lives with friends and family." The moment she said family a ghost of sadness swiped across her face.

To hide the sadness, she leaned her head back and drank more of the water.

"You okay?"

"Yes, except..." She began looking all around her. "I really have to use the bathroom."

CHAPTER 19
Bathroom Break

Devina

"Oh shit. Do you think you can hold it for a few more hours?"

"Hours?" I'd just drunk a liter of water. "Don't they have bathrooms here?"

Tyton shook his head with a small grin. "Yeah, but here's the dilemma. There's one area dedicated to women and you can't go in there with you being disguised as a boy. That leaves one of the men's bathrooms which are more like a large row of urinals with a few stalls."

"All right, then I'll just take one of the stalls."

"You sure you want to do that?" Tyton looked skeptical. "They're disgusting and if I can, I always hold it until I get back home."

"I just have to pee."

He scratched his ribs and the contact between the gray t-shirt and his skin made the fabric moist. Clearly, I wasn't the only one sweating from the heat.

"We could take the drone and fly to a private place."

"You mean your house?"

"No, that's too far. I mean somewhere quiet like a field or bush where you can relieve yourself without anyone watching."

"Except for you."

He gave me a wry smile. "I promise to turn my back."

"I don't know… it sounds like a lot of work to fly away. How about we try the bathrooms here first?" I was here on an adventure and seeing a nitty-gritty detail like the toilets at a bridal tournament seemed like solid research.

Even with Tyton's warning, I was still hit by the strong stench of ammonia in the bathroom. At least twenty men stood in a long row and peed down a long metal-colored basin of sorts. I hadn't understood what he meant by urinals since standing up while peeing was a new thing to me. My dad and brother had always sat down like normal people. I knew because with one bathroom and eight of us in the house, it hadn't been unusual to have a family member come in to pee while I was taking a shower.

For a moment, I stared at the way the men held their penises in their hands and then shook them before tucking them back in their pants.

"Stop staring." Tyton elbowed me and it made me move past the men to a stall. As soon as I opened it, I backed out again. The stench was unbearable and made me want to gag.

I tried the two other stalls, but they made me hold my breath and cover my nose with my sleeve.

Keeping my right hand down I hurried to the only sink in the room and washed my hands. Having touched anything in this place gave me the creeps. Tyton came and pushed at my side, signaling for me to give him space to wash his hands too.

"Feces isn't supposed to smell like death and rot. It's all the animal-based products you people eat."

"Ha, and now you want me to believe that vegan poop smells of wildflowers and roses?"

I ignored his comment and frowned. "Why is there only one sink for all these men?"

"You're asking the wrong question. Do you see people lining up to use the sink?"

I looked back over my shoulder and only a few were waiting to wash their hands.

"You people really need to work on hygiene."

Bending forward and taking time to scrub his hands clean, Tyton muttered. "I guess they didn't grow up with germophobic moms who taught them the importance of washing their hands."

"And you did?"

"Uh-huh. Joan is all about hygiene."

When we left the bathroom, I held my head down and avoided eye contact. I'd been trying to hold my breath for most of the time in there and now that we came back out, I was feeling overheated and dizzy. "I'm so hot."

"I know, but you can't take off your shirt. Come on. Emmerson's fight is about to start, and I gambled half of my savings on him."

"Is Emmerson the one Wilma was hoping would make Champion?"

"Yeah, he's among the youngest of the fighters and a charming lad, but he's up against a strong finalist who made champion in the last tournament with me and Frederick. That's why the odds are against him and I can make a fortune on his victory."

"What happens if he loses the fight?"

Tyton groaned. "Ehh... my sister will be disappointed, and I'd lose thousands of dollars."

"At the last tournament... how many fights did you win to make champion?"

"Five."

I leaned my head back to look up at him. "And still it wasn't enough?"

"No. In the end, Starr chose Frederick."

"Do you know why?"

He shrugged as we walked to the nearby arena. "I've wondered about it, but it's bad manners to ask such questions of a woman, so the truth is that I have no idea."

"What time is it?"

"Nine forty-five."

Tyton stopped by the entrance to arena four where a guy was selling snacks and beverages "Do you want some more water?"

Men of the North – FORBIDDEN LETTERS

"No. I still have to use the bathroom, remember."

He frowned. "But you can hold it, right?"

"I'll try."

"Look, if you can hold it for this fight, we can take off and find a spot where you can also get that thick hoodie off for a little while.

Rolling up my sleeves, I looked up at the sun. We had found seats that were in the shade from the cover of the arena, but it was only a matter of time before the sun would move and leave us bathed in the pressing heat.

When Wilma arrived with the rest of her family, everyone stood up and bowed their heads to her.

Like a princess from a forgotten time, she waved her hand and smiled at them while keeping her back straight and her head high.

"Is that Frederick?" I asked when a man pulled out a chair for her.

"Yes. Next to him is his wife, Starr, and then there's my middle sister Claire behind them with her husband, Lucas. And the last couple is Marni and her pain of a husband, Henry."

"Where are all their children?"

"The only one old enough to come is Marni's son Knight, but he got in trouble with Henry yesterday so they're probably punishing him by making him stay home with his younger brothers."

"Did you say his name was Night?"

"Yes, but with a k in front."

"Ahh, like a king's knight. I get it. You Nmen have the most peculiar names, but I'm happy to hear that at least you don't submit young children to watching public killings."

Tyton rolled his eyes. "No, typically, we wait until they're twelve years old."

A large man came out in the fight arena and was received with cheers. A presenter introduced him, but I didn't catch his name. From Wilma's reaction to his opponent as that one stepped up in the arena and raised his hands to the audience, I knew the large man had to be Emmerson.

"Didn't you say he was young?"

"He's twenty-six."

From our seats back in the arena, he looked older with his enormous size, beard, and all those tattoos on his bare suntanned torso. His shoulder-length hair was braided close to his head and he stood with such confidence that I already felt sorry for his opponent, who looked to be at least ten years older.

"I can see why she likes Emmerson better," I whispered.

"Yeah? And why is that?" Tyton squared his shoulders and straightened up in his seat.

"He's younger and better-looking."

Despite Tyton's being quiet, I sensed his displeasure, so I turned my head. "What's the matter?"

"Nothing."

"Then why do you look like I dunked your head down one of those disgusting toilets that they have here?"

"I don't."

"You're angry about something. Did I say something that upset you?"

"I just don't appreciate you pointing out your attraction to other men when I'm around."

I stared at him like he'd lost his mind. "I've never been attracted to a man in my life." Somewhere in the back of my mind a little voice began questioning that, because there had been that erotic dream the other night.

"Okay, but then be honest. If you were to choose between me and Emmerson, who would you pick?"

I laughed and shook my head.

"Who would you choose?"

Since it was clear as glass that this meant a lot to Tyton, I went with the polite answer. "I would choose you of course."

"You would?" There was such relief in his almost boyish smile that it made me laugh, and people turned around in their seats to see what was going on.

Tyton and I had been so engulfed in our bubble that we hadn't noticed people coming close enough to hear us.

The moment we realized that several were watching us, I closed my mouth and shrank in my seat.

"Hey, boy, what's so funny?" one of them called out.

I ignored him and kept my eyes on Emmerson and his opponent, who were preparing for the game by riling each other and the audience up.

"Aren't you hot with that thick sweater on?" the same man asked. "Who wears a hoodie when it's this hot?"

Tyton leaned forward, blocking the man's view of me. "The boy has a condition. It's nothing for you to worry about."

"What kind of condition?"

"His skin reacts to sun, so he has to cover up at all times."

"That sucks. How old is he?"

"Fourteen."

"All right, well, you enjoy the fighting now," The man turned back to face forward and watch the action himself.

I kept quiet and suffered through another round of fighting as brutal as the first one. Midway through, the sun reached us and the men around us stripped out of their shirts.

Tyton was half into taking off his shirt when he asked, "You don't mind if I take it off, do you?"

"No. I'm just envious."

"Do you have anything on underneath?"

"Yes, a top and a t-shirt."

"Can't you take that off at least?"

It was a bit of a trick to get the t-shirt off while still wearing the big hoodie, but because it was so baggy, I managed without anyone but Tyton noticing.

"Better?"

"A little, but I wish I had a fan." I threw a nod to the VIP section, where Wilma and seven other women sat with electric fans in front of them.

"Let's hope Emmerson knocks out his opponent and gets a quick victory."

With a sound of agreement, I leaned back and since I had zero interest in the fighting, I studied Tyton's broad shoulders and back. It was incredible how large all these men were compared to our men at home. He was resting his elbows on his thighs and even without flexing there were still bumps of muscle on his arms.

My mind was occupied by taking mental notes and putting words to all the strangeness around me.

The large turkey legs that men chewed on and ripped pieces off with their teeth. The large cups of beers that they drank like it was water, and the group to my left who smoked something with a spicy smell.

I watched how they shared things, like when one brought back six beers and handed them to people around him or when the man who lit up the strange device that he used for smoking passed it around to others around him.

At one point when Emmerson threw a mean punch, a man nine rows down from us stood up and called Emmerson a long row of curse words. It provoked another man in the audience who had been cheering for Emmerson and he threw the bone from his turkey leg at the critic but hit a third man instead.

The three of them now stood across a sea of people and shouted obscenities at each other.

"They're missing out on the fight," I said after having been silent since the whole thing began.

Men of the North – FORBIDDEN LETTERS

"You're right, but the later in the day, the more fights break out among the audience members. People get drunk and stupid."

When others rose from their seats and shouted for the three men to sit down, Tyton leaned in and whispered, "I don't like this. Unless security comes to calm them down, we'll have to get out of here. I don't want to get caught in a massive brawl."

"I wouldn't mind leaving now. I'm melting from the heat." I'd been wanting to ask him if we could leave but was afraid of sounding whiny.

Tyton kept staring at the fight, where Emmerson and the other man were going at each other. I envied Wilma, who sat in a short-sleeved dress with a fan in front of her. She was in the shade and still hot. I was in the blazing sun and felt like dying.

"Just hang on for a minute." Tyton was invested in the fight and had bet a lot of his money on it.

For another five minutes I sat in agony. With my sweat dripping down from my wet hair into my eyes, I was worried about the glue of the fake eyebrows. Joan had given me extra glue in case I needed it, but I would need a mirror to apply it.

When I felt dizzy and weak like jelly, I touched his arm. "Tyton, if you take me to a cold place, I'll be forever grateful. I'm so hot."

"Yeah, I will, just... I think Emmerson has him now." Tyton wasn't looking at me but focused on the fight.

I couldn't wait for Emmerson any longer. If I didn't get out of here, I would faint from overheating. Even now, I was worried that I would fall down the stairs if I tried walking.

"Tyton..."

"Uh-huh?" He kept his eyes on the fight.

My voice was weak when I spoke in desperation. "If you get me out of here, I'll let you massage me."

"Say what?" He swung around to see me, but by then I could hardly keep my eyes open.

"Holy shit." His eyes grew big when he saw what state I was in. "Why didn't you say something?"

"I can't breathe." It was the last thing I said before my eyes rolled back and my body went limp.

CHAPTER 20
Emergency

Tyton

I'd been so occupied by the fight that I'd failed to see the state Devina was in.

She was over heating and I needed to cool her down, right now.

My instinct was to pull off her shirt, but that would lead to a disaster. If I asked for water and poured it on her, others would get involved and pull her hoodie down.

My only choice was to put her over my shoulder and carry her out of there.

"What's wrong with him?" people asked as I pulled Devina over my shoulder and began making my way to the stairs.

"Someone alert the paramedics," I heard people call out, but I didn't stop. With a firm grip around her, I ran down the stairs and kept going despite all the shouting asking if I needed help.

Rushing to the VIP area, I was led in by security.

"What happened?" one of them asked with concern.

"Oh, just a fight. He got knocked out, but it was well deserved. The boy can be cocky." It was hard keeping my face straight and sounding nonchalant about it when I was worried out of my mind.

"Ahh..." The two security guards nodded with understanding.

As I passed a bar area, I grabbed a large bottle of water from an ice-bucket and continued to my drone.

After getting Devina inside, I cranked up the air conditioning on full power and buckled her in.

"Let's find you a cool lake," I muttered and took off.

As we lifted from the area I didn't even look to see if Emmerson was still standing down in the arena. Money and fights meant nothing to me right now. If Devina died of a heat stroke, we would have a big fucking problem on our hands and I would never forgive myself. What kind of protector would miss how much she had meant it when she had told me she was hot?

I was so used to Wilma's fussing and whining that I hadn't taken Devina seriously. Once again, I was reminded about how different Motlanders were from us Northlanders.

As the drone took us away from the tournament, over fields and toward a large forest area, the cabin was cooling down fast.

"Devina, wake up." I reached out my hand and shook her shoulder, but only weak moaning sounds came from her and her head still hung down to one side.

Lake Mino, a favorite spot for tournament-goers, was close but many came here to bathe and we would need somewhere private.

"We're almost there," I promised her and flew as fast as I could.

A minute later, I set down the drone in a meadow Frederick had shown me during the tournament where he won Starr. Pulling Devina out of the drone I carried her in my arms and kept talking to her. "Come on, wake up, pixie."

I saw her eyes flicker and roll back in her head as I moved fast toward the small creek. It ran along the edge of the meadow in the shade of the trees and ever since I'd first visited this place four years ago, I'd loved the tranquility of it. Now it would help me save Devina.

I kicked off my shoes and set her down on the brink of the water before I jumped down into the stream. It was

Men of the North – FORBIDDEN LETTERS

low water and only came to my knees, making my pants wet. "Come on, let's get you cooled off."

I didn't take off any of Devina's clothes before I brought her down in the creek with me.

As soon as the cold water washed over her and soaked her clothes, she opened her eyes and sucked in a breath.

The confusion on her face made me tighten my grip around her body. "You're fine. You just overheated and now I'm cooling you down."

For a while she didn't speak. She just let the cold water run over her and then she lifted her hand and used it as a bowl to drink some of the water and spit it out again.

"It's clean. You can drink it."

"You sure?"

"Yes."

"How did we get here?"

"I carried you."

She looked up at me. "I'm sorry."

"Why? *I'm* the clown who didn't get you out of the sun in time. You told me you were hot, but I just didn't understand how bad it was."

Closing her eyes, Devina leaned her head back. Her long hair had been tied back in a ponytail but she removed the hairband and let it out. "This is nice."

"I know. But it soaked your clothes so now you don't have anything to wear when we go back."

The sun was peeking out from the trees around us and blinded her for a moment. Shielding her eyes with a hand she kept her body submerged in the shallow water. "Can't we let it dry in the sun?"

"Ehh... we could but..." I looked around. "The problem is that I lost both our t-shirts when I carried you to the drone."

She didn't respond or look worried.

"What I'm trying to say is that if you take off the hoodie I don't have anything for you to cover yourself with."

133

"It's okay, I still have my top on underneath."

"Good." I pointed to her shirt. "If you take it off, I can wring out the water as much as possible."

I tried not to ogle her when she stood in her pants and a top that covered only her breasts. Instead I used all my strength to get the water out of the blue hoodie.

"Tyton, would you mind if I take off my pants to dry them as well?"

"No, of course not."

"I'll keep on my panties since nudity makes you so nervous."

I was in the process of placing her sweater and my shorts in the sun and looked down at her in the creek. "I never said that nudity made me nervous. I'm just unfamiliar with female nudity, that's all."

Devina stayed in the cold stream for minutes.

"Are you feeling better?"

"Yes."

"Do you want to come up and dry?"

The creek was low, and she sat on the bottom with her chest covered by the water. "Do I have to?"

"No. But if you wanted me to wring out the water from your pants, you'll have to give them to me."

"It's fine. I'll be up in a second." She stayed another few minutes before she stood up and stepped to the edge. "Will you pull me up?"

I took her outstretched hands and helped her out of the creek and up into the meadow full of wildflowers.

My eyes wouldn't listen when I asked them to look away as she stepped out of the baggy boy pants right in front of me. She was naked except for her plain black top and panties, and I couldn't stop admiring her soft curves and slim waist.

Her attempt at wringing the water out of her pants was pitiful so I stepped forward with my pulse racing. "Here, let me."

"Thank you. I feel weak still."

"No wonder. Only fifteen minutes ago you were passed out from a heat stroke. Did you drink a lot in the stream?"

"Yes."

"I wish I'd brought some food, but I didn't think of it."

"What about towels? Any chance you have some in your drone?"

"I'm afraid not. Sorry."

She shrugged. "It's okay, the sun will dry us."

Like a fragile old person, she got down on the ground with slow movements. "Tyton."

"Mmm?"

"I'm so sorry that I took you away from the tournament. I know how much it means to you and you have a lot of money on the line with Emmerson. Did he win?"

"I don't know. But it's okay. Don't worry about it. As long as we're back for the ceremony tonight, we'll be fine."

"What time is that?"

"At eight."

"Okay." Devina lay down on her stomach, using her hands as pillows. "Does that mean we have time for a nap while our clothes dry? I haven't slept much these past nights and I'm tired."

Seeing her lying on a bed of wildflowers had to be the most erotic sight of my life, but I was determined not to scare her again.

"Sure, you can take a nap."

I wanted to ask about the massage she had mentioned, but no part of me found it okay after she had just been passed out. Instead, I lay down beside her and closed my eyes listening to the calming sound of the stream and the subtle wind playing in the trees.

"This is a nice place."

"Uh-huh."

I was on my back when she turned on her side and moved a little closer.

"Can I tell you something, Tyton?" Her voice sounded drowsy, like she was close to falling asleep.

"Sure."

"I miss my family a lot." She paused but I sensed there was more that she wanted to say. "I miss their hugs and kisses. Sometimes I would cuddle up with one of my siblings and we'd sleep in the same bed. Now, there's only Nellie."

"Your dog?"

She nodded. "Does your family kiss and hug you a lot?"

"Not really. Not since I was a child."

"Do you ever miss it?" She yawned. "Physical contact, I mean."

I hesitated before telling her the truth. "Yeah, I miss it, but I'm a grown man. Who would I cuddle with?"

"My youngest sister used me as her pillow. I would play with her hair and draw on her skin. It was one of my favorite things."

Noticing how her voice broke a little, I lifted my head and looked over at Devina, who had her eyes closed. "Are you crying?"

"I'm sorry."

My lungs felt constricted because I couldn't stand seeing her upset. "Do you want me to get you something or tell you a joke?"

"No." She rolled to her back and dried her eyes with her hands. "But would you hold my hand?" One of her fake eyebrows was hanging loose and the other one was crooked.

"Of course I will."

"I think these need to dry too." Pulling the eyebrows off she sat up and leaned over to place them on top of her pants, which lay in the sun.

Our bodies were still cold from the water in the creek, but it felt perfect to me.

Holding out my hand to her I watched her with curiosity. It was the first time she had asked me to touch her and it excited me.

Still sitting up, she turned to me. "If you want you can use me as a pillow."

"Ehh... How does one use you as a pillow?" I asked.

"Hannah would find the softest place to rest her head." She patted her stomach and lay back down again.

Turning my body, I lowered the back of my head to rest on her stomach. At first, I was careful and tense, but then her fingers began weaving through my hair and I closed my eyes and relaxed.

"Every time Hannah and I did this she would say the same thing."

"What did she say?"

"Promise not to fart." Devina gave a small laugh but with the way her voice shook I knew nothing about this was amusing to her.

"I'm so sorry you lost them."

"Me too. I don't think I'll ever be whole again."

It was tempting to try and distract her from her sadness, but I sensed that she needed to remember them, so instead, I encouraged her by saying, "Tell me about your family."

For a long time, Devina told me about them. Her grandmother, who had been a healer, and her biological mother, who had a fierce temperament for a Motlander and who had loved antique romance books.

The other mother in the family unit had been an amazing cook and spoiled all the children.

All the while, talking about her siblings, she was emotional. Some stories made her cry while others made her laugh a little. She had been present when her youngest sister Hannah was born and told me about her pride when the doctor asked her to cut the umbilical cord. Her fingers kept playing with my hair and for the most part I said very little.

Being this close to another person was new to me. I loved my family, but we didn't curl up and talk about things that made us cry. For her to share such a vulnerable moment with me made me fall even deeper in love with her.

Rolling to my side, I faced her but kept my head on her stomach. "You know what fascinates me about women?"

Devina had been quiet for a while but opened her eyes to look at me.

"The fact that you can give life." I placed my hand on her stomach next to my face. "A person can grow inside you, and it freaking blows my mind how big of a miracle that is."

She wrinkled her forehead. "I'll have to look into that soon. I promised my nana that I would have a child."

"You mean in one of those clinics?"

"Yeah." She yawned again. "But I'll finish my book first, I think."

"What if you didn't go to a clinic?" I should keep my mouth shut, but it spilled out of me.

"My family tree would die out. I promised her not to let that happen."

"But what if instead of going to a clinic and having an anonymous donor, you had a child with me?"

Devina still had her eyes closed and covered her mouth when she yawned again. "You want to donate your sperm to me?"

"Any time."

"Hmm, we should use that in the book. Mark could get Deidra pregnant like back in the old days. That would fit well with the romance genre, but I'd have to write the book under a pen name or I would get angry letters."

"Why?"

"Because of... you know..."

I lifted my head a little. "No, I don't know."

"The clinics guarantee the healthiest outcome since they make sure there aren't any unwanted chromosomes that could result in syndromes and that sort of thing."

"Ahh..." I lowered my head to her stomach again. "I still prefer the old-fashioned way of creating life. The thought of impregnating a woman is the biggest turn-on to any man. If you would let me be the father of your child, I would be the happiest man on earth."

I waited for her response but her heavy breathing told me she had fallen asleep.

There was something magical about being in one of my favorite spots in the world with a gorgeous woman who trusted me enough to fall asleep in my presence.

She had been scared of me after her first visit, but the writing we had shared and the hours at the tournament had made her lower her guard around me.

Feeling afraid that my head was too heavy on her stomach, I turned and lay on my back next to her. She looked peaceful as her chest rose and fell with deep breaths. Her lips were slightly parted and being so close to her, I could see how long her dark lashes really were.

It was tempting to trail a finger along the bridge of her nose just like I used to do with Wilma when she was little, but I settled for holding Devina's hand like she had asked me to.

Closing my eyes, I surrendered myself to the peaceful tranquility of the murmuring and bubbling sounds from the creek mixed with chirping birds in the distance, and that calming sound of the tree tops swaying ever so lightly from the wind.

"Thank you," I muttered low because even though Devina was fast asleep and wouldn't hear me, I felt a deep sense of gratitude in my heart that she was here with me.

CHAPTER 21
Dreams

Devina

The comforting sound of my brother's soft snoring made me smile. I had missed being close to Justin and was quick to cuddle up against him. He made a small sound of protest when I arranged my head on his shoulder and swung my legs over his thigh.

"Mmm." It felt so nice to be close to him again. We had done this often when he was little. Justin had been the biggest snuggle-bug of all of us, but lately he'd complained he got too hot when we cuddled, and I didn't visit my family as often as I'd like to. With him being sixteen he was bigger than me. My hand rested on his chest and part of my brain registered that it was harder than I remembered. And since when did Justin have a dusting of hair on his chest?

Opening one eye, I saw that my dream of cuddling up with Justin had resulted in my wrapping myself around Tyton but when I stiffened, he turned his head and kissed the top of my hair.

"Ehh... I dreamed that you were my brother," I explained and tried to pull away.

"Don't stop." His arm came around me. "I dreamt that you were my wife."

"Is that why you kissed me?" I should be moving but despite the initial awkwardness it felt nice to be this close to him.

"Uh-huh."

"And what did I look like in your dream?"

"You had large brown eyes and long thick lashes." His voice was hoarse from sleep.

"I have that in real life. I thought you said you dreamt of your wife. Don't you have some imaginary dream woman?"

"Yeah."

"Tell me about her."

"She's my age."

"But I thought all brides were fifteen?"

"They are, but we're talking about my dream woman."

"Okay, go on."

"She's intelligent and we can have real conversations, but the best part is that we're more than husband and wife. We're friends."

I smiled a little and didn't think about it when I raised my leg higher on his body.

With a hand on my thigh, he stopped my leg. "You don't want to go any higher than that."

The feeling of his strong hand on my naked thigh made me almost purr from the delightful sensation that spread inside me. I had read some of my mother's steamy romance novels and found them funny when they described arousal but being this close to Tyton, felt nothing like being cuddled up with my brother or sisters. My pulse was faster than normal, and I was aware of his body in a different way. The scent of him suddenly made me want to bury my nose against his skin.

Something was happening and like an automated part of me took over, I pressed a little closer to him.

In response he tightened his arm around me and began stroking my arm up and down.

"Tyton."

"Yeah?"

The way his heart was beating fast under my hand made it clear that I wasn't the only one affected by the situation.

"Does this feel weird to you?"

He stiffened. "Unusual would be a better word."

"Do you like being this close to me?"

"Uh-huh." His voice sounded raw.

"You know they say that physical contact is good against depression and it improves your immune system. That's why massages are encouraged."

"I didn't know that."

"So, in a way we're doing each other a favor." I made my tone light and cheerful as I let my fingers play with the hair on his chest. "What time is it? I left my watch at your house. You mom said it didn't go with the outfit."

Instead of removing his arm from under me, Tyton pulled me closer against his chest to see his watch, one that looked much more advanced than any watch I'd ever seen. "It's almost noon."

Afraid that he would say it was time to go back, I attempted small talk. "Your watch looks high-tech."

"It's a small computer. It's weird to me that you people have chosen to distance yourself from technology."

"It could change. Who knows, in a few hundred years we might be far ahead of you. We're just very cautious about technology. Maybe if our ancestors had been critical as well, we could have avoided the mass destruction of the Toxic War. To create technology with the power to annihilate the planet was…"

He cut me off and stirred under me. "I don't want to hear about us men being the villains again."

"All right. Then what about that massage you promised me?"

Again, he stiffened. "Ehh… you want me to massage you?"

"If my choice is between going back there to see more violent fighting or staying here and getting a nice massage, it's an easy choice. I'll even give you a massage too, if you want it."

This time Tyton sat up. Placing his hands on my shoulders he looked deep into my eyes. "Don't mess with me, Devina."

I laughed to ease the tension. "A massage isn't that big a deal."

"It might be the most natural thing in the Motherlands but trust me: to me it's a big fucking deal."

"Relax. You did fine when we snuggled up together, so just try and think of massage as a physical immune-system booster between friends."

His eyes widened. "You see me as your friend?"

"You've been very kind to me today and I've forgiven you for what happened when we first met."

Tyton shook his head like he had a hard time understanding what was happening.

"You've never had a female friend, have you?"

"No. Not unless you count my sisters."

I gave him a wide smile. "Then I'm proud to be your first."

The way his ears grew red and he swallowed hard made me tilt my head to the side. "Did I say something wrong?"

"No, not at all. I would be proud to be your first as well."

"My first Nman friend?"

"Yes..." He looked away.

"Since you have little to no experience massaging, how about I start with you, so you can get a sense of it?"

"Okay."

"It would be better if we had some lotion."

"I have some sun blocker in the drone. Will that work?"

"Sure."

Tyton got up and jogged to the drone. It allowed me time to watch his strong legs and back. Wearing only briefs, he was like something out of an old novel or movie.

Now that I'd seen hundreds of Nmen, I could see how well-proportioned he was and how he wasn't as pumped as some of the others. When he returned, he carried a bottle of water and the lotion.

"How tall are you?"

He stopped in front of me, squinting his eyes because of the sun. "I'm six foot five."

"We measure in meters, not feet."

Reaching out his hand, he pulled me up. "Then let's measure my height against yours. How many meters are you?"

Thinking I was being funny, I answered, "Twenty-two."

"Okay." He positioned himself up against me and used his hand to mark my height. "You reach my collarbone, so I'm about one and a half head taller than you. If you're twenty-two meters tall then..."

"No one is twenty-two meters tall. I was trying to be funny, but since you really don't know about meters, it fell flat."

"Oh. Then how many meters are you?"

"I'm one meter and sixty-three centimeters."

"Hmm." He scrunched his mouth. "I liked it better when you were twenty-two meters. That number was easier to calculate."

When he tapped his watch, which he'd said was a small computer, I cut in. "It doesn't matter. You're the tallest of my friends and close to two meters, I think." I took the lotion from his hand. "Now get your tall body down on the ground and let me give you your first massage."

Tyton's lips pursed. "Normally, I don't like taking orders, but this time I'm happy to comply."

I spread the lotion on his shoulders and began massaging him. Every part of his body was firm and with

Men of the North – FORBIDDEN LETTERS

some curiosity I took more mental notes to describe how Deidra would feel when she touched Mark in my book.

We didn't speak as I massaged his arms and fingers. He turned his head and I felt his eyes on me when I intertwined our fingers as part of the massage. "Do you like it?"

"Yes." For a moment we smiled at each other and another burst of butterflies made my stomach tingle.

After massaging both his arms, I moved on to his feet and then up his shins and thighs. "You're very tense; maybe you should get massages more often?"

"Maybe."

I skipped the part of his body covered by his briefs and moved up to the small of his back.

"Do you mind if I sit on you? It makes it easier for me to reach."

"Sit on me all you want."

We laughed about that and I crawled on top of him to sit astride his back.

"Is this how you massage at home?"

"Yes. It's good, isn't it?"

"And you want me to do the same to you?"

"If you want."

"No, for real, Devina. Are you sure you want me on top of you the way you're on top of me right now?"

"It's the best way to give a back rub."

He didn't respond so I kept going. "I'm almost done with your back and then you can turn over and I'll do the same to your front."

"Fuuuck." A low groan sounded from him

"Unless you don't want it of course."

Twisting his neck back to look at me, he narrowed his eyes. "Are you going to sit astride me if I turn around?"

I frowned, not sure what the problem was. "Do you mind?"

He gave an incredulous chuckle. "You have no idea how men work, do you?"

"I had a brother and a father. I'm not clueless."

"Oh yeah? So what happens when you sit astride your male friends and massage them?"

"I can only think of two friends that I've done it with and they were fine. We do this in school, you know."

"No fucking way."

"Yes, massaging is part of school. It's a good way to make children feel comfortable, relaxed, and accepted."

"You people are the weirdest bunch."

Getting off his back, I repeated, "If you turn over, I can massage your front."

"I can't right now."

"Why not?"

Turning his head, Tyton squeezed one eye together and wrinkled his nose. "Because I don't want you to be scared."

"Of what?"

"Of my major boner."

The look of confusion on my face made him elaborate, "You know what an erection is, right?"

By then, I understood, and I felt stupid for being so slow. "Yes, I know what it is."

"I get that this isn't sexual for you, but I can't control that I'm turned on by your closeness and your touch."

Again, that wild swirling inside my stomach made everything tingle and I involuntarily smiled. "You're turned on by me?"

"Very."

Having a man desire me was a first and it surprised me how a dormant female pride stretched and smiled inside of me. Tyton had already proven that he could be trusted. He had been alone with me in a secluded area for a few hours now and he hadn't taken advantage of the situation.

"I don't mind."

He stared at me. "That's because this all means nothing to you, but I'm not going to turn around and have you on top of me. If I do, I'll fucking come in my briefs."

"If you're so bothered by it, then you can massage me."

Closing his eyes, he gave a short nod. "Okay."

I got off him and he rolled away, letting me have his spot. Closing my eyes, I used my hands to rest my head on.

"Do you prefer it if I keep my top on?"

"Would you normally take it off?"

"Yeah, but I don't have to if this is hard for you." I turned and noticed his hand shaking a little when he pushed his hair back.

"Or I could take it off while you do my back and then I'll put it back on when you do my front. Would that be okay?"

"Uh-huh."

Because he couldn't look me in the eye, I asked again, "You sure?"

He looked serious when he nodded.

Pulling off my top, I closed my eyes again.

"Okay, Tyton, use those strong hands of yours." It was meant to be funny, but he was so tense that I felt a little bad for him. "Relax."

"I am relaxed."

"No, you're tense and serious. I get that it's the novelty of the situation, but on the other side of the border this is just an everyday thing."

Brushing my hair to one side, he began massaging my shoulders.

"Remember the lotion, it makes it easier."

"Oh, right."

It was clear that he had paid attention when I massaged him because he moved from my shoulders down my arms, fingers, and then down to my feet. Because we weren't talking, I listened to all the sounds of nature.

"How would you describe the sound the wind makes?"

"I don't know."

"When I studied to be an author, they taught us about onomatopoeia, which is a real fancy description of words that phonetically imitate a sound. Like a pig says oink and a cat says meow."

"I can't even pronounce it. What was it again – onamoto... something."

I laughed and said it slower this time. "Onomatopoeia."

"Pretty and smart."

"What did you say?"

"I said that you're both pretty and smart."

"That's funny, since twenty minutes ago, you thought I was clueless." I could have kicked myself for bringing back that awkward incident with his erection.

"You're just very innocent in your thought patterns. You trust people without knowing them for years, and it tells me you've never been exposed to much cruelty."

"I haven't."

"It's fascinating to me, and I'm both flattered and alarmed that you would put yourself in this situation."

I turned my head to look at him. "I trust you."

"I know. But I'm not sure you should. At the moment I'm not even sure I can trust myself."

"If you wanted to hurt me you would have done it already."

"See, you're doing it again. You have no idea how beautiful and tempting you are to me. It blows my mind that you're so fearless around me."

"You're pretty fearless around me too."

He chuckled. "Why wouldn't I be?"

"What if I decided to abuse you while you slept?"

"I wish."

"Bad example then, but I could have stolen your drone or something."

He was massaging the back of my knees and moved up to my thighs. "You're too sweet for that and it wouldn't work anyway."

"Why not?"

"Because you don't know how to fly a drone and you need my thumb print to start the engine."

"Oh, well, never mind then, but I'm just saying that you seem to trust me too."

"Because you can't hurt me."

"That's not true. I could have drawn attention to myself at the tournament and told them that you touched me. Remember your words from this morning about not getting you killed?"

He sighed. "Fair point."

Because he was massaging my inner thighs, I automatically spread my legs wider to give him space. It made him lose his rhythm and groan a little.

"You were right, Tyton."

"I'm always right, but what are you referring to?"

"Your hands are great for this. I'm enjoying it."

"Good." He kept massaging me and then he asked in a low voice. "About that in and out thing. Do you want me to do that?" His hands went higher, and it was starting to do funny things to my body.

"This is weird."

"What is?"

"Just now, I felt a tingling." I laughed because it felt silly that I'd react so differently to a massage I'd had hundreds of times before.

"You mean when I did this?" He had a firm grip on the outside of my thigh and let his other hand slide all the way up my inner thigh, only to stop before touching my most sensitive spot.

"If feels different when you do it. Maybe it's because I'm not just another client to you."

"Fuck no."

"I'm trying to use this for the book. I'm thinking Deidra and Mark could have a massage that goes into something more."

"That would be hot."

"I'm just not sure Motlanders would see it like that. I mean massages are so common and non-sexual that they might not think anything of it."

"Even if he goes this high?" Tyton's hand stopped all the way up with the tip of his fingers touching my panties.

"You're not doing anything but touching the fabric there. Maybe we've been desensitized but I feel like it would take a lot more before my audience would think of it as something sexual."

"Then he could remove her panties."

"I don't think that would matter. People are naked during massages back home.

"What if he pushed her panties to the side, like this?" I felt Tyton move his finger up under the fabric of my panties.

"I don't know."

His breathing changed, and he got bolder, squeezing my thighs tighter and pushing my legs apart. "Or what if he tasted her?"

My brow rose up and I kept looking at him. "Tasted her?"

"Yes, tasted her." As he said it, he lifted his finger to his mouth and licked it with a slow movement.

A surge of what could only be pure arousal shot through me. "They wouldn't expect that."

"Then why not let Mark turn Deidra around like this..."

I didn't resist when he turned me around, nor did I try to cover my breasts. I just listened as Tyton continued, "...and have him lick her cute pussy." His eyes were roaming over my body with burning desire and like something out of an antique novel, he hooked his arms around my thighs and pulled me to him. He gave me plenty

Men of the North – FORBIDDEN LETTERS

of time to protest when he dipped his head and kissed my pelvic bone.

I watched and promised myself that I'd remember all the amazing emotions going through my body at that time. "Wait."

Lifting his head again, Tyton looked stubborn like he wouldn't be pulled away from his favorite meal just yet.

"I think that could work, but isn't it weird if Mark does that to her, without their having even kissed first?"

"Would a massage involve kissing?"

"No, but it wouldn't involve this either." I pointed to him between my legs. "They could kiss in an earlier scene, before they get to this point."

He looked down at my panties and seemed reluctant to leave. "Are you asking me to stop?"

"No, I'm asking you to kiss me... as research for the book."

Moving up my body, Tyton lowered himself on top of me and looked into my eyes. "Just for the record. You might think of this as research, but I don't."

Lifting my hand, I let it run along his jawline and closed my eyes when he pressed his lips against mine and held them there for seconds. I'd been kissed plenty of times by family and friends, but Tyton's kiss felt different and the nerve endings on my lips reacted with a glorious feeling of curiosity and pleasure. Just when I thought he was going to end our kiss he instead deepened it and licked my lower lip.

Another tingle at my core made me spread my legs wider to accommodate the large man between my thighs. Tyton pushed a little higher and a hoarse growl reverberated from his chest. Surprisingly it ignited some primeval instinct in me. Opening my mouth, I let his tongue in. His words that he wasn't doing this for research, combined with the feeling of his weight on my body, his tongue raking over my lips and twirling around my tongue, made it feel like he was tearing away the map of the world that I'd carried with me my whole life.

Who knew that kissing could feel this good?

It was almost like there was a different dimension to life where loneliness and pain didn't have a place.

As if I were afraid he would stop kissing me, I lifted my legs and wrapped them around him. His moan told me he'd noticed, and he retaliated by fisting his hands into my hair and pressing himself harder against me.

Our kisses intensified as he grew more demanding, and I loved it when he moved from kissing my mouth to my ear and all the way down my neck to my breasts as if he wanted to taste and feel every part of me.

A sound of ecstasy rumbled from Tyton's throat when he began kissing and suckling on my breasts. "God, this is the best day of my life."

Lifting my hands up in a sort of surrender, I enjoyed watching the way he played with my nipples like they were a source of wonder. He pushed my breasts together and buried his head between them before licking and sucking some more. All the while I wondered how I'd gone from being scared of him to feeling completely safe with him in such a short time.

Missing his lips on mine, I pulled him back up. "We're not done kissing."

Those words fired him up and he tilted his head and gave me a deep and sensual kiss that felt like an invitation to once again probe, lick, and taste the most intimate part of him. I responded by tightening my arms around his shoulders and meeting his tongue with mine. With my heart beating, I welcomed the feeling of our bodies melting together and our breaths becoming one. With a small moan, I arched my spine up against him.

"Fuck!" Tyton's body was shaking with need and he kissed me with a ferocious hunger that eradicated all worry and grief from my mind.

"Yeees." Letting my hands move over his strong shoulders and back, I kept my eyes closed. It only enhanced every sound and touch.

"This feels like a wedding night." Moving his body up and into alignment with mine, he put weight on my midsection and it made me open my eyes and gasp.

The sensation of his erection pressing through his briefs against my panties felt like a small bombardment of my erogenous zones.

"Why didn't we know about this?" I whispered.

"Know about what?"

"How good sex feels?"

He bit into my neck and the touch of his teeth on my skin felt delicious and erotic.

"Mmm."

It was bliss to be this close to him, and as if our bodies were calibrating for something more to come, we found a rhythm of moving our hips back and forth against each other.

I didn't want it to end, but at the same time I was finding it hard to breathe. "You're crushing me," I moaned into his mouth.

In a smooth movement, Tyton turned us over and was now below me. His hands were on my behind and he was rotating against me while his eyes closed. "Fuck... this feels amazing."

With my hands on his chest, I saw his jaw tense and his facial color redden.

"Fuck, Devina, you don't know what you're doing to me."

"Do you need a break?" I was hoping he'd say no, but his chest was rising and falling and suddenly he picked me up and moved me to my back again. He didn't ask before he removed my wet panties, spread my legs, and placed kisses along my inner thighs.

"Ahhh…" It felt wonderful and then his kisses moved to the center and he began circling my sensitive spot with his tongue. "Oh, Tyton."

"Say my name again."

"Tyton. Yes… it feels so good."

He licked and sucked and even though I wanted to take mental notes for my book, all I could do was enjoy it.

His fingers spread my moistness around and he made a comment that I was wet for him.

"Look at me, Devina."

I propped myself on my elbows and watched as he had requested.

"You will watch when I penetrate you for the first time."

There was something foreboding in the way he said first time, but I was aroused and bit my lip. "I'm watching."

Sliding his finger inside me, he lowered his head and suckled on my clit again. I let my head fall back and moaned out in pleasure. "Ahh…"

"Say my name!"

"Yes, Tyton."

My previous in-and-out massages paled compared to the way he fingered me. Moving up my body he went back to kissing me while letting first one and then two large fingers work in and out of me. "Look at me," he kept demanding as if seeing my pleasure gave him fulfillment.

He was rougher than a normal masseuse and it made images of him taking me with more than his hands enter my mind.

Tyton kept at it, whispering how sexy I was and how tight my pussy felt. No one had ever spoken to me that way and I should be appalled, but the truth was that I loved listening to his dark voice talking dirty to me just as much as I loved the scent of his large masculine body.

In our state of lust and closeness, we had gone to a place that belonged only to Tyton and me. Nothing felt wrong or embarrassing here. Not his dirty talk. Not the moans I made, or the way I begged him to keep licking me. There was no shame or judgment in our special place. Just desire, acceptance, and raw emotions that felt like they had always been here, just waiting for us to arrive.

"Yes... Yes... Oh yes..." My body shook, and my insides convulsed around his fingers when I came in an orgasm much stronger than ever before.

He kept going but I squeezed my thighs together signaling that I couldn't take any more. "Stop," I whispered against his shoulder.

"Did you just come?"

My eyes were still closed and my body absorbing all the glorious endorphins that had been released. "Yes."

"I made you come?"

"Yes." It was sweet how proud he sounded.

"For real?" He pushed at me and my eyelids felt heavy when I opened them and smiled at him.

"Best orgasm of my life."

Rolling on top of me, he kissed me. "Women can have multiple orgasms; we don't need to stop now. This was just foreplay."

"What about the tournament?"

"Fuck the tournament! This is what they're all fighting for. I'm not going anywhere."

We smiled at each other and kissed again.

"Will you make love to me?" His question was sincere, and his eyes shone with hope.

Nuzzling his hair, I admitted, "Just before I came, I imagined another part of you inside me."

"Please, Devina. I'll give anything to make love to you."

I smiled. "I always thought of sex as weird and outdated, but now I wonder why people gave up on it."

Lowering his forehead onto mine, he whispered. "You didn't answer me."

"First, tell me this. If Mark and Deidra have sex, what does it mean to him?"

Tyton began rocking back and forth in slow movements. "It would mean *everything* to him." His hands were caressing my shoulder. "It's a sort of mat–"

I didn't hear the rest of his sentence because he gave a sudden growl of irritation.

"What's wrong?"

"It's not you. My wristband has been vibrating for the last twenty minutes. My family is trying to reach us."

"Then answer them."

"I don't want to. This is more important."

"But they might worry."

Tyton gave another low growl. "I'm afraid that if I answer I'll lose my chance of making love to you."

Caressing his face, I smiled. "Family comes first!"

CHAPTER 22
Mating

Tyton

The moment I answered the incoming call, I regretted it. My family had searched for us and found out from the security guards that I'd taken off with a boy who had been in a fight.

I would have preferred to stay in the meadow with Devina for the rest of the day, but it looked suspicious that'd I taken off with a young boy during my sister's tournament. We had to go back.

Picking up Devina's hoodie, I held it out to her. "It's still damp."

"That's fine. Maybe it will make it more bearable to wear it. Can you help me?"

"Sure." I took the fake eyebrows from her and glued them on top of her own.

"What about the glasses?"

"We lost them when I carried you out of the arena. When we get back, I'll look for them." I took a step back to assess my work.

"Approved?"

"Yeah." I sighed. "I wish you could dress like a woman and I could hold your hand."

"Why?"

"Because it would make me proud to show the world that you're mine."

Devina stood in front of me, expressions flashing across her face so fast that I wasn't sure what she was thinking.

"I know we aren't married, but what happened between us bonded us, don't you think?"

She gave a small nod and relief filled me. So, it had meant as much to her as it did to me.

The flight in the drone was too short and when we returned to the tournament and landed in the VIP area, my entire family were waiting for us.

"You just missed out on two spectacular fights," Henry, husband of my oldest sister Marni, said and scowled at Devina. "Your parents told us about your new worker getting in trouble. I hope you gave him a whipping for being such a pain in the ass."

Devina kept her head down.

"I took care of it," I assured them. "Devin understands and will keep close to me. There won't be any more problems." I tried to appear annoyed that I'd had to leave.

"Is it true that you missed the last of Emmerson's fight?" Henry's question to me was followed by another scowl in Devina's direction.

I nodded. "Did he win?"

"Yeah, he fucking won, and it was spectacular." Henry went into a detailed description of Emmerson's impressive victory and how he'd fought off an audience member who had managed to break through security to attack him.

"You should have seen it," Wilma's eyes shone with excitement. "The man attacked Emmerson from behind and he got so enraged that he turned around, picked up the man, and threw him through the air like he was nothing but a child." She laughed. "The idiot landed in the first row of spectators and everybody laughed at him."

"Why did he attack Emmerson?" I asked.

My dad shook his head. "Who knows? Maybe he wanted a minute of fame or it could be that he was upset for losing money on Emmerson's victory. Most people believed he would lose. Anyway, Emmerson is a confirmed champion now and so is Wayne, and Scott Thomas. There are two more finals and then the wedding can begin."

Scott Thomas was at least five years older than me and I'd been surprised to see him sign up for the tournament. He was a strong warrior, but I was sure my sister's silly ways would be exhausting to him. If she chose him, I feared it would be a lonely marriage with their having nothing in common.

"Shit, did Emanuel loose to Scott Thomas?"

My mom furrowed her brow. "I'm afraid so. Wilma was disappointed, but at least there's Emmerson and Wayne."

Devina and I spent about forty minutes in the VIP section eating food and talking to my family. It was hard for Devina since only Frederick, Wilma, and our parents knew her true identity and we were always surrounded by others.

"Devin, do you mind a word," my mom had the tone of someone scolding a boy for being naughty and had a strict face on when the two of them walked away from the crowd.

I knew my mom well enough to know she would find a quiet place to make sure Devina was okay, but my sisters Marni and Claire exchanged a look.

"You shouldn't have brought that troubled boy. I can't believe he ruined those fights for you and now Mom has to use her energy on giving him one of her lectures."

"It's the empty nest syndrome," my dad joked. "With Wilma leaving us today, there will be no more kids left to fuss about. Taking in a troubled teen is a way for her to feel needed."

"Oh, that makes sense." Marni nodded. "But if you need more life in the house, I'm happy to send over my boys. Henry and I would welcome the break."

"Frederick, I lost Devin's glasses and my shirt when I removed him from the… ehh… fight. Do you know if there's a lost and found?"

"There is. Come on, I'll take you." Turning to our father Frederick asked, "Can you cover for us for a few minutes?"

Pushing out his chest, Henry gave a look of importance. "We've got this, don't worry."

Frederick and I were happy to have a few minutes to ourselves.

"What the hell happened?" he muttered as we moved out of the VIP area and got swallowed up in the masses.

"It was a heat stroke because of that stupid hoodie."

"Yeah, there's been several cases of heat stroke today. They've been telling everyone to hydrate and seek shade. It's too fucking hot."

"Tell me about it."

"So where did you take her?"

"To the meadow."

Frederick raised an eyebrow. "My meadow?"

"I would claim it's mine now."

We walked shoulder to shoulder when we weren't stopping to let people pass us.

"What do you mean, your meadow?"

With an arm around his shoulder, I pulled him in and whispered in his ear, "I mated with her."

Smiling, I continued walking, leaving him behind.

My brother was quick to catch up and spun me around. "Tell me everything."

I grinned from ear to ear and after looking around, I gestured for us to step to the side for privacy. "She's a goddess. So wise and innocent at the same time. There's nothing but pureness and kindness in her."

"And you had sex?"

"Yes, but not full intercourse. We were about to when you and Dad wouldn't stop calling me."

Frederick jerked his head back. "You left the meadow before you finished bonding?"

"Yes, but she confirmed that we've bonded, so it's fine. I even said that she was mine and she didn't protest."

"Still... why the hell didn't you go all the way if you had the chance? What a moron would give up on a chance like that?"

Rubbing my forehead, I felt stupid. "She had already given me so much. I don't know... Dad's call just fucked up the moment, you know?"

Frederick was looking at me with large green eyes, similar to mine. "But what are you going to do? She's a Motlander. It's not like you can ever truly be together."

"I know, but..." I let my hands fall down. "There has to be a way."

"Do you love her?"

I grabbed his shoulders and stared into his eyes. "It's like we were made for each other. She's so much more than a young bride could ever be."

"How old is she?"

"A year younger than me and completely different from brides like Wilma who think they are the center of the universe." I spoke fast. "Devina is smart and kind. I don't always get her humor but it's not her fault that she was born as a Motlander."

"Hey, Starr was a young Northlander bride and I love her."

"I'm sorry, I didn't mean to bash your wife, but you know what I mean."

Someone in the passing crowd shouted Frederick's name and he raised a hand to wave back. "Later, okay?"

The man got the message and Frederick turned his focus back on me. "Tyton, listen. It doesn't matter how amazing she is. You can't move there, and she can't move here. Period! If it was possible it would have happened at some point, but the wall has been there for almost two hundred fucking years. You're risking your life here and you have to stop it!"

"That's easy for you to say. You have Starr."

"And you'll have Tamara in a year."

I took a step back and drew my eyebrows close together. "I'm not fighting in Tamara's tournament."

"You have to!"

"Didn't you hear me? I just mated with Devina."

My brother gave me a look of pity. "This isn't going to end well, and you know it."

The rush of euphoria that I'd felt after my time with her in the meadow was wearing off and the reality was showing its ugly face. We were close to a fence and I let myself slide down with my back to it. "Fuuuck!"

"Don't. Drunk people might have pissed here last night." Frederick pulled me up.

"I know it sucks," he told me, "but at least no one knows about this but us. Tonight, when you say goodbye to her, consider yourself lucky that you got away with it and pray that you'll be blessed with two women in your lifetime."

"I can't marry Tamara."

"You can't marry Devina either. If you do it's going to be the loneliest marriage in the world with the two of you being on different sides of the border."

"But if we could find a way..."

My brother leaned in and with a hand around my neck he spoke in a no-bullshit tone. "You think her country is going to let her go? And even if they did, are you naïve enough to think King Jeremiah will be okay with you claiming her without a fight? There are ten million men who would feel cheated and once it gets out how you met, bottles and letters from this side will litter their side."

He let go of me and I pulled back with deep frown lines on my forehead.

"You have to stop dreaming like a fucking school boy."

Men of the North – FORBIDDEN LETTERS

I hated that he was right.

Walking next to him, my head was in chaos and I just followed along as he retrieved the glasses for Devina's disguise in the lost and found area and helped me pick out a new t-shirt at one of the vendors.

When we got back to the VIP area, Devina was in the shade with a bottle of water in her hands so I figured she'd told my mom what really happened.

When she saw me, she smiled, but it faltered when I didn't smile back.

She was so beautiful. Even though she was dressed as a boy, I could still see the extraordinary woman who had called my name when she came in my arms earlier.

If only I could knock down the border wall and claim her for mine, I would. Seeing her be so close and yet out of my reach was fucking painful.

Frederick said, "How about you stay with Starr and the others and then I'll keep an eye on the little rascal? We'll meet up with you all later."

I was unable to respond but watched as my brother gestured for Devina to come with him. She looked at me over her shoulder with confusion but followed Frederick out of the VIP area. My hands folded into fists and I wished I could have gone into the arena and smacked someone around. Anything but this awful feeling of being powerless.

"Are you okay, son?" My dad patted my shoulder.

"Yes." I forced the word out and moved away. I didn't need him to pity me like Frederick had.

The two fights were endless. I sat next to Wilma and watched large warriors fight for her.

"Who do you think I should choose of the two?"

"Only one will win. It's not your choice."

"I know, but I meant *if* I was to choose between them."

"They are both great warriors."

"But don't you think Ruben is more handsome?"

I stared at her. "You're going to choose a man on his looks?"

"And his charm."

"What about his strength, personality, or his intelligence?"

"Oh, Tyton, why do you have to be in such a bad mood? You're ruining my day."

I looked away, feeling the unfairness of it all pressing me down. I'd found a woman to love and because of politics I couldn't have her.

"If you hated protecting Devina so much, you could have just said it. It's not my fault you had to miss out on some of the fights. Mom told me Devina had heat stroke."

"I fucking told you it was a bad idea to bring her," I sneered low. It was childish, but I couldn't stand everyone being so happy around me when my happiness had just been torn from me. "Excuse me." Getting out of my chair, I walked off, needing to get away from the bride-to-be and her happy entourage.

I couldn't go and sit with Frederick and Devina so I chose a seat where I could see them.

Devina looked bored and in a way, it fitted her disguise well. She was wearing the glasses again that we had retrieved from the lost and found area, and she kept drinking from her bottle. We had both emptied our bladders before we left the meadow, but with the rate she was drinking she would have to go again soon. Would Frederick know how to handle that?

As I watched her, she turned her head and found my eyes. My heart rate picked up. Across an audience of hundreds of people, she had felt me reaching out to her. *So that's what it means to have bonded with someone.*

It reinforced my decision that I'd never fight for Tamara.

Devina was my mate and if I couldn't have her, I didn't want anyone else. Claiming Tamara would be wrong when so many men would worship her despite her youth. To me, the girl would always pale compared to the woman I'd fallen in love with.

Locking eyes across the sea of people, I swallowed hard. Tonight, when it was time to take her home, I'd have to talk to her about our future together, or rather – our future apart.

CHAPTER 23
Wilma's Wedding

Devina

On the stage in the largest of the arenas, five large warriors stood side by side facing Wilma.

Two of them had black eyes and one had a swollen eyebrow. Another had a finger wrapped, but they all looked like they would go another round to protect her.

On large screens above us, close-up images of Wilma, the champions, and the man standing between them showed.

"That's our king," Frederick whispered to me. "He's an asshole, but we can't say that."

I studied the man with the opulent clothing. "What's his name?"

"King Jeremiah. He kills for his own amusement and would rather sit on a golden throne than feed his people."

The man in question held the audience captive when he asked the biggest question of the night. "Wilma Green, which of these fine warriors will you choose as your husband?"

Wilma's eyes darted between the five champions, who all had hopeful expressions on their faces.

"I choose..." She paused and tapped her lips.

"She has doubts," I muttered.

"Nahh, she just likes the suspense and drama."

My eyes were fixed on Wilma, who had the poor men holding their breath.

"Emmerson. I choose Emmerson."

With a loud howl of victory, the large man raised two fists in the air and fell to his knees with his head leaning back.

Frederick chuckled. "I remember that moment like it was yesterday."

"When you won your wife?"

"I was sure Starr would choose Tyton, but for some miracle she picked me."

"Do you know – why is Tyton keeping his distance from me?" I had wanted to ask that question since we got back from the meadow, but I assumed Frederick didn't know what had happened between Tyton and me, so I'd kept quiet.

"It was my suggestion." Frederick lowered his voice. "Tyton is smitten with you."

"What does smitten mean?"

"He's in love. But I talked to him. There's no future for you two and we can't allow him to give up his chance of having a family to pursue a dream that is doomed from the beginning. Tyton needs to be in next year's tournament and fight for Tamara."

I kept quiet and looked away.

"If you care about him, you'll help him see that. He's strong and we all want him to experience the joy of fatherhood. Only Tamara can give him that."

My stomach twisted in pain as I avoided his burning gaze on me.

"He says that you're the kindest person he's ever met, so I'm counting on you to be selfless."

Frederick and I were standing against the wall behind the others in the VIP section. My whole body shrunk as I imagined that in only a year it would be Tyton on that stage marrying a young bride.

Good for him.

I looked down, not able to fool myself with positive thinking. I hated the idea of my going back to being alone in the Motherlands and his moving on to be with someone else here. What had happened today in the meadow had felt healing to me. The feeling of being wanted and desired by Tyton was addicting and I had hoped we could do more of it tonight.

I watched Wilma and Emmerson take a stand across from each other and then King Jeremiah spoke about a husband protecting and loving his woman, and a wife honoring and obeying her husband.

"Did he say obeying?"

"Yeah." Frederick nodded. "If a dangerous situation arises, she must be willing to follow instructions. How else can he protect her?"

"So, it doesn't apply to all situations?"

Frederick chuckled. "I'd like to say yes, but Starr can be a ball-buster at times. Northlander women are strong, and they don't tolerate weak men."

"I now declare you husband and wife." The moment King Jeremiah said it, Emmerson stepped in and kissed Wilma. When he pulled back, she beamed up at him and laughed as he picked her off her feet and swung her around. They were glowing with happiness and it was impossible not to smile.

And to think I wanted to save her from this.

If Emmerson was as good to her as Tyton had been to me today, then all my worries for her had been a waste of time.

Feeling burning eyes on me, I turned my head to the left and saw Tyton sending me a longing glance.

We didn't smile. We just stood there and even though there were hundreds of people between us, I could read his mind. He wanted to marry me just like Emmerson had married his sister. The thought was crazy because we didn't know each other that well, but then again, compared to Emmerson and Wilma, Tyton and I knew each other intimately.

Men of the North – FORBIDDEN LETTERS

The newlyweds didn't stick around for more than an hour before they flew off in a drone. I wondered when Wilma would have time to write me again and if Tyton would keep his promise and deliver her letters.

Watching the drone disappear in the distance with Wilma in it, the dreadful feeling of loss made me tear up again. After my family's death, Tyton and Wilma had been my distraction from my grief and a lifeline of sorts.

I looked down to hide my tears but still sensed when Tyton moved closer to me. Frederick's words of reason had made it clear to me that what I'd found with Tyton today had been nothing but a fleeting moment of happiness.

"What's wrong?" he asked with a worried expression.

"Can you take me back to the beach now?"

Frederick was close enough to hear and answered first, "Let me do it."

Tyton sneered low. "No. *I'm* taking her."

Frederick crossed his arms. "You think that's wise?"

"Make sure you take Dad and Mom home," Tyton instructed his brother and threw a nod for me to follow him.

Frederick called out for us to stop, but that only made us walk faster as we headed straight for Tyton's drone. When we took off, I leaned against the window and looked out on the lights below. Neither of us spoke, and it was like a wall of sadness and frustration had built itself between us.

Taking off the glasses and the fake eyebrows, I rubbed my face.

"Are you tired?"

"Yes."

"Did you get all the research you needed?"

I turned my head and looked at him, not sure what to say.

"Devina…" He sighed. "What happened between us today… It was amazing and…"

Without waiting for his "but" I cut him off. "Yeah. Frederick already gave me the lecture. We're from different worlds and you have a tournament coming up in a year."

He wrinkled his brow. "No. I'm not fighting."

"You have to. It's your only chance. Didn't you just see Emmerson's and Wilma's happiness?"

Tyton's chest rose and he gave a noisy exhalation as he turned to look straight ahead. "I'm not marrying Tamara. It wouldn't be fair to her."

My knees were bobbing up and down and my chest felt tight, like someone was sitting on me. Wrapping my arms around myself I fought the tears that welled up in my eyes again. "Who said anything about *fair*? It wasn't fair when Maria died, or when Caro, Justin, Hannah, my parents, or my nana died. Why should any of this be fair?"

"But we bonded today. I can't marry someone else when I'm bonded with you."

"Bonded? What does that even mean?" I was half laughing and half crying.

"I should have never answered that stupid call. If my family hadn't called us back, I would have claimed you as mine. Hell, in my mind, I did claim you."

I shook my head and gave him an incredulous stare. "There's no such thing as claiming another person."

"But I told you we bonded, and you agreed."

"Tyton, I didn't understand what you meant. Where I'm from, we bond with our teammates in sport and with our friends. It's not a binding or legal bond, but a way of growing closer as friends." Throwing my hands up in the air, I sighed. "I'm not saying that what happened between us wasn't special, but how did we even get to the point of talking about claiming and bonding? You're an Nman and

I'm a Motlander. So what if we shared an experience based on mutual curiosity?"

"It was way more than curiosity."

"You were longing for physical contact and so was I." Sniffling loudly, I dried my nose. "You have no idea what it's like to lose your whole family and be the only one left in that big house full of all the memories. It's the loneliest place in the world – and there you were, making me feel loved and cared for. For a short while you took all my worries away, and I'm grateful for it. I don't regret what we did and I'll use every bit of it in my book."

Tyton reached out for me. "I hate seeing you crying."

"Then it's a good thing you don't live with me. These past months I've cried buckets." I sniffled again and used the backs of my hands to dry my tears away.

He looked down and spoke in an earnest tone. "I don't want to stay away from you. Can't we find a way to see each other? You've been here twice in one week. Maybe I could visit you and we could spend nights together. We can write each other. It's not hopeless."

"I can't stay in that house. There's nothing for me here, Tyton."

"So, you're leaving then?"

The pain in his eyes made me look out the window again. "I have to."

"When?"

"I don't know. It will take me some time to pack everything and there's the book. I would still like to finish it here. It makes sense to be close to the border and..."

"And me?" He said it for me and when I nodded, he added in a soft tone, "Will you still let me read it?"

"If you want to."

"It's my book too. You included my writing, remember?"

My lips tugged up in a sad smile. "Yes, I haven't forgotten, and I'm counting on you to deliver the steamy scenes in the rest of the book."

"Steamy scenes are my specialty."

We were moving toward safer ground and using my sleeve, I dried my eyes and gave him a small smile. "I could probably write a scene based on what happened between us today."

"Do that! I would love to read how it felt for you."

With my shoulders weighed down by sadness, I looked away. "I don't know any words that could describe how good it felt."

Tyton reached for my hand and squeezed it. He didn't say anything, but his eyes shone with gratitude and it made me feel like my words had mattered a great deal to him.

"Will you take me straight to the beach?"

"Only if you ask me to. I would prefer to keep you at my place for the night."

"That's probably not a good idea."

"No one would know."

"We would know and spending the night together would only make it more painful to part."

He frowned. "I'm willing to suffer the pain for the pleasure if you are."

Back in the meadow I'd been happy for the first time in months and it was tempting to say yes. "I crave the pleasure. No one has ever made me feel the way you did."

He lit up. "So, we're doing it?"

"We can't! I want it as bad as you do, but I'm already broken up with grief for my family. I can't take any more pain and loss."

"But what if we allowed ourselves just one night?"

I shook my head. "You know one night wouldn't be enough."

With a deep sigh, his head fell forward. "Yeah, I know."

We sat in silence for the rest of the flight, both processing our own grief of having found something precious only to have it ripped away from us.

CHAPTER 24
Letting Go

Tyton

When we reached the beach, I wished it had been another hour away so I could have spent more time with Devina.

"Thank you for flying me back here."

"My pleasure."

The twilight had descended into night and once again we were back on the beach with only the moon above us. As soon as we got out of the drone, she backed away and raised her hand to wave at me, but I wasn't ready to let her go yet.

"How are you getting home when you get to the other side?"

"I have a bike."

"Good." Tucking my hands in my pockets, I looked out to the fence in the water that was only dimly lit by the moonlight. "I've seen the other side."

She stopped. "You have?"

"Uh-huh. We were teenagers and Frederick dared me to cross over."

"How far did you go?"

"I swam out far enough that I could see what was on the other side, but I never walked onto the beach or anything."

"It looks like this side."

"I know, but as kids we used to fantasize that on the other side there would be thousands of women sunbathing without clothes on."

"But you saw none."

"That's right. I had all my childhood fantasies crushed."

"If it's any consolation, people do sunbathe naked. We just do it further down the beach."

I narrowed my eyes with suspicion. It was hard to tell when she was joking.

"I'm serious. It's only about fifteen minutes that way. The sand is nicer down there and the fence doesn't block the panoramic view."

"But people aren't really naked, are they?"

She gave me a puzzled look. "How else would they sunbathe?"

"In a bathing suit."

"You put on a suit when you tan? That defies the purpose, don't you think?" She shook her head. "You men are a weird bunch. Why is it so hard for you to accept your bodies? We're born naked and it's natural."

"Whatever you say." I chuckled and suppressed a million questions in my mind, not least the image of Devina's curvy body naked from earlier today.

"I need to find my bag." Jogging away from me, she went to retrieve a dark green bag in a smooth material.

"Waterproof?"

"Yes."

"All right. Let's do this." I pulled off the t-shirt Frederick had helped me pick out at the tournament and let it drop to the ground.

"What are you doing?"

"I'm coming with you."

"To the Motherlands?" She was squeezing her eyebrows together in disbelief.

"I won't go onto the beach. I'm just making sure that you get there safely."

"Why? I can swim back by myself. I did it the last time."

"This is different. It's been a long day and you're tired."

"But..."

Arching a brow, I gave her my *it's not up for discussion* look. "You fainted today and there's no way in hell I could ever forgive myself if you drowned on my watch." Kicking off my shoes and stepping out of my pants, I was down to only my black briefs again.

"Tyton, you don't have to do this."

"Yeah, I do."

With a shrug, she opened her bag and pulled off her black hoodie before pointing to a stone. "Do you mind checking to see if my underwear from this morning is still there?"

I looked left and right as I searched. "It's not here." The lights from the drone were illuminating the area with the stones clearly, but the rest of the beach was only dimly lit by the moon and I couldn't see any clothing lying around.

"Oh bother, then the wind must have moved them, hopefully out to sea, or some Nman will be confused when he picks up a pair of women's panties down the beach."

"I'm pretty sure he'll treasure them." I walked back to her, admiring her soft shape and then I sucked in a breath and stood transfixed for a second. "What are you doing?"

"I'm taking off my top. I'll need dry clothes on the other side."

Even though I'd seen her breasts in the meadow earlier today, I was still blinded by how perfect her natural teardrop shape was. As I watched, the wind made her nipples contract and point at me. Acute desire in my body mixed with immense pride that she felt so at ease around me.

"Stop staring. They're just breasts, Tyton. There are billions of them in the world."

I blinked my eyes and swallowed hard. "What did you say?"

"You've seen my breasts before."

"Yeah but..." There was no way I could explain to her how I'd fantasized about being with a real woman for as long as I could remember and that today had been the highlight of my life. Taking in her beauty, I promised myself that I'd memorialize every detail in my memory vault.

"What about the clothes that I borrowed from your mom and Wilma? I know I should give it back, but do you think I could borrow it? It's just that my own clothes are at your house and I would hate to bike home naked when I get to the other side."

"Keep it."

"You sure?"

"Of course. I don't even know where they got it from."

"Okay, thank you." With a short nod, she used her thumbs to push down the baggy boy pants. It was just as arousing as when she did it in the meadow but this time, the moon peeked out from behind a cloud in perfect timing to glow down on Devina's feminine shape when she bent down to put the hoodie and pants in the bag.

Once she was done, she tied the rope around the slim waist that complimented her wide hips so well.

"You're swimming back like that?"

"Uh-huh." She picked up the bag in her arms and moved into the water. "It's sweet of you to offer, but you don't need to come. The water is cold."

"I'm coming!" I followed her and caught up to her when she stopped to pause. "Do you even know how gorgeous you are?" She was like some magical mermaid with the way her brown hair flowed down her shoulders and the moon lit up her outline like she was a piece of art to watch.

"You're just saying that because I took off those bushy eyebrows."

"No, I've never seen anyone more beautiful than you."

"Tyton, you're making this harder for both of us."

I was about to reply when her arm reached out to silence me and her eyes looked up. "Shhh..."

"What is it?"

Her head tilted like she was listening. "Did you hear that?"

"Hear what?" It was hard to concentrate when she was touching me, and every part of her above water was naked.

"There was a sound. There..."

This time I heard it too. "That's a wolf but it's not close."

"Is it on my side or your side?"

Again, we heard a distant howl.

"I don't know. It's rare for wolves to come to our lands but it happens."

"I shouldn't say this about another living being, but I hate wolves. They scare me."

"Do you want to go back to my drone? We can go to my place until the morning."

She looked tempted but shook her head. "No, it's okay. I'll just hang out on the beach until the sun comes up. I don't want them chasing me through the forest."

I didn't like the image of anyone chasing Devina. "Has anyone been killed by wolves on your side?"

"Not recently, but I'm not taking a chance."

"We could fly my drone to your side of the beach and I could wait with you."

"No, it's too risky. I'm sure if you crossed over in your drone there would be an alarm of some kind going off."

"Wait here." I ran back to the beach, turned off my drone, and picked up my clothes and shoes before returning to her. "Open your bag."

"Are you coming with me to wait on the beach?" This time I didn't sense a rejection but rather relief from her.

"It would make more sense to wait in my drone, but since you're insisting on waiting on the beach, I'll wait with you."

When she held out the open bag to me, I leaned forward to put my clothes in. My pulse picked up from how close my face was to her chest.

"You ready?" She closed the bag.

"I'm ready."

We walked shoulder to shoulder further out in the ocean. Devina took ten quick inhalations before getting her shoulders under water.

"You don't like cold water?" I began swimming next to her.

"No one likes cold water."

"You loved the cool stream in the meadow."

"Because I was over-heating and it was so peaceful there." She kept swimming, always holding her head above the water. I followed close by, making sure she was closest to the wall and had me between her and the large ocean. The ocean wasn't calm like the first time she had done this, and I could tell she was worn out from the long day.

"You've got this," I encouraged her when she swam against the current and seemed to get nowhere.

Once we reached Devina's side of the beach and we could walk the rest of the way, she wrapped her arms around her body to shield herself from the wind that felt so cold against our skin.

Her teeth were chattering and her fingers stiff when she untied the bag's rope from her waist.

I was in awe of her. Devina was a decent swimmer, but no expert, and it made her willingness to swim to our side of the border to save Wilma that much more impressive. For her to walk into a dark ocean, swim against the current, only to run into a foreign territory where she was convinced there was danger was the craziest thing ever.

"How long did it take you to plan your first rescue mission?"

"You mean my mission gone wrong?"

"Ah, come on, give yourself some credit here. It wasn't a complete failure, was it? I mean you saw for yourself that Wilma wasn't being forced to marry."

Devina put the hoodie back on. It was long enough that she could remove her wet panties without showing anything.

"Here." She handed me my clothes from the bag. When I put my foot through the leg of my pants, she made a "tsk" sound. "Why would you put your dry pants over your soaked briefs?"

"Ehh..." The idea of stripping naked in front of her was strange, even with what had happened between us earlier. "Are you saying that you wouldn't mind if I removed my briefs?"

"If I were you, I would take them off." She picked up her things and left me to stand alone, balancing with one foot inside the pants.

Okay then.

I got rid of the wet briefs and put on my clothing before following her.

Devina sat on the ground next to something I'd only heard about.

"Is that a bicycle?"

"Yes."

"Is that what you meant when you said you had a bike?"

"What did you think I meant?"

"Something with a motor. Not that! Fuck, you people really are serious about living basic lives, aren't you?"

"You say fuck all the time, do you know that?"

"So, what? Does it bother you?"

She pulled her knees up in front of her and wrapped her arms around them. "We try to avoid foul language. It's unnecessary."

I snorted. "Sorry, pixie, but I talk the way I want to talk."

"My brother used to curse sometimes too, but it's a bad habit and now the Council is talking about making it illegal."

Sitting next to her, I leaned back and planted my hands in the sand behind me. "That's ridiculous. You can't make words illegal."

"Apparently, you can."

"But how would they police it?"

"I'm not sure, but someone said that the idea is for all of us to help each other out by reporting improper communication."

I narrowed my eyes. "Is this your twisted sense of humor or are you serious?"

She turned her face to me and there was a smile that made her face softer and prettier. "I wish it was a joke. As an author I like the variety in words, accents, and speech patterns. I don't swear much myself, but it makes things more interesting."

"Fuck yeah!" I laughed and felt pride in my chest when she smiled again. "But tell me something; why did you swim instead of jumping the wall?"

"It's much too high for me and there are mines on this side of the border."

"Mines?"

"Yes. That's why I swam to this part of the beach." She pointed in the direction of the wall, which was about a hundred and thirty feet away. "I never go all the way up to the wall. There are signs that warn about mines."

"And you believe them?"

"Why wouldn't I?"

I chuckled again. "Pixie, come on."

"What do you mean?"

"Think about it. You have wolves, but what about bears, cougars, elk, and moose? Do you have those too?"

"Yes. And a lot of wild horses and goats too."

"Okay, and have any of them been blown to pieces?"

She frowned.

"If there were mines, don't you think some animals would have been blown up by now?"

"You think they've been lying to us?" Her eyes widened. "No. They wouldn't do that. Our society is based on integrity and trust."

I laughed out loud. "You're so sweet and innocent."

"Don't laugh at me."

"I've just never seen anyone trust in authority the way you do."

"You think I'm naïve."

"I know you are, but it's one of the things I like about you. You're so damn pure."

For a moment we sat without talking and then I leaned forward and drew a circle in the sand with my finger. "If there was a way, would you consider living with me in the Northlands?"

She took time before she answered. "Our cultures are so different, Tyton. Maybe we got carried away for a moment, but all my friends are on this side. I'll see them when I go back home."

"Where is home?"

"Blue Valley City. It's around four hours southeast from here. It's where I went to university and it's where my friends are… or were."

"Were?"

"There are still some left, but many of them have moved to other places by now."

Brushing my hands off on my pants, I ignored how cold I was. "So why go back there?"

Devina rocked back and forth. She was cold too. "There's nothing for me here. This area was always rural, but the epidemic wiped out a lot of families. That's why…" She looked away.

"Why you can't stay?"

"Maybe I'll stay another month or two to grieve and work on my next book, but I made my grandmother a promise that I intend to keep."

"Ah, that promise?"

Devina's teeth were back to chattering a little. "Yes, it was my grandmother's last words that family is everything, and then she made me promise to have a child."

"Your grandmother sounds like a wise woman."

"Tha... thank you."

"Wow, you're really cold. Your lips are turning blue. Maybe sitting on the beach all night isn't the brightest idea."

"But the wolves."

"I haven't heard them since we got here."

Devina turned her head to look over her shoulder with deep frown lines on her forehead.

"How about I'll accompany you home and then you'll draw me a map so I can find my way back here when the sun rises?" Getting up from the beach, I stood in front of her. As if it was the most natural thing in the world, Devina reached her hands up to me.

We clasped our hands together and I helped her up. It was still strange and a bit surreal to me how different she was from any woman in the Northlands and how natural touch seemed to her.

"If I did this to an unmarried woman in the Northlands her protector would kill me for it."

"Hmm." She made a sound revealing that she thought I was exaggerating.

"It's true. You said that on this side you have one man per twenty women, but on our side, we only have two hundred and five women in total. With ten million men that makes for fifty thousand men per woman. The only way to protect them is to have ironclad laws that make it illegal for any man to touch or even address a woman without permission from her protector."

"I'm sorry to hear that. Did you have to kill anyone for touching Wilma?"

"No. It's instilled in all of us Nmen from early childhood not to touch women, and no one has dared approach her. But then my father, Frederick, or I were always there when she left the house and now that responsibility falls on Emmerson."

"I can't imagine being that restricted. I'm used to going everywhere by myself, which reminds me..." Devina pointed to the bike. "Do you know how to ride one of those?"

"No."

"It's not so different from the hoverbike, you just have to keep your balance and pedal your feet at the same time. I would offer that you can sit behind me, but you're too heavy for that."

"How about you ride that thing and I jog next to you? It would help me get warm again."

"All right. I won't go too fast. The trail through the forest is bumpy so I always take it slow."

As I looked on, Devina secured her bag to the bike and turned on a lamp in the front and one in the back. Then she pulled it to a dirt trail close by and swung one leg over the seat. "Ready?"

I began jogging ahead, eager to see where she lived.

CHAPTER 25
No Time for Bed

Devina

Tyton ran the whole way from the beach to my house and kept up a steady pace next to my bike.

Only twice did we hear wolves howling in the distance and both times, he distracted me by asking questions about something unrelated.

"What are you going to say if we meet someone?"

"We won't meet anyone out here at this hour. The few people who are left in this area are sleeping or at least inside."

"Yeah, but still. What would you tell them?"

"I don't know. Just that you're my friend from Blue Valley."

"Would they believe you?"

I turned my head and looked at Tyton's well-muscled body with his wet hair pushed back and his stubble.

"No. You don't look like any men I've met on this side of the border. And no one would wear a t-shirt like yours."

"What's wrong with my t-shirt?"

His light blue t-shirt had a glass of beer with foam on top and the text, *I make beer disappear, what's your super power?*

"Alcohol is illegal here, but it's not just your t-shirt. You're too big and hairy and you have an accent."

"An accent? I don't have a fucking accent."

"Yes, you do. All you Northlanders speak with an accent."

"Huh. You don't sound that different from us when you speak, except that you pronounce all the words more clearly maybe. We have a guy on the News who speaks a bit like you. Real proper, you know?"

"Take a left here."

Tyton, who was a bit ahead of me, complied and ran up the dirt road to my family home.

Stopping in front of the entrance, he turned to me. "Is this a typical Motlander house?"

"For this area it is."

Nellie was in the window barking like crazy.

"The dog is old and a little grumpy, but she won't bite."

"Don't worry. I'm great with dogs."

"We'll see. Oh, here she comes." Using the dog door, Nellie came running out to sniff Tyton.

"Hey, sweetie." He reached down his hand and spoke to her in a soft voice. "I'll bet you're confused. Devina told you she was bringing back a girl from the Northlands, didn't she? And I'm probably the ugliest girl you've ever seen."

I smiled at his humor.

"You didn't think she'd bring home a large Nman instead, did you?"

The moment he said it, I stopped and stared at him. "That's not even funny. Think about how this would look to others! You're an Nman and the first time I met you was a nightmare. And here I am bringing you to my house. People would think I'm crazy."

Tyton was squatting and stopped petting Nellie when he looked up at me. "Screw what others would think. What matters is that you know I wouldn't hurt you. You trust me, right?"

My chest rose in a deep intake of air. "Yeah, call me naïve, but I feel safe with you."

"Good!" He rose up to his full height and stood in front of me.

Leaning my head back I pondered out loud, "Besides, if you wanted to kidnap me you would have done it the first time I came to the Northlands. I know from experience that you're crazy strong." Opening the door wider, I walked in and heard him close it behind us.

Turning on lights, I walked through the house. "Told you it was messy. I'm packing and organizing everything."

"Wow, you weren't exaggerating. This makes my place seem tidy."

In the open kitchen, I turned to him. "Would you like something to eat or drink?"

"Just water." He followed me and when I poured water into glasses, he was close behind me. "Are you still cold?"

"Yeah. That ocean water was frigid."

"A day of extremes, huh? You've gone from overheating to freezing." The edge of his lips lifted.

"You could say that. All I want now is a warm shower and a bed."

A slow, mischievous smile spread on his lips. "That sounds amazing."

Oh, not again... Just like back in the meadow, butterflies took over my stomach and the sheer look of lust on his face made me want to do everything we'd done earlier today.

His hand slid up my arm. "I could warm you up."

He already was, as heat was spreading in my body and my hands were shaking, so I set my water down and saw him do the same.

"Look, Tyton, we talked about this..."

The way his breathing picked up made it obvious that his heart-rate was racing just like mine, and when his eyes lowered to my lips, an electric impulse ran up and down my spine. The pull between us was stronger than my will power and when he kissed me, I kissed him back like it was a matter of survival.

My hands squeezed around his waist, pressing myself against him while his hands were in my hair holding me in a tight grip as he kissed me with an intense hunger that matched my own.

All the rational details of why we shouldn't do this were washed away, and my sole focus was on feeling and tasting this massive man who made me feel so deliciously wanted.

"Fuck, Devina. There's no way I'm leaving here without claiming you. You're mine!" His words were pure nonsense but at the same time the most arousing ones I'd ever heard.

I was smiling as our tongues did another round of seductive dancing around each other.

"Say you want this too." His hands were sliding up under my shirt and it made every nerve ending on my naked skin feel like an erogenous zone.

"My bed is upstairs," I managed to get out between moaning and kissing.

"I don't have time for beds." With a growl of arousal, Tyton picked me up and carried me to the dinner table. His eyes were hooded when he set me down and pushed me back with a strong hand on my shoulder. "I want you naked."

I watched in awe as he tore at my pants to get them off.

Slow down. It was right there on my tongue, but the truth was I didn't want him to take it easy. I wanted him as much as he wanted me and so I lifted my behind to make it easier for him to get the baggy boy pants off of me and was rewarded with another sexy growl when he tore them off me.

A desperate need to touch him made me reach out to lift his shirt, indicating for him to take it off.

With a hand behind my neck, Tyton raised me up to sit in front of him and then he pulled off his t-shirt and stood like an oven of body heat in front of me. He was broad-chested and while he investigated my body, I did the same with his. I registered his hands lifting my breasts as if he wanted to feel their weight, but I was busy sliding my fingers down his abdomen with deep fascination. There were six squares under his strong chest and a line of light brown hair that led from his navel down to his pants.

"Gorgeous," he muttered and leaned down to take one of my nipples into his mouth.

"Take off your pants."

"What?" The word was muffled because he'd filled his mouth with my left breast.

"I want to see where the line leads."

"What line?" He straightened a little and looked down at himself.

"That line in the middle of your lower squares." I pointed to the hairs under his navel.

"Squares? You mean my six-pack?"

I nodded to his pants again. "Take them off."

"Oh wow, who would have thought Motlanders could be so demanding?" His smile was cheeky when he opened his pants and pushed them down a little.

My fingers trailed down the line until it hit more hair, but he would need to push his pants lower so I could see everything. "More."

He laughed. "You want more?"

"Yeah. I want to see all of you."

"Then you do it." His voice was hoarse with arousal and, biting down on his lower lip, he raised his hands. "I'm all yours."

It was like a challenge and moving further out on the edge of the table, I sat naked with my fingers pushing down on his pants.

"Fuck, you don't know how hot it is to have you undress me."

We locked eyes and then I tugged him closer to me. "I never got to see that part of you in the meadow."

"I didn't know you wanted to."

"I'm a curious woman."

His fingers pushed a lock of my hair back and he gave me a lopsided grin. "But if nudity really isn't a big deal to you, then you must have seen lots of dicks."

"Never one that was hard." Without breaking eye contact, I slid his pants all the way down. He had nothing on underneath since he'd left behind his wet briefs on the beach.

His lips were parted and he breathed faster when my hands slid over his naked and very firm behind.

Slowly, my eyes lowered down his strong chest to his navel and along that trail of hair that ran all the way to his crotch.

His penis was enormous and pointing right at me.

"Don't be scared," he whispered and used a finger to lift my chin and meet his eyes again.

"I'm not scared."

"Then why did your eyes just double in size?"

"I was just surprised at the size, that's all."

"Do you want to touch it?"

"Uh-huh."

Kissing me and nibbling on my lower lip, I could feel him smile. "Go ahead then."

Tyton groaned with pleasure when I stroked my fingers up and down his long shaft.

"You call your penis Dick? Is it normal for men to give that part of their body a name?"

He pulled back to see my right hand investigate his erection.

"It's another word for it, not a name. I prefer cock or dick but there are a million words for it."

"Oh, I see."

Careful not to hurt him, I closed my hand around his shaft but he was too large for my fingers to reach all around.

Men of the North – FORBIDDEN LETTERS

When I rubbed my hand up and down on his shaft, he closed his eyes with a sound of pain in his throat. Fearing I was doing something wrong, I let go.

"No, don't stop. It felt amazing." Taking my hands, he brought them back and showed me how to hold on even tighter.

"You sure I'm not hurting you?"

"Yeah, I'm sure…" He pushed the words out and tensed his jaw and then he began rocking his hips back and forth while keeping my hands around the tip of his cock.

His mouth was open and his eyes fixed on my breasts. And from the way his breathing became shallow and fast, I knew this felt good to him.

"You like my hands on you?"

"Uh-huh." His answer was strangled, and I was fascinated at the redness that spread up his neck and the way his face tensed up.

He dipped his head and kissed me while moving his hips faster. "Oh fuck, I should… Oh… this is… Devina… I…" Every syllable was pushed out like his brain was fighting a battle to communicate, and then his eyes squeezed and he moaned out in a long deep sound. "Ohhhh."

I felt something wet on my chest and looked down to see the head of his dick pumping out semen.

Earlier today, I'd orgasmed in his arms and there was a warm sense of pride inside me that I got to return the favor.

When he opened his eyes, I smiled at him.

"That's not how I wanted this to go." He rubbed his face, but I kept smiling at him.

"You gave me an orgasm and now I gave you one. That's good, isn't it?"

His eyes fell to the semen on my chest and stomach. "I've jerked off a million times myself, but to feel your soft hand on me was divine."

"Divine, huh?" My smile grew bigger.

He leaned in to kiss me again. "Devina and divine sounds the same anyway."

Reaching for some tissues, I dried myself off. Tyton took another one and helped, and soon we were back to kissing and exploring each other's bodies.

"You never asked me what position I wanted to try the most," he mumbled.

I was still sitting on the edge of the table and felt his fingers squeeze my hips only to slide down and lift my legs up. My heart beat faster with excitement.

"There are two that I'm dying to try." Tyton pulled back from kissing me. "Lean back."

Trusting him, I laid back, propping myself on my elbows, curious to see what he was going to do.

With intense desire radiating from him, he lifted my legs up and placed them against his strong chest before aligning our bodies and using his thumb to rub over my clitoris. "This is one of them."

I bit my lip.

"You're so damn wet." Using his fingers, he opened me up and inserted a finger inside me. I closed my eyes and moaned a little.

"Open your eyes." His tone was demanding. "I want to see the expression in your eyes when I claim you."

I smiled but now wasn't the time to point out that claiming was a thing of the past. I was a modern woman and no man could ever... I didn't have a chance to finish my thoughts on the matter before something much larger than a finger pressed against my core.

"Look at me!"

Tyton had his hands hooked under my knees, holding them up while I pushed up from my elbows to let my hands support the weight of my torso.

"Are you seeing this?"

Men of the North – FORBIDDEN LETTERS

"Yes." I looked down to see him push against me. His cock looked enormous and I frowned, doubting that it would work.

He intensified the pressure and the plum-shaped tip of his cock moved inside me.

"Oh, Mother Nature." This was like five fingers at the same time and somewhat painful.

He pulled back a little, only to push in more, and when his entire crown was inside of me, he rocked back and forth.

Lowering myself back to my elbows, I locked eyes with him again. "We're really doing this."

His eyes were glowing with pride. "You're mine now!"

I closed my eyes taking in the sensation of being stretched by Tyton.

He kept going and what had felt like too much at first became pleasurable.

I followed his lead when he lowered my feet and pulled me to stand only to move me around and push me down over the table.

"Lift your knee." He touched my right hip and I complied, lifting my knee up on the table. "You look fucking gorgeous."

I held onto the edge of the table when he squatted down behind me and licked me like I was his favorite candy.

We were back in that special place of ours where nothing else mattered. His sounds of hunger as he kept kneading my behind and licking me made it easy to relax and enjoy the sexual pleasure that I hadn't known until I met Tyton.

Squeezing the table harder, I closed my eyes, moaning out loud. "Yes, Tyton. It feels amazing. So good."

I was like clay in his hands and he kept pushing me higher and higher until my insides began contracting in that same delicious way they had in the meadow today.

"Mmm..." My moans grew deeper and just when I was about to let go, he got up and pushed inside of me. It was an exquisite feeling of joy that overtook me as the table shook from his moving in and out of me.

"Yes. Yes... oh, Tyton, yes."

His fingers were boring into my hips and we were both panting but I didn't want any of it to stop. I was soaring above all worries and no grief could reach me this high up in our special place.

"More... yes, Tyton... this feels so good."

"You're mine now. Mine!" His hips slammed against my behind as he kept pushing in and out of me.

My orgasm felt like a ball of fire growing in size until it exploded and spread as euphoria in my bloodstream. I couldn't hold back the scream that followed. "Oh, yes, that's it. Yes!"

Tyton growled low, wrapped his arms around my waist, and held me in a firm grip. The guttural sounds that came from him sounded like "I'm coming."

He was coming inside me. I knew it and the romantic part of me welcomed it. This wasn't what Nana had meant when she told me to get pregnant, but it felt right.

As soon as I moved, Tyton's hold on me tightened to an iron grip. It felt so primeval and in my state of post-orgasmic bliss I pushed back against him like a nonverbal assurance that I was okay with his filling me up with his semen.

He leaned over me and kissed my spine with a deep sigh of satisfaction.

CHAPTER 26
Constant Stream of Letters

Tyton

Three weeks after my night with Devina, I sat against a tree in our garden with Lilo and Rocky lying next to me. The two Newfoundland puppies had been a gift from my dad to my mom now that she had no more children to fuss over, but I was the one who spent the most time with them and they were exhausted from running on our estate all morning.

In my hands were the latest chapters to the book and once I'd made my last comment, I picked up the letter Devina had attached this time and read it again.

Dearest Tyton,

Here are the last three chapters. I've included the scenes you wrote and I have to say that I loved Mark's inner thoughts on his relationship with Deidra. I cried when he spoke about his desire for intimacy. To feel her and to be felt by her. To dare being naked, vulnerable, and flawed. To find acceptance and safety and to be a haven of love for her. It was so beautiful when he admitted that the intimacy that he had found with Deidra was better than what he had imagined it could ever be.

For Mark to be willing to live in the Motherlands in order to have a family is the most romantic thing ever and I think readers will love the dramatic ending to the book. I know I cried when I wrote it, so hopefully it will touch them as well.

This morning I woke up wondering if Mark's thoughts about intimacy were your own. Were those your thoughts that night we spent together?

I wish I could see you again, but I stick by my decision that it's better if we stay apart. Although often, when I'm in my bed trying to sleep, I come up with all sorts of crazy plots in my head to find a way for us to be together.

Part of me wants to ask you to come here, like Mark did in the book, but we've been over this so many times and the chance we took by you coming here the last time was reckless.

I couldn't hide you in the house forever and once the authorities knew you were here, they would hand you back to King Jeremiah, who would kill you for breaking the law of never crossing the border.
Even if we could beg the authorities to let you stay, we wouldn't be together. I guarantee that they would submit you to long-term evaluation in a closed facility.
I can't bear the thought that you'd come to resent me in time for coming between you and your parents, siblings, nephews and nieces. You're always so protective of me, but this time, I'm also protective of you.

May your day be filled with sunshine and good thoughts,

Love, Devina

With a sad smile, I trailed my fingers over the last two words, *Love, Devina.*
Is she saying that she loves me?

I wasn't sure how much to put into it, but it was the first time she'd used the word love, and there had been a constant stream of letters going back and forth between us.

I had brought a pen and pad and wrote my answer to her while the puppies lay sleeping on the grass next to me.

Dear Devina,

We will see each other again and we will repeat that night. It's all I think about!
I hate these last chapters of the book – simply because they are the last.
My only hope is that your editing phase will be long and keep you here. My life has come to revolve around our letters and the answer to your question is a big yes.
Being with you exceeded everything I'd ever envisioned intimacy could feel like.

Love, T

PS: I'm enclosing a flower from my garden. It's called mountain phlox and is one of the wildflowers that grew in the meadow. For the rest of my life, at least once a day, I'll close my eyes to remember you on that bed of flowers in the meadow. Also, Wilma sent you a letter that I'm passing on.

I folded the paper and plucked one of the small purple flowers beside me. Picking up Wilma's letter, I read it one more time.

My sweet Devina,

So sorry that I've only written you a few letters but I can't tell you how busy I am as a married woman.

Emmerson is on me all the time and we're learning about marriage together. I'm not saying it's easy because there are days when he annoys me more than Tyton with his know-it-all attitude. Like for instance, he postulated that all women in the Motherlands have short hair and look like men. Since I'm the only one with a Motlander friend, I consider myself an expert and I told him that you have long hair and that you're very feminine, but guess what; Emmerson thinks that I made you up, and you want to know why? Because Tyton and my parents shook their heads like they had no idea what I was talking about when I asked them to confirm that you came to our wedding. Can you believe that shit?
Emmerson thinks it's cute that I have an invisible friend and when I showed him your letters as proof, he suggested that I'd fabricated the letters myself out of boredom or because I long for a female best friend.
Do you know how stupid that makes me look now that I'm sitting here writing you?
Anyway, men can be fools and that's why I'm happy I have a sound friend in you who knows how real you are and that I'm not crazy.

I love you, my dear friend, and I hope you understand that once the weather permits it, you must swim over again so I can prove to my husband that not all Motlander women have short hair.

Big hugs and lots of kisses,

Wilma

It was a good thing that my parents had kept to our agreement of never telling anyone about Devina. Wilma seemed to think of their friendship as something that gave her bragging rights, but people talked and there was no reason to let the rumor reach our unstable king, who was unpredictable, dangerous, and greedy.

A woman was worth more than all the gold in the Northlands, and who knew what twisted ideas he would have when it came to Devina?

As I threw over the letters, I felt a pang of fear in my chest that one day Devina would pick up and move on from our letters and me. She had told me from the beginning that she wouldn't stay forever, but I couldn't bear the thought of losing our connection.

CHAPTER 27
Editing

Devina

My steps felt extra slow and heavy when I walked to the border that morning in December. Brushing fallen leaves off the catapult, I noticed how the wood had turned greenish and slimy from months out here in the forest.

I squatted down next to the catapult in the same spot where I'd found Wilma's first bottle and stared at the border wall. I hated every brick that kept me and Tyton separated.

Nellie sat down next to me with her tongue hanging out and her eyes watching me. It was cold and her breath was showing like a cloud of moisture.

"Don't look at me like that. It's been three and a half months since I saw him. This has to be done."

Sending this bottle off would feel like letting the catapult rip my heart apart. This was the letter Tyton feared the most. It was my goodbye.

As a way of prolonging the moment before I had to send what felt like an arrow straight to his heart, I read my letter one last time.

My dearest Tyton,

As I already told you, I've never written a book as fast as I wrote Forbidden Letters from the North.
With our love story as inspiration and our constant stream of letters, it felt like the story wrote itself.

With all the times you've offered to come to me, the temptation grows. But the wall was never what truly separated us. It's our difference in culture and the fact that you would be feared on this side and I'd be auctioned off on your side.

I wish we could find the same kind of happiness as Mark and Deidra found in our story of them. But then Mark paid a high price and even if you were willing to give up on your family, the warm welcome Mark received in the Motherlands was fictional.

The truth is that for the last months, I've edited the book again and again. The glimpses of happiness when I'm picking up a letter from you has made it a precious time in my life. But I can't lie to myself any longer. It's clear that I'm searching for things to edit so I can justify staying a little longer although I know it's long overdue for me to go.
Loving you is like loving a ghost that I can sense but never touch.

My publisher loved the script I sent her and I'm bringing her the final version today.
I'm not taking Nellie with me to the city. She wouldn't like it there, and the forest ranger has agreed to adopt her. She already has three other dogs that Nellie likes to play with.

I'll be back to give over the house on December 30th. I doubt a new family will move in anytime soon since most considered us crazy for being willing to live this close to the border in the first place.
Letting go of the house with all the memories of my family and our night together is going to be the hardest thing I ever had to do, but I can't keep holding on to it.

Tyton, I don't know how to say this and I've written at least fifteen versions of this letter, but once I close down the house and leave, I can't promise you that I'll ever be back.

I hope to find a last letter from you when I return on the 30th, but I fear that you'll be too mad at me to write me back. In that case, I want you to know that I'll carry the memory of you with me forever and that no matter what happens in my future, I'll never forget you or the love we shared.

Love, Devina

Standing up, I took a long breath to steady my heart. My throat was itchy from the tears running down my cheeks and my hands trembled when I placed the letter in the bottle and sent it off with the catapult.

Long after the bottle was out of sight, I stood motionless, rooted to the ground by the immense pain that filled me from knowing my words would hurt the man I loved.

And then I heard it in the far distance. A long howl of sorrow with the word "Nooo" screamed out like someone was ripping out Tyton's soul.

He had read my letter and even if I'd wanted to scream back, I couldn't with the way my throat closed, and I couldn't breathe.

My tears clouded my vision and Nellie whined next to me when I fell to my knees and sobbed.

"Noooo..." The distant roar from Tyton was cutting my chest open and making my heart bleed.

Holding my hands to my belly, my shoulders bobbed as I sucked in air between sobs.

I had lost so many in the last six months and now I was losing Tyton too. He couldn't guarantee my safety on his side of the border and the only thing that I could guarantee on my side was that I would love him. I didn't for one second believe that would be enough when everyone else would loathe everything he represented. In the book, Mark had faked his own suicide in order to live with Deidra, but the pain that would inflict on Tyton's loved ones made that unthinkable.

Ever since I found out that I was pregnant, I'd wanted to tell him so badly. But if Tyton knew about it, he would have climbed the wall and refused to ever leave me.

I should have told him, the selfish part of me blamed myself but in all his letters he'd talked about fishing with Frederick and his father, hiking and racing with his friends. Tyton was social and had people he loved and who loved him in the Northlands. I couldn't fill all their shoes and if there was anything I understood, it was loneliness.

There was a reason no Nman and Motlander lived together. It was simply because it only worked in a romance.

CHAPTER 28
Publishing

Devina

"This is outstanding work, my darling." My publisher, Ebony, had her short curly hair under control with a yellow hairband that contrasted with her dark skin. "When you first spoke about an Nman, I thought you were joking, but this story is like something out of the olden days. It's like you're writing with a completely new, fresh, and unique voice, and the steamy scenes were so unexpected."

"Do you think the audience will like it?"

Ebony leaned back. Resting her elbows on the side of her chair, she let her fingertips meet and form a triangle in front of her. "They will either love it or hate it. It's one of those books. Oh, but don't look so scared, I was up reading it all night, and I've already passed it on to three people here at the office. If they are as impressed as me, we'll go all in and push this baby so far into the world that *everyone* will know about *Forbidden Letters from the North*." Ebony narrowed her eyes. "This could be your big breakthrough."

"You think?"

"Yes! I don't want you to get your hopes up, but I'm thinking of swapping your release date with Anisa's. She's on a mountain somewhere meditating and I'm not convinced she's up for the press tour."

My eyes found the pictures of Ebony with Anisa, one of the most famous authors in the Motherlands. The two women were smiling at some book-signing event.

"Okay."

"If we work fast, your book could be going out to librarians next week. If they like it, they'll share it with the reading groups and we'll be golden.

"Why rush it? You always said it's better to take our time."

"I know, but when you have something like this, it's too good to sit on." Pursing her lips, she gave me a mischievous smile. "We're so close to beating the other publishers, and your book could be our winter miracle."

"All right." It was all going so fast and I'd never seen her so enthusiastic about any of my books. "That sounds good."

"Great!" Standing up, she moved around her table. "But I have to ask you. How in the world did you come up with the idea of mixing romance with an Nman? It's so bold. I mean, you might as well have written about a demon or Lucifer himself."

"Maybe Nmen aren't as bad as we think."

"Ha!" Ebony shook her head. "As long as they stay on their side of the border, I don't mind playing pretend games, but if I saw one in real life, I'd run for my life."

I furrowed my brow. "You wouldn't even give him a chance before you ran?"

"Nooo. Can you imagine?" She laughed.

"So what if, on a hypothetical level of course, my book wasn't based on my imagination but on an actual experience? What if I knew an Nman and wanted him to live here with me?"

Ebony stared at me like I was talking in a dead language.

"What if I was in love with an Nman?" I specified.

Her whole face fell and she walked over to take my hand. "Darling, this happens sometimes, you know. All great authors have artistic souls and your characters feel real to you. I should have known that being alone in that forest for so long wasn't healthy for you. Especially after what happened to your family." Lifting her hand to her collarbone, she looked ridden with guilt. "How awful that we didn't insist on your coming back here."

"I'm fine."

"Okaay…" She dragged the word out and it dripped with skepticism. "Then you understand that Mark is just a character, right?"

I pulled my hand back. "Of course."

"Good."

"I'm just asking you if you think our society could embrace and welcome an Nman if he decided to live here."

"In theory, yes."

"But in reality?"

She shrugged. "Well, as long as he was willing to shave and fit in with the rest of us, I suppose it wouldn't be impossible. But he would have to give up everything that makes him an Nman and where's the fun in that?"

"But Deidra accepted Mark for who he was."

"What would it matter, if the things he enjoys are illegal here? He couldn't fish, hunt, eat meat, or wear leather. And he would have to give up alcohol, which he seemed very fond of in your book."

"Yes, but they would have each other."

Ebony sat down on the edge of the table. "You know what, when readers ask you, just stick with the answer that it's possible. It's better if you don't get too realistic. Let them love the fantasy of Mark as the dangerous demon."

"He's not a demon. He's a man."

"Who can hurt you." Ebony winked. "I felt almost filthy for loving the book so much but I suppose even we modern women can dream of fixing corrupted men."

Pushing the chair back, I got up from my seat. "He's *not* a demon!"

"All right, calm down. I didn't mean to upset you." Ebony rose to her feet and took my hand again. "You seem stressed. Why don't you go and get a massage? That helps."

I wanted to scream that I could never have a massage again without being reminded of Tyton and it would hurt too much.

"See your friends and go out a little. It'll do you good, my dear. Once we've had an internal meeting about your book, I'll tell you what the plan is and we'll get you all set up for the press tour."

A few hours after I'd left Ebony's office, I met up with two of my author friends whom I'd studied with. After the initial kissing and hugging we caught up and talked about their current projects and when it was time to talk about me, I suddenly got uncomfortable.

"Didn't you say you had a meeting with your publisher this morning?" My friend Tina blew her nose and it made her large blonde curls bounce around her head. "I'm so sorry but my nose is stuffy. I thought about canceling, but it's been so long since we saw you and I've missed you."

I smiled. "I missed you too. And you're right, I met with Ebony today."

"And did it go well?"

"I think so. She was excited about the book and called it fresh and unique."

Amber, who had been in an accident as a child and sat in a wheelchair, leaned in. "I'm dying to know what it's about."

"It's a romance."

"A romance?" The surprise on Tina's face was followed by Amber's wrinkling her nose up and tossing her many thin braids over her shoulders. The bright colors of pink, yellow, green, blue, and purple yarn in her braids complimented her caramel-colored skin.

"Who writes romances nowadays?"

Taken aback by Amber's negative tone, I arched an eyebrow. "I do."

"But why? Is there even an audience for that?"

Tina shushed Amber, and focused on me. "What's the book about?"

I told them about *Forbidden Letters from the North* and Tina moved further to the edge of her chair. "And then what?"

"Then Mark's brother follows him and climbs the wall too. He's jealous and waits until Mark goes home that night and then he sneaks into Deidra's house."

"Oh no." Tina gasped while Amber covered her ears. "If he hurts her, I don't want to hear about it. This is getting scary."

"Relax, it's a romance. They always have happy endings."

"What kind of happy story involves a woman in danger? I'm surprised your publisher didn't tell you to remove that part."

"A little danger can hook your audience." I blew down at my cup of tea, which was too hot for me to drink.

"You mean traumatize them."

"Amber is right. You have to be careful not to write something too upsetting."

I stared at them. "What's wrong with you two? I've been gone less than six months and you talk like you've forgotten everything Professor Maddison taught us at the university: good writing makes your blood boil, your head spin, or your pulse speed up. You may hate what you read, but if words can affect you that much, the author did well."

When they just exchanged a wary glance, I groaned. "You do remember those words, right?"

Amber fiddled with the armrest of her wheelchair. "I'm not sure I believe those words anymore. The Council has been collecting data on the effects of emotionally loaded entertainment and it's alarming. I mean people used to love horror stories and now everyone knows that they are toxic for your brain."

"Still. Isn't it our very job as authors to provoke and excite readers? How can I write a book if I'm scared of upsetting their feelings?"

Amber shrugged. "Tina and I both write mystery novels, and we've had to adapt after the ban on horror came out. Now we just make sure it never gets too much."

I frowned. "So, you're okay with the Council censoring our writing?"

Amber nodded. "I think they have to. I would be devastated if I traumatized or upset anyone."

Leaning back, I sat down my tea and hooked my hands under my thighs. "That's bonkers."

Tina lowered her voice. "Careful. You don't want anyone to report you for improper communication."

"Very funny."

When they didn't smile back at me, my laughter died and my lips disappeared in a single flat line. "Don't tell me that the Council went through with the communication law?"

"You didn't know? It was on the News. There's directions on WiseShare."

"No, I didn't know!" I looked around as if everyone in the restaurant might be taking notes on my every word. "And I can't say bonkers anymore?"

Tina looked to Amber. "I don't know, can she?"

"I'm not sure either. The list of offensive words is so long."

Running my hands through my hair I felt like I was suffocating. "Excuse me, but I need some fresh air."

I got up and walked outside the restaurant, where I looked up at the gray December sky. Now, it was a given that Tyton could never be happy here. He would get reported the moment he opened his mouth.

Looking down the street, I saw two men biking while talking. They looked pretty with their red lips and braided hair. I couldn't hear what they were talking about, but one of them laughed out loud.

These men were nothing like Tyton, and he could never fit in as one of them. Tears streamed down my cheeks and I stood in limbo feeling too changed to fully belong here with the direction my country was taking.

The men noticed me crying and their brakes squeaked when they came to a halt. "Are you hurt? What's wrong?" the tallest of them asked with concern on his pretty face.

I didn't try to hide my tears; instead a question burst from me like I was some kind of rambling idiot, "Are you happy living here?"

"What do you mean?" They exchanged confused glances.

"Do you ever wonder if you'd be happier living in the Northlands?"

"What is she talking about?" the shorter man asked his friend as his hands went to check on his hair and make-up.

"I don't know." The taller of the two got off his bike to place an arm around me. "Do you have a friend we can call for you? You seem a little stressed out, dear."

"My friends are inside." I sniffled and used my sleeve to dry my eyes.

"Okay, do you want us to take you to them?"

I shook my head but he insisted and walked me to the entrance of the café. Before the door closed behind me, I heard his shorter friend call out to him:

"What did she mean about our wanting to live in the Northlands? Do you think she was hinting that we looked uncombed and savage?"

"I hope not."

Their quiet chatter faded as I went back to my friends.

As soon as Tina saw me, she got up from the table to hug me. "Sweetie, I can't believe you didn't know about the proper communication law. Are you afraid for your book? Is that why you ran out?"

"Yeah," I lied because telling them that I loved a man who swore all the time wouldn't do.

"Oh, I'm sure readers will love your book. Romance might be a tiny genre, but that gives you the chance to do well in it. I'll read it if that helps."

"Thank you, Tina. It might be the only copy that gets downloaded."

Sitting back down, I sipped from my now cold tea while trying to hide the heavy sadness that made it hard to breathe. Tina and Amber were some of my best friends, but still I didn't feel like I could tell them about Tyton, or even Wilma for that matter.

While growing up, I'd asked my nana many times why we lived in such a rural area and she had repeated over and over that being alone and feeling lonely are two different things. She had insisted that it was possible to feel lonely while surrounded by people, but I'd never understood the significance of that until this moment. I couldn't trust my friends with my secrets, and it made me feel like there was a physical barrier between us.

Tyton had been a bright spot of healing light in a pitch-dark time in my life. To hear Ebony talk about Nmen as demons and for my two best friends to worry about petty stuff like saying the wrong words made me feel lost among my own people.

For twenty-eight years I'd thought of us Motlanders as open-minded, educated, and kind-hearted. Now I wasn't so sure. I longed to talk to Tyton or read more of his fearless chapters that always made my heart beat faster. He wasn't afraid of offending others and he liked to provoke. I used to see those as faults in him but the more I reflected on it, the more I realized that they were some of the most refreshing and liberating qualities about him.

Tina touched my arm. "I'm going to get some cake. Do you want anything?"

I shook my head with a polite smile, but in my head a loud voice boomed. *Yes, I want Tyton.*

HAPTER 29
Cut Off

Tyton

I'd been on edge ever since Devina'd moved away. She had warned me this would happen, but the pain of being cut off was still gnawing at me every time I thought about it, which was all the fucking time.

I missed her letters with our daily discussions about the story line in the book and the cultural differences between Northlanders and Motlanders. It was entertaining to me how little she understood about us Nmen, and all our correspondence had made me reflect on things that I always took for granted.

She had assumed that I'd be angry with her for moving away and she was right. She had left me powerless on this side of the wall with no way to reach her. Even though all her arguments about why we could never be together were valid, I wasn't ready to accept it.

Devina was the most spectacular woman I'd ever met and living the rest of my life without any contact with her was not an option for me. That's why, after reading her goodbye, I'd roared out my despair, crumpled up her letter, and known one thing for sure: on December 30th when she would be back one last time to close up her house, I'd be waiting on her doorstep!

Without her daily letters it felt like a part of me had been amputated. Several times a day, I stopped what I was doing and looked in the direction of the wall. It was always the same strong pull to see if by some miracle a letter was waiting for me. Ten days had gone by with my checking at least three times a day. Nothing!

By now, it felt torturous to get my hopes up only to have them crushed over and over again.

With my head bowed and my chest tight from missing Devina, I was walking back from another unsuccessful visit to the border when shouting voices and the sound of glass splintering made me stop for a split second before I set off into a full sprint.

Inside the house, I saw Frederick smashing another glass against the wall while screaming.

My dad looked just as agitated as Frederick and my mom sat on the couch bent over with her hands in her hair while Starr was rubbing her back.

"What's going on?"

Fredericks's nostrils were flaring when he turned to me. Holding up a hand he gestured that he was too amped-up to speak.

"What the fuck is going on?" I repeated, and this time Starr answered me with tears dripping down her cheeks. "It's King Jeremiah." Her eyes fell to a ripped-up letter on the floor.

I picked it up and put it together to read it.

Starr's voice broke, "It came today. I already talked to Marni, Claire, and Wilma. They all got the same letter."

"But what does it mean?"

Frederick sneered out loud, "It means the sick fucker has decided he wants a wife and every husband of a beautiful young woman is in danger."

My eyebrows drew close together as I read the letter again. "He's saying that he claims the right to marry a woman should she become a widow."

My mom's crying intensified.

"But that's not how it works," I exclaimed and looked to my dad. "A widow has the right to choose her own husband."

"Since when did King Jeremiah let laws stop him from getting his way?"

My mom lifted her head. "No woman in her right mind would ever choose him. He's mentally unstable and his breath alone is enough to make people keep a distance."

Frederick paced the floor. "Did you see how he ogled Starr at the tournament? If he decides he wants her, I'm a dead man."

My dad stood with his feet spread and his arms crossed. "It was the same with Claire and Wilma. He wants a young wife so he can have an heir."

"Then he should have fucking competed in a tournament when he was younger," Frederick stopped and growled while I fisted my hands.

"No woman deserves to be forced into marriage. I would rather die than marry him." Starr kept rubbing my mom's back.

I wasn't married myself, but this affected my whole family. Holding out the pieces of the letter, I looked to my brother. "Did you talk to anyone about it?"

Frederick gave a short nod. "The others are on their way."

Within the next hour the house filled up, with my three sisters and their husbands adding their voices to the speculations that within a year King Jeremiah would arrange for a beautiful young woman to become a widow.

"We have to fight this." Emmerson was livid. "We all know that he'll go after Wilma with her being a new bride and not yet a mother."

"No. I'll kick him before I let him touch me," Wilma declared.

"Claire isn't a mother either." My eyes went to my sister, who stood pressed up against her husband, Lucas. "You and Wilma would be his obvious choice."

Claire paled. "You think he'll kill Lucas to get to me?"

Lucas gave a low sneer. "Let him try. I can defend myself. Jeremiah is no match for me."

Frederick snorted. "Don't be a fool. He's not stupid enough to go up against any of us man to man. He's sneaky and he'll make it look like an accident."

I propped my hands under my armpits. "Not if he has an accident first."

There was a moment of silence in the room and then Emmerson lifted his chin. "Keep talking."

Over the next hours we plotted the death of our king. Our best chance was at one of the upcoming Christmas parties where he would be eating and getting drunk.

"You men won't get any weapons past the security, but I can smuggle in a dagger under my skirt," Marni offered.

"What about poison? I could have some in my bra," Wilma added.

"Whoa, we're not leaving it to you women to protect us!" Emmerson frowned.

"None of you are killing the king. I am!"

The room went quiet and they all stared at me.

"You sure, Tyton?" Henry asked. "If anything goes wrong, you're dead."

Despite the pressure in my chest, I nodded. "You women are too valuable and I'm the only single man in this room. If anything goes wrong and I die, I won't be leaving a widow for him to prey on. It has to be me!"

My father, Henry, Lucas, and Emmerson all bowed their heads to me and Frederick grabbed my shoulder. "You won't be alone. We'll help you."

"Yes, whatever you need," Marni added.

"As long as you distract his guards like we talked about; I'll need the time to get close to him."

CHAPTER 30
Killing a King

Tyton

The annual Christmas party at the royal palace was an affair with tight security. Our family had a prominent place in society, which put us on the guest list, but we weren't close to the king and were seated in the other end of the large banquet hall.

The plan was simple. We would wait for the king to get drunk and start bragging like he did every year. Once he began wandering through the room to make sure we all heard him boast, I would challenge him to a drinking contest and hand him a glass with beer that was poisoned.

If it worked, I would have ended the tyranny of our worthless king.

If it failed, I would be executed.

Marni's original plan to smuggle in a dagger under her skirt had been shot down by us men. The previous years, women had been exempted from walking through security scanners like us men, but rumors were that King Jeremiah was getting more paranoid.

As the night progressed, the voices of the two hundred people in the room grew louder. Music played and men were erupting in drunken laughter here and there.

Our king was surrounded by his supporters during dinner but as anticipated he grew tired of their company and began shouting to people at other tables, lifting his glass and drinking like there was gold on the bottom of his glass.

We watched him push up from his chair and scream profanities at random people.

"Here he comes," Frederick whispered.

According to plan, I'd pretended to drink heavily and acted drunk for the last hour. "I'm ready," I slurred, keeping in character.

With King Jeremiah attracting attention, no one saw me slip the powder in a jug of beer.

Raising my beer in the air, I shouted across the hall to Jeremiah. "Oi, you think you're so good at drinking… Come prove it."

His skin was reddish and his forehead sweaty, which made his thin hair stick to his forehead in a peculiar fashion. Swaying a bit, he watched me and lifted his chin with a frown. "Tyton Green."

I made a stunt of almost tripping when I got up from the bench I was seated at. "I have to take a piss, but before I go why don't you come here and show us how good of a drinker you are?" My speech was slurred and as planned, my dad and Frederick reached out to reel me in, shushing me. I batted their hands away. "It's fiiine! He's a man. I'm a man. We drink beer."

People had gone silent around us, watching our king as he staggered toward us. "You think you can down your beer faster than me?"

"I know I can." I hiccupped and used my hand to support myself against Frederick. "I can fucking take on all of you." My finger pointed to the entire room and men began to laugh.

"Tyton, sit down!" my dad hissed.

"Are you game or not?"

Frederick took the jug with poisoned beer and filled his own glass. Just as he lifted it to his mouth, I reached for it and handed it to Jeremiah. "Get ready to lose!"

I didn't wait for him to accept but lifted my glass and just as I'd hoped for, he took the bait and drank.

It was like the man had no gag reflex and just swallowed the content in one go.

"Bloody hell," I exclaimed when he finished before me. Jeremiah gave a loud burp but then his facial color changed from red to pale white and his cheeks bobbed out.

I glanced at Marni, who had supplied the poison from her friend who was married to a pharmacist. It was supposed to be a slow-working poison but Jeremiah looked like he was going to be sick.

Frederick pulled me back just as a projectile of vomit spewed from Jeremiah.

"What the fuck?" Some drunken men laughed and joked that he couldn't hold it in, but Jeremiah was a proud man and took offense.

"There's nothing wrong with me. The beer was stale and tasted like shit." Lifting his hand, he pointed at my table. "You people pissed in my beer."

"No!"

Some of his security came over and pressing his almost empty glass into the chest of his guard, Jeremiah dried his mouth and ordered, "Take this to Bernard. Tell him to test it. If I drank piss someone is going to die!"

I swallowed hard. "I assure you that's not necessary."

"You laughed at me." His eyes narrowed as he swayed back and forth while pointing with uncoordinated movements. "All of you laughed and *no one* laughs at me."

"Your highness, we never laughed," my father tried to say, but the room had gone silent and a filthy stink from King Jeremiah's vomit made a few women turn their heads with disgust.

"Arrest them!" Turning on his heels, Jeremiah swayed as he walked back to his own table while shouting over his shoulder. "Arrest every man at that table. I won't be ridiculed in my own house."

Like a group of killer bees, armed guards surrounded our table. Squaring my chest, I stepped in front of my mom to form a wall with my dad. Around us Emmerson, Lucas, Frederick, and Henry did the same."

"Don't fight back. We are unarmed and outnumbered. If they shoot, they might hit one of our women," my dad said loud enough for all of us to hear it.

Still, I elbowed the guard who pushed at me. With a hand to his bloody nose, he raised his gun to point it at my head, sneering, "Move motherfucker."

Henry and my dad moved forward with their hands up, while Lucas, Frederick, and Emmerson fought back like me. We all knew that if Bernard, Jeremiah's personal doctor, tested the content of the glass he'd find something much worse than urine.

Jeremiah's captain who had been at the high table and was drunk himself, waved his gun around and fired a shot against the ceiling. "Move or I'll decorate the walls with your brains." Screaming at his guards he gestured to the door. "Just get the filthy traitors out of here."

As we were pushed out of the room, Jeremiah sneered one last thing. "Don't worry. We'll take good care of your women."

Being locked up in a small cell with the others gave me too much time to worry.

We were hungry and on edge.

Six protectors unable to protect our women were like an explosive bomb of violence waiting to happen, and twice a fight broke out between Lucas and Emmerson. It took Frederick, Henry, my dad and I to separate them.

When the captain finally turned up, he only spoke to us through a square hole in the door.

"Where are our wives?" Frederick asked.

The captain looked amused by our misery. "Your wives are here in the palace. The king is entertaining them."

"Can we see them?"

"Yes. On New Year's Eve you'll see them."

"That's in eleven days. Is he going to keep us here for eleven days?" Henry's voice was full of disbelief. "I didn't do anything."

"That's the king's order."

"Will we at least get something to eat and drink? It's been two days and we've had nothing."

Snickering low, the captain joked, "The king said that since you're so fond of piss, you can drink your own."

"There was no piss in that beer."

"No, we know that."

I held my breath. "Then why are we still here?"

"You know why you're here. You tried to poison the king."

My head was exploding with panic and my eyes went to Frederick and my dad. They knew. This was bad!

"As I said, you'll see your women one last time on New Year's Eve since they will be there at your public execution."

With an aggressive growl, Emmerson ran against the door and slammed his shoulder against it.

The captain stepped back and closed the latch in the door.

"I should have fucking broken Jeremiah's neck when I had my chance." I groaned out loud and let my thoughts go to Devina.

My plan of being at her house when she came back was nothing but an impossible dream now. I'd been so sure that we would succeed. Now I wished that I'd at least left a message for her to find when she came back. The thought that Devina would leave for good thinking that I was too mad at her to write her back made me sick with sorrow.

My only consolation was that she wasn't here in the palace to see me being executed and that I'd left a small mark in this world by creating a book with Devina that people in the Motherlands would read.

I might be dead soon, but at least the story of Mark and Deidra would live on.

CHAPTER 31
Best Seller

Devina

Sitting on the windowsill of my apartment, I leaned my head against the window frame and looked out at the people walking the streets below me.

Those people had places to be, jobs to do, and friends and family to visit. A pair of women were walking close with their arms linked by the elbow. They were laughing and talking like they had no care in the world. I felt a pang of envy.

I used to be like them but now I felt detached and lost.

My book had caused a storm. The media hated it, but the more they talked about it, the more copies were picked up by readers around the world.

The critics used harsh words like "this was a waste of time," "worst book ever published," and several accused me of having a disturbing imagination.

I'd done interviews but even though the reporters had been polite and nice to me in person, their articles had been critical of my choice of topic.

Ebony had been right: Nmen were considered demonic monsters and my book had become a guilty pleasure no one would admit to reading.

When my phone rang, I considered ignoring it, but being a Motlander, I was too polite for my own good and so I answered it. "May peace surround you."

"Devina, I have bad news." It was Ebony and her voice sounded brittle, like she'd been crying.

"What happened?"

"Did they call you yet?"

"Who?"

She sighed. "Oh, sweetie, I don't know how to tell you this, but we've been ordered to unpublish *Forbidden Letters from the North*."

"Why?"

"Because according to the Council, it's a dangerous book that preys on the naïve and instills dangerous fantasies in the minds of fragile people."

I closed my eyes but didn't say anything.

"Devina, are you still there?"

"Yes, I'm still here.

"It's a great book, sweetie. It practically sells itself, but the Council is concerned and want it shut down."

"What exactly are they concerned about? It's just a book."

"I asked them the same question and it turns out that some readers have been going to the border searching for bottles and attempting to throw over bottles themselves. The council has had to increase the border patrol and put up more cameras and signs to remind everyone that there are mines. Yesterday a woman took it a step further and instead of throwing over a bottle, she got caught while trying to climb the wall. Unfortunately, she fell down and broke both her legs."

"Oh no!"

"Yeah, and according to the Council we're to blame for putting dangerous ideas into these people's minds."

"They told you that?"

Ebony sighed again. "They suggested that I should take some time off to reflect upon my part in all of this." Her voice broke again. "I don't have time to be away from my business and I don't want to be by some lake contemplating my part in the universe. I want to be where my friends are and have fun publishing books."

"I understand."

"They already dismissed the librarian who according to them made the mistake of approving the book and now they're going to contact you too."

I felt all blood sucking out of my face. "They said that?"

"Yeah."

"Because they think I'm crazy?"

"They didn't use the word crazy, but they worry that you're delusional and need help."

Turning my head, I looked to my entrance door. "How long do I have?"

"Not long."

"Ebony..."

"Yes?"

"Thank you for letting me know."

She sniffled. "You're probably going to be in reflection for months, so as your publisher I urge you to write a book while you're there. You'll have all the time in the world."

"If I write more about Deidra and Mark, they'll never let me out."

"No, don't do that. Maybe you could write a mystery novel under a new pen name or something."

I answered on the exhalation, "Yes, maybe."

"I'll contact you when things settle down."

"That's fine."

"Again, I'm sorry, Devina."

"I'm sorry too."

When I hung up, I sat for a second watching the people down on the street, wondering if any of them had read my book and whether they'd loved or hated it.

What am I going to do?

I had felt lost for a long time, but now I was falling into a dark pit of hopeless despair. In desperation, I reached out for a lifeline and called up Tina.

"Hey, love, Amber and I were just talking about you. Are you okay?"

In a loud and clear voice, I heard Amber call out to me in the background, "They just talked about your book on the News."

"Ebony called me. They're unpublishing my book." It flew out of me.

"I'm so sorry about that," Tina began before Amber interrupted: "Told you romance was a risk."

"Someone got injured climbing the wall to the Northlands, and they're blaming me for it."

"Yes, we saw on the News. It's horrible." Tina's tone was empathetic.

"Can you believe that a woman broke both her legs?"

Amber gave a small outburst. "It was because of your book."

The blaming in her voice made me defensive. "I never imagined my book would make people try and get to the Northlands. That was never my intention."

Amber wasn't helping. "See, this is why it's so important that we're responsible as authors. Our words inspire people to do either good or bad. That's why we need censorship."

"What did they say about me on the News?" My question was for Tina, but again, Amber answered and my irritation with her grew with every syllable that came out of her mouth.

"They used your book as an example to explain the Council's latest bill that expands the ban on emotionally charged entertainment."

"What does that mean?"

"You know that horror is banned, but now there will be a complete ban on all entertainment that evokes dangerous emotions such as terror, anger, or lust."

"A ban. No, they can't. Books are sacred."

"Well, would you rather have people break their legs or, worse, kill themselves because they believe in some far-fetched fantasy?"

Amber might as well have punched me physically. I gasped out loud and blinked my eyes. My throat was feeling like a cactus was stuck down there and speaking would hurt.

"Amber, that was harsh," Tina whispered but I said nothing. I couldn't!

My lifeline had failed and there was no one left to pull me out of the dark pit I was falling into. My nose tickled from the sobbing that wanted out, and once again, I felt grief hit me like a panic attack.

I couldn't see Tyton and tell him how awful I felt about a woman's getting hurt because of my book.

No phone line could ever reach my mom and let her tell me that things would be all right. And there was no going back to the house for one of Nana's wonderful healing sessions.

If only I could curl up with one of my sisters and share my worries for a while or get a bear hug from my dad. I suppressed the sob in my chest, closed my eyes, and remembered how he would always kiss me on the top of my hair and call me Miss Freckle.

They were all gone!

Justin would never prank me again and we would never celebrate another birthday in our family.

I didn't even have Nellie anymore.

"Devina, are you there? Is there a bad connection?" Tina sounded like she'd said my name several times, but my body weighed a thousand kilos and I had no strength to answer her.

Ending the call, I let my chin fall and gave in to the despair I felt. If I died this very minute, no one would miss me.

Two hours later, there was a knock on my door.

I had expected it and had calmed down enough to open the door with a polite smile that never reached my eyes.

Two women stood outside and introduced themselves as Leonie and Marcy, asking if they could come in.

Opening my door all the way, I gestured for them to go ahead.

"We've been wanting to talk to you for a while about your book." Leonie angled her head and gave me a sugar-sweet smile. "As you might have heard, it has had an unfortunate effect on many of your readers who now seem to think that Nmen are kind and wonderful people. With our history of their kidnapping and enslaving our women to breed for them, you can see why that's unfortunate, can't you?"

"That was more than a hundred years ago."

"Still, by painting a picture of them as heroic and evolved men, you've inspired many women to try and go there. Several have been hurt in the process but at least so far, we've managed to save all of them from actually crossing the border."

I didn't speak.

Leonie folded her hands in front of her and sat up straight. "As of today, the Council has requested that your book be banned."

"Yes, I've heard."

"Would you mind telling us what inspired you to write the book in the first place? You used to live close to the border, correct?"

"Yes."

"Have you ever had any contact with someone from the other side of the wall?"

"Do you mean if I exchanged letters myself?"

"Yes."

"What would it change if I did? You've already decided that you're banning my book."

They looked a bit surprised by my confrontational question.

Men of the North – FORBIDDEN LETTERS

"We're just trying to understand more about the situation. Can you confirm that you went to your doctor three days ago?"

"Yes."

"We've obtained your medical records and it shows that you're four months pregnant, yet you've had no visits to an insemination clinic. Can you explain how that's possible?"

My heart was beating fast. "I was impregnated by a man, of course."

Both women shifted on the sofa and exchanged a glance. "Can you direct us to him?"

"No."

"And why is that?"

Because it's none of your business. It was right there on my tongue, but I just shook my head.

"Can you give us his name at least?"

"Look, I had a short encounter with a man and it led to my pregnancy. I didn't see him after that and I don't want you to contact him."

Marcy cleared her throat. "Devina, we understand that you've gone through a difficult time with the loss of your family. It's easy to see how the book was created from the longing to be close to another person. Grief makes people do irrational things, but we feel that you would be better off taking some time to reflect and heal in a tranquil setting."

"How long?"

"As long as you need."

I looked away. "No thank you."

"You look like you've been crying. We're not here to punish you but to help you feel better."

My mind was numb except for one persistent thought that I clung to. I didn't want to accept censorship and laws banning books. I didn't want to be okay with the Council taking away our freedom of speech. I couldn't stand the thought of going to a place that served the Council and submit myself to constant reflection on how I had done something wrong when I hadn't!

Readers loved my book for a reason. It made them feel and dream of being loved themselves.

Marcy, a woman with a short dark bob, cleared her throat again. "Would you like to come with us now, or do you need a bit of time to make arrangements?"

My body stiffened as I understood that I wasn't being given a choice. One way or another, they wanted me in a place of reflection.

"We could give you a few days, if you need it."

I met Leonie's eyes. "I'm closing down my family's house in four days. I can go after that."

"Four days, that would be December 30th?"

"Yes."

"All right. Here's a list of the different facilities that you can chose from. Just let us know which one suits you the best and we'll make the arrangements."

Getting up from my chair, I bowed my head. "Thank you."

They got up too and by the door, they offered me their hands in a formal goodbye.

Leonie squeezed my hands and looked deep into my eyes. "Sometimes we make unfortunate choices and need help getting back on track. That's why we're here."

As soon as they were gone, I pressed my back against the door. My mind was racing to find a way out of the mess I was in.

Only one solution came to mind.

CHAPTER 32
The Mind of an Author

Devina

I had packed my few belongings and was closing the door to my apartment when Tina showed up out of breath and with a bag in her hand.

"Devina, where are you going?"

"Back to my family's house."

"I figured you might." She fell into step with me as I walked down the hallway to the staircase. "You're mad at Amber and me. I get it. When you hung up, I felt awful and then when you wouldn't pick up your phone... I was afraid that you'd never speak to me again."

"I have a lot on my mind."

Tina followed me outside the building to the self-driving community car that I'd ordered. When I got in, she was quick to get in with me.

"You want me to drop you off on the way?" It was the polite thing to ask even though I felt a little annoyed since Tina lived in the opposite direction.

"No, I'm coming with you." Her tone was matter-of-fact.

I scrunched up my face. "You can't come with me."

"You're going to do something wild. I know you."

I sighed. "You think that because I wrote an outrageous book, I only do wild things?"

"Tell me the truth." Her eyes fell to my belly. "Mark is real, isn't he?"

I'd told my friends that I had an experimental encounter with a man, but no one had questioned whether he was from the Motherlands.

My hesitation made Tina widen her eyes. "I knew it!"

"No, it's…"

She cut me off. "I couldn't tell you while Amber was there, but I read your book in one night. It was amazing. You made me feel like I was right there. Mark was so different, and I want to know how you came up with someone as fascinating as him. You have to tell me everything."

I turned my head and looked out the window as the community car drove down the street. "There's nothing to tell, Tina. I'm an author like you and we make up stuff."

She leaned back in her seat and gave me a scrutinizing look, but I didn't budge.

Then she leaned against me and whispered into my ear. "You're afraid our conversation is being recorded, aren't you? It's okay. You can tell me later."

My mind was reeling. I could use a friend, but would Tina try and stop me from executing my plan?

"It's a four-hour drive to the house. How about I take you home?"

"No thanks. If only we had one of the drones you described in your books… I'll bet the journey would be much shorter then."

I ignored her complaint. "You wouldn't like it at the house. I've packed up everything and I'm only going back to hand over keys and say one last goodbye."

"And then where will you go?"

"I've been asked to spend some time in a place of reflection."

Tina took my hand. "Maybe that wouldn't be such a bad thing. You've suffered a lot with the loss of your family. It would be a place for you to find peace again."

"Maybe, but..." I couldn't tell her that what I feared about going to a place of reflection was to be subjected to lectures about how disturbed my book was. My memories of my time with Tyton were precious and beautiful. I couldn't bear to let anyone poison them by planting doubt in my mind.

Tina was still stroking my hand. "I took a class on grief, you know."

"You did?"

"Yes. That's why I've never tried to cheer you up. Haven't you noticed?"

I moved in my seat. "What's wrong with cheering people up?"

"It doesn't help. People giving you advice on how to get over your grief by focusing on the positives are just making it worse. I've learned that the best thing we can do when someone is grieving is to acknowledge the pain they're in and walk next to them as they go through their darkness. It's not our job to take away their grief, and we couldn't if we tried."

"Yeah." I looked out the window. "I know I'll be grieving for the rest of my life."

"Of course you will. You lost your entire family." Tina weaved our fingers together. "Do you want to talk about it?"

"The worst part is the guilt that I wasn't there to help. Maybe I could have eased their suffering by reading to them or making sure they had food and water. I'm not saying that I could have healed them of the virus, but as the only survivor of my family, I keep thinking, why me?"

For the next hours, Tina listened as I talked about my family and my grief. She asked questions and let me go back to happier times for a while. It was nice to have someone to talk to about it, but when she suggested for the second time that maybe the place of reflection wouldn't be so bad, I shook my head again.

"No. I'm not letting anyone tell me what to think or feel. My book wasn't sick or twisted. It was a love story between two people who had been taught to dislike each other. If anything, it was a beautiful story of acceptance and tolerance."

"I agree. I loved every page of your book. I'm so sorry the Council couldn't see how wonderful it was. It's because they don't understand how the mind of an author works."

Her kindness and praise of my book made me squeeze her hand and give her a sad smile. "Tell me about your latest book. I would like to think of something other than my worries."

Tina did her best to entertain me with her gift of storytelling. She published mystery novels but had dabbled in a romance for her own amusement, although she had no hope of getting it published now that there was a ban.

When we arrived at the house in the forest, we got out and before we had unlocked the front door, the self-driving car had already left us.

"Aww, the house looks cute. It's exactly how you described it."

I walked inside with Tina at my heels and felt an instant surge of grief wash over me. Setting down my bag, I walked over to turn up the heat.

"There are blankets on the couch. Feel free to curl up under one."

Tina plunked herself down on the sofa and covered herself with the white throw-over that my dad knitted a few years ago.

"Let me just turn on the fireplace. That will warm up the living room fast."

Tina waited until I had lit the fire and joined her on the couch. "Here." She lifted the blanket and gestured for me to let it cover my feet. "You want to tell me the truth now?"

Again, I hesitated.

"Come on, Devina. The frenzy your book created with all the people dreaming of an Nman themselves happened because you're an amazing author. It's not right that they're banning your book."

"Why didn't you say that when Amber was around?"

Tina bit her lip. "Because people are going crazy these days and Amber has changed. I'm not sure, but I think she reported one of her sisters for improper communication."

"Are you saying that you're afraid of Amber?"

"Of course not. It's just that she's become quite judgmental. If I told her how much I loved your book, she might..." Tina trailed off and lifted her shoulders in a small shrug.

"She might think less of you. Is that it?"

"Mmm, with the way people have treated you, do you blame me for not wanting a piece of that?"

"I could have used someone in my corner."

Tina leaned forward and reached out her hand to me, her white unruly curls pointing in all directions. "I'm here now!"

My lips tugged upward in a tiny smile.

"So, tell me, is there a real Mark or not?"

I gave a single nod.

A shriek came from Tina, whose eyes glowed with excitement. "Tell me everything."

"His name isn't Mark. It's Tyton."

"Tyton... wow that sounds very Nmannish."

"Just like Mark in the book, Tyton runs a large family business overseeing their estate with its fields and woods."

"Is he a landscape architect like Mark?"

"No, I just made that up because Tyton likes to garden and he's outside a lot."

The heaviness in my chest lifted a little just from speaking about my deep secret. "Things happened much like in the book except it was his sister, Wilma, who threw over a letter and her that I began corresponding with."

I told Tina how I'd believed Wilma was in danger and how I'd gone to save her.

"Oh, Wind and Water, you're the bravest person I've ever met. Weren't you scared?"

"Terrified!"

"So, what happened?"

"I tapped on what I thought was Wilma's window and out of nowhere, Tyton attacked me from behind and carried me to a hay barn. I tried to get away from him, but he thought I was a danger to his family, so he was furious. He assumed I was a boy and wanted me to explain myself." I didn't tell Tina how Tyton had thrown me around and punched me.

She had her hands to her mouth and her eyes fixed on me as I told all the other details from that night.

"Why didn't you get on his bike?"

"Because I didn't know him!"

"Yeah, but if he was anything like Mark, he would have protected you."

"You're only saying that because you read my book, but to me, Tyton was a large and very scary Nman."

Tina's eyes lowered to my abdomen and a small triangle formed between her eyebrows. "Be honest. Did he rape you?"

"Nooo!!!"

She smiled. "Did he give you a book of tantra sex? Is that what happened? Like Mark did to Deidra in the book."

"No, that part was all fiction and written by Tyton."

"What?!"

"How would I know how to write sensual scenes like that? In the beginning he did it to mess with me but then we worked together to create a romance between a Motlander and a Northlander."

"That's crazy. I can't believe that you wrote the book with a real Nman."

"Yup."

"And when did you fall in love with him?"

I jerked my head back. Tyton and I had never spoken the words that we loved each other. At least not out loud.

"I mean you must have made love to him at some point."

I placed a hand on my belly. "The last time I was there, he took me home and stayed for the night."

Tina's voice sank to a whisper. "Was it as good as you described it in the book?"

"Yes. A thousand times yes." My eyes teared up when I said it.

"Then why didn't you beg him to stay with you? Why would you ever want to be apart from him?"

Blinking my tears away, I shook my head. "This isn't some fiction book, Tina. The Council won't even allow a book about an Nman. In what world do you think they would allow him to stay here?"

"But Mark..."

"Mark isn't real!"

"I know that. But Tyton is real and you're having a child with him. What did he say when you told him?"

I swallowed and looked down.

"You didn't tell him?"

Shaking my head, I blinked away more tears. "I wanted to but family means everything to him and it would have driven him mad to know he had a child on this side of the border that he couldn't raise."

Tina was quiet. "What if you went to the Northlands?"

My heart sped up. "It wouldn't be safe. They have a mad king and Tyton is convinced I would be auctioned off in a tournament."

"But then he could fight for you, couldn't he?"

"And what if he loses? I've seen their tournaments. It's brutal and inhuman. Men die, Tina."

"They die?" She scrunched up her face. "Do you mean *die* die?

"Yes. I don't want men fighting for me. I only want Tyton." It flew out of me with some force.

"Then what are you going to do?"

I looked away, unsure if I could trust her with my deepest secret.

Tina touched my leg. "Devina, what are you going to do?"

"I've made a decision." My eyes stayed downturned because I didn't want to face the shock in her eyes.

"Yes?"

"I'm not crazy and I don't want to spend months in a place of reflection. Tyton lives on an estate and I'm hoping he can hide me there somehow."

"What do you mean hide you?"

"If no one knows I'm there, we can raise our child without the mad king knowing about me."

Tina brushed her hands through her curls and frowned. "Devina, that's never going to work. You can't stay inside forever."

"I wouldn't have to. They have land and I could move around. If we go out, I'll dress as a boy. I've done it before."

"And your child. How would you explain your child?"

Throwing my hands up in despair, I sighed. "I don't know. I haven't figured out everything and that's why I need to meet with Tyton. We have to find a way to make it work."

Tina's face softened and her hand landed on her chest. "Aww, that's just like Deidra and Mark."

"Except we're not them." I tried to bring her back to reality.

"Okay, okay, but..." She looked around. "What's the plan then?"

"I'm going to write him a letter and hopefully, he'll answer right away. I can only stay here a few days before the officials will insist that I check into a place of reflection."

"And if he doesn't answer?"

Scratching my arm, I thought about it. "I don't know. I expect him to be angry with me for leaving so suddenly. Nmen are proud. Tyton might be too upset with me to answer."

"Then you have to tell him about the baby. I'll bet he'd answer then."

"Maybe."

While Tina stayed under the blanket, I got a pen and pad to write my letter.

Dear Tyton,

I'm back early and hope you're getting this letter.
Our book became an instant success and sold more copies than any of my other books. The good thing was that the Press spoke about the book a lot, which provided exposure, and boosted the sales. Almost three hundred thousand copies were sold and that's unheard of for a romance. The bad thing is that the Press hated it and called it a toxic book. Today, I was told that our book has been banned and that I'm considered a danger to the innocent minds of my readers.
I want to meet with you, Tyton.
Please write me back as soon as you can.

May our souls find a way to break down the wall between us,

Devina

When Tina and I walked through the forest to the border, we arrived to see new signs warning of mortal danger and a new security camera on top of the border wall.

"This is bad." I frowned and watched the camera to determine if it was a prop or the real thing. It didn't move and there were no lights in it to signal it was on.

Searching the ground for bottles, I was disappointed to see that there was nothing waiting for me.

Either Tyton had been too angry to respond to my goodbye letter or whoever had set up the new signs and the camera had found the bottle before I got here.

The catapult was still hidden under the branches where I'd left it, but it was slippery from moss.

"You think they'll record you on the camera?"

"Maybe, but what are they going to do about it?" I pulled my scarf higher over my nose to hide my face. Just as I was about to send off my letter, a small drone came flying along the border wall.

"Hide." I pulled Tina back and saw the tiny thing continue to the right along the wall.

"You never mentioned border drones in your book," she whispered.

"Because I've never seen one before today," I whispered back.

Tina scratched her nose, which was red from the cold. "Well, the News did say that the Council has increased the security along the border."

We waited a while before I sent off my letter. My heart was pounding. "I think we're good."

Tina helped cover up the catapult and just as we were about to walk away, the drone returned. This time it spotted us and a red light turned on.

"This is a restricted area and you must move away."

We turned our backs on it and jogged to get out of the way.

When we returned an hour later, we sneaked up, running from tree to tree.

"This is so exciting." Tina grinned. "I can use this in one of my mystery novels. I could have someone spying or avoiding being seen." The way she made herself small behind a large tree had me smiling.

She beamed back at me. "It's good to see you with color in your cheeks and a smile on your lips. I was worried for a while."

There was a moment when we just smiled at each other and then I whispered. "Thank you for coming with me."

"I wouldn't miss it for the world." As soon as she said it, she ran the next distance and pressed herself against another big tree.

We managed not to get detected by the border drones, but even though we checked for Tyton's reply four times that day, there was nothing.

When there still wasn't a bottle the next day, I wrote another letter.

Dear Tyton,

I understand that you're angry with me for leaving, but please, I need to talk to you.
Won't you answer me?

Devina

For two more days there was nothing but silence and Tina kept pushing me to tell him I was pregnant.

I resisted because I feared it would only upset him to find out that I hadn't told him about the pregnancy.

To Tina this was like another entertaining chapter in *Forbidden Letters from the North*, but for me there was nothing fun or exciting about Tyton's hating me. I longed for him and I physically hurt on the inside from worry that I might never see him again. Memories of our night together kept me above water and every time I walked to the border it was with hope in my chest.

When three days had passed without a sign of life from him, I sent him another letter.

Dear Tyton,

Tomorrow is New Year's Eve. I'm giving over the house at noon and then I have to leave. You don't know how much I wish I could stay and wait for your anger to cool down, so we could talk.

Please forgive me for causing you the pain that would make you hold a grudge so deep that you continue to ignore me and refuse to write me back.

For what it's worth, I think of you constantly, and I meant it when I said that I love you.

Devina

Tina stood by my shoulder when I sent off the letter.
"Did you tell him about the baby this time?"
"No."
"Why not? I'm sure it would make him write you back."
"I have to tell him in person."
"How? He won't even respond to your letters. I hate to say it, Devina, but maybe he doesn't love you the way Mark loved Deidra."
My throat felt like someone was pouring down boiling hot tea and it hurt.

"I'm not saying it to upset you," she continued. "But tomorrow is our last day here."

"I'm not going to a place of reflection."

"What choice do you have?"

I closed my teary eyes and leaned my head back, sucking in a breath of fresh air. "I could go there and demand that he speak to me."

"How? You'd die from hypothermia if you swam. It's December and freezing."

"I could dig a tunnel."

Tina angled her head. "Don't be silly. You can't dig a tunnel in a day."

"Then I'll climb the wall."

"They have cameras and border drones. Even if you got over there, they would demand you were returned and it could start a war. Not to mention that you're four months pregnant and could lose the baby if you fall down. How would you even get over that wall? It's at least twelve meters high."

Fat tears were rolling down my cheeks as I stood powerless, hoping for a bottle to come across that wall.

"I love him." My words were low and weak.

Tina rubbed my back. "I know, sweetie, but it doesn't seem that he loves you back."

CHAPTER 33
Head on a Spear

Tyton

We were like caged lions clawing the walls to get out of our imprisonment.

Even my father, who was known to have a calm personality, was losing his shit and had to be stopped when he banged his head against the wall in frustration.

"We're not helping anyone by hurting ourselves." My eyes fell on Lucas, whose knuckles were hurt from when he hit the door two days ago.

"Our women are out there, unprotected! If anything happens to Claire..." Lucas' jaw tightened.

The somber atmosphere permeated the cell we were in, and the fact that it was smaller than my bathroom with only three thin and dirty mattresses for six people meant that we were all sleep deprived, sore, hungry, and worried out of our minds.

We didn't talk much except for the initial declarations that we would kill King Jeremiah and anyone who supported him as soon as we had a chance to.

Unfortunately, our time was running out fast as we were starving and losing strength by the hour. Eleven days with a minimum of food had left us dizzy and weakened. On the evening of the second day, we were brought water, but when the guard laughed and told us that he suspected the king had poisoned it, none of us wanted to touch it at first. My dad declared that we needed to drink and as the oldest he would go first. When he didn't develop any symptoms of poisoning, we greedily shared the jug of water.

The almost two weeks in that room had felt like years and we'd all lost weight. On the morning of New Year's Eve, the captain returned and opened the small square in the door.

"We need food and water. We're starving," Henry complained.

"Aww, are you hungry?" The captain's tone was mocking. "Then I have good news for you."

"You brought us food?" My dad moved closer to the door.

"No, but your hunger is about to end." There was something sinister in the captain's tone that made Frederick and me exchange a worried glance.

"King Jeremiah has invited his favorite subjects to witness his New Year's Speech, which will be broadcasted to the people. Your public execution will be a treat to the viewers and a highlight of the year. Everyone is excited to see six traitors get what they deserve."

I stepped forward, repeating what I'd already said several times. "*I* was the one who poisoned the king's beer. The others had nothing to do with it."

The captain shrugged. "The king sees it differently, but don't you men worry. Your wives will be taken care of. In fact, we'll have five weddings at midnight and I'm happy to announce that I've been rewarded by the king and will be married myself."

"The hell you will!" We all stormed the door, sneering and growling.

The captain stepped back and gave a cocky laugh. "Come on, don't ruin my wedding day by being difficult. I'm sure your wives will mourn you a little but we'll make sure to keep them busy, if you know what I mean."

"Don't you fucking touch them!" Emmerson sneered and hammered his fist against the door.

"Oh, I assure you, we'll *touch* them. The king has first choice and he's meeting up with the women right now to get a better look at them. I'm hoping he leaves Claire for me. Unlike you, Lucas, I would have her with child within a month."

"I'll kill you!" Lucas spat through the small opening in the door and the captain looked down at the saliva that had landed on his foot.

For a second, he just stood there, and then he gave a sardonic smile. "This gives me an idea. I think I'll start off my wedding night with Claire by having her go down on all fours and clean my boot. While she's down there, I'll have her stay on her knees and then I'll have her open my pants, reach her sweet little hand in, and take out my massive cock that I'll have her lick from the root to the top."

While he was talking about all the vile ways that he would rape my sister, we men cursed at him and threw our bodies against the door.

"Save your energy, boys. We'll need a little feistiness for your execution this afternoon. It makes it so much more entertaining."

After the captain left us, Lucas sank to one of the mattresses and buried his head against his knees. He looked as powerless and broken as I felt.

Twenty minutes later, the slide in the door opened again and a guard gave us a whole loaf of bread and a large bowl of potato soup.

"This is your last meal so you'd better enjoy it."

My dad tore the bread in six parts and then we used it to soak up the soup. It was amazing to feel warm food in my stomach again.

"When they take us out for the execution, we'll kill him," Frederick muttered while chewing on his bread. "We only have to kill Jeremiah and then the others will bow to us. It's the way of the Northlands."

"Uh-huh." Emmerson nodded.

I said nothing because I knew we wouldn't get a chance to come near King Jeremiah. He was counting on us fighting for our lives and he'd make sure that there were plenty of armed soldiers between him and us. The man would enjoy the show without putting himself in danger.

Like a thousand times before, my thoughts went to Devina. I would never get to talk to her again or to laugh with her about some of the differences in our cultures. She had been right when she said that we were brutal savages. For our king to execute us and force my mother, Wilma, Claire, Marni, and Starr to marry again before the day was over was cruel and barbaric. This wasn't what we Nmen stood for and my only hope was that good men in our country would rebel and start a revolution. If only I could live to see King Jeremiah's head chopped off.

I sighed. *No, I would give up that satisfaction to write Devina one last letter and tell her of my attempt to save the people I loved. I wish I could tell her that the hours I spent with her were the best hours of my life.*

The sound of Frederick's soft sobbing made me reach out a hand and rub his back. My brother was strong and tough and I hadn't seen him cry since he was a small boy. The others looked away, swallowing their own despair while I felt my own tears well up and the enormous ball of emotions in my chest spilling over as I leaned against my little brother and cried with him.

In that moment, I didn't care about my male pride. In a few hours we would all be dead anyway. I cried for the cruel destiny that awaited my mother, sisters, and Starr.

Two hours later ten guards came to get us. They threw in handcuffs through the small square in the door and ordered my father to put them on us.

With my hands cuffed behind my back, I watched the guards open the door and turn my father around in a rough movement and put handcuffs on him too before they shoved us forward.

"Fuck, you men reek," one of them said and wrinkled his nose up.

Lucas gave a sarcastic reply. "The shower facilities were lacking."

"Stop talking to them," the captain barked at his men.

We were in a line surrounded by eight armed soldiers. I wracked my brain to find a way to overcome them, but with our hands tied behind our backs and them outnumbering us, I would be dead as soon as I attacked one of them.

We were led in the direction of the banquet hall where we'd been when we were arrested, but instead of going into the large hall, we were shoved into a room with large windows overlooking the river that ran behind King Jeremiah's palace.

The king stood in front of a long table and to the left my mother, sisters, and Starr stood in a close group. They were staring at us men, and seeing how disheveled and dirty we looked they moved toward us with sympathy on their faces.

Claire managed to touch Lucas before they were torn apart.

"Stand back!"

I protested when the women were forced back with guns to their heads.

My mother sank down on a chair looking pale with her cheeks sunken like she had been starving as well. Wilma took her hand and stepped in front of our mother with fire in her eyes blazing in the direction of King Jeremiah.

Starr and Claire were hugging each other and crying, while Marni held her head high and stood with stoic calmness that seemed out of character for my sister, who was always yelling at her rowdy sons.

To the right of the long table were three men that I recognized as some of Jeremiah's strongest supporters. One was Carl, a corpulent man in his early sixties who was hated across the country for pulling in taxes with violent methods when needed. The other was an opportunistic bastard called Eli. He grew up with Jeremiah and did his twisted bidding without question. The third man, Bruce, spoke to the captain who strolled over to join the little group. Bruce had been the servant of our previous ruler, Lord Theodore. It was because of him that Jeremiah had gained access to Theodore's bedroom where he had killed him in his sleep. Mean rumors speculated that Bruce had romantic feelings for Jeremiah, and that's what made him betray his lord, but I'd never seen them touch.

"So good of you to join us." King Jeremiah held out his hands and smirked at us. "I've had a lovely time getting to know the ladies and I can tell you that they're all dying to know which one of them will be the lucky lady who gets to be my queen."

The women remained quiet but from the way Wilma narrowed her eyes, I knew she was holding back her loathing for him.

"It's not an easy choice with so much beauty and charm among them." Jeremiah moved over and stood in front of my mother. "A woman my own age with grace and wisdom would make a regal queen." Turning his head to my father he asked, "Don't you think so, William?"

My father swallowed hard and refused to answer.

Jeremiah took a step to the left. "Marni has the strength of a true Northlander woman and I don't sense a strong bond between her and you, Henry. Of all the women I think she would grieve the least, but it's such a shame to kill off four healthy sons."

Marni's chest rose and fell fast, revealing her pulse was hammering.

"Obviously, no king can allow any competition to his own offspring, so four strong big brothers won't do." His eyes moved to Starr and Claire.

"I've considered taking two brides because the sweetness of you two is astonishing. Of course, Starr has a son as well and he's so young that some might object to my killing him." He gave a theatrical sigh. "That means the choice is really between Claire and Wilma, who aren't mothers yet." With his hands at his back, Jeremiah walked leisurely toward us men and stopped in front of Emmerson and Lucas. "My doctor assured me that should either be carrying a child the pregnancy can be terminated so we can start afresh."

Emmerson's growl rose to a roar and he pulled four guards with him when he tried getting to Jeremiah.

The captain pulled his gun and fired a warning shot that made the women scream in fright.

"Relax!" Jeremiah backed to the large table and stopped when his backside bumped into it. "I understand your frustration, Emmerson. You just won Wilma and now you won't get to see the fruit of your hard work, but let's be honest here; you would do the same if you were in my shoes."

"You're a fucking sick bastard!" Emmerson spat out and was knocked on the head with a gun by one of the guards. That only infuriated him and he looked dangerous with a split eyebrow that bled down over his eye.

"Tsk, tsk, tsk." King Jeremiah waved a dismissive hand. "You're just jealous and why wouldn't you be? I'm the most powerful man in the world and tonight I'll be inside my chosen queen."

Pivoting around, King Jeremiah looked straight at the women. "Enough with all this anticipation. I've made my decision and I'm choosing the youngest and most fertile of them all."

My mom sucked in air and gasped. "No."

"That's right. Wilma is the lucky one who gets to carry my heir in her womb."

Wilma was staring at the floor with her whole body frozen in a rigid stance when Jeremiah addressed her:

"I can see it would be difficult for you to express your excitement with Emmerson still in the room, but I wanted the men to die knowing that you women would be taken care of by good men."

"Bullshit!" Marni exclaimed. "You wanted to rub it in their faces because you're an evil sadist."

Everyone was looking at Marni and Jeremiah raised an eyebrow. "Now you're making me almost regret not picking you. I would have enjoyed breaking a feisty woman, and it's funny because rumors have it that Henry has been trying for years." Turning to his four friends, Jeremiah chuckled. "Who is up for a passionate and feisty wife?"

Before they got a chance to respond, Jeremiah swung around and clamped his hand around Wilma's wrist. "Why don't we start the celebrations a little early? I want you in that chair." He pointed with his free hand to a large chair in the middle of the table made for two people. "Don't worry, I'll join you in a minute and we'll enjoy a nice roast while we say goodbye to your troubled past."

Seeing the psychopath force Wilma around the table and push her down in the largest of the chairs made my piss boil with anger. For him to lay his filthy hands on my sister like that made me want to kill him even more.

"Unlike you traitors, my friends over here are smart enough to be loyal to me and as a reward, they too will be marrying tonight." I watched in horror as Jeremiah waved Eli over and paired him with Claire.

"Eli is my oldest friend and a good man. Unlike Lucas, I'm sure he can give you the children that Lucas clearly hasn't been able to produce." Jeremiah took Claire's hand

and placed it in Eli's. She tried to pull her hand back but Eli locked his grip on her.

"Now Starr, you'll be happy with my loyal man, Bruce. He might not be as handsome as Frederick but he's loyal to me so at least you won't have to see two men executed."

Starr backed away but was pushed into Bruce's arms and he too locked his hand around her wrist to keep her close.

"Marni, you've proven to be feisty and I know the captain is used to dealing with difficult prisoners. Not only will he make a good obedient wife out of you, he'll enjoy the process."

Marni spat at the captain's feet when he used force to make her stand next to him. As a result, he twisted her arm back.

King Jeremiah laughed. "Ah, I see the fun has already begun. Your marriage will be full of passion."

Turning to my mother, he smiled. "Now, will you fight too or will you go to your new husband, tax collector Carl?"

My mother didn't move but Carl walked over to stand next to her.

"Go ahead and join your next husbands at the table while we let the traitors say their last words to you."

All the women looked sick to their stomachs as they were sat down in chairs like a jury lined up to be entertained. Each one with her appointed man next to her watching over her.

"Why don't we start with Tyton? No, wait..." Holding up a hand, Jeremiah gestured to a server by the door. "Bring in the food and wine before the entertainment starts."

Four waiters came in with wine followed by trays of meat, roasted potatoes, vegetables, and baskets with bread.

Jeremiah filled both his plate and Wilma's, encouraging her to eat.

Her spine remained glued to the back of her chair and her lips closed.

"Oh well, maybe you'll get some more appetite once you hear what the traitors have to say." Without looking at me, Jeremiah stuffed his mouth and gestured for me to speak.

I cleared my throat. "Wilma, I need you to tell what happened to *anyone* who might be interested." I hoped she knew I meant Devina.

Wilma met my eyes.

"The best day of my life was your tournament." It would make no sense to anyone but Frederick, my parents, and Wilma, who were the only ones who knew I'd spent that day with Devina. My eyes went to my mother, who sat next to Carl. She looked petite in the massive chair as large tears were falling down her cheeks.

"I'm sorry we failed you." My words came out like thorn bushes ripping my throat up with regret and despair.

"Yeah, yeah, enough of that." Jeremiah pointed to Emmerson. "Do you want to congratulate Wilma before she is crowned my queen tonight?"

Emmerson and Wilma stared at each other and the strong man spread his legs and squared his shoulders as much as he could with his hands cuffed behind his back. "Babe, don't ever forget me."

Wilma breathed in and moved her lips but there was no sound. Still I could tell she mimed, "Never!"

"Next." Jeremiah pointed to Henry. "Make it short, will you?"

Henry swallowed hard and looked at Marni. "I've done so many stupid things that I regret in our marriage. Please forgive me and protect our boys. I love you all."

Marni's nostrils were flaring as if she was holding back tears but she nodded her head to him.

Next came Frederick, who declared his eternal love to Starr, followed by Lucas, who recited a sentence from a poem that made Claire burst into tears.

My father apologized for not being able to protect my mother from the evil in this room and swore to come back as a ghost and haunt Carl for forcing her to marry him and to find a way to kill Jeremiah.

"Ha! You should have thought about your duty to protect your wife before you decided to try and kill me." Jeremiah shrugged. "Everyone agrees with me that you don't deserve the privilege of being a protector."

"I did it, not them!" I repeated for the umpteenth time.

"Yes, and for that, you'll go first!" Jeremiah pointed to a window behind me. "As soon as we're done eating, we'll continue this lovely day in the courtyard, where we're having a public execution. You'll have to excuse me but I've always had a taste for the macabre, so when we get down there, you'll see six spears. One for each of your heads."

My mom's eyes rolled back and then she went limp in her chair.

"Mom!" Claire was closest and reached over Eli. "Mom, are you okay?"

Jeremiah laughed. "Oooh, I see not everyone enjoys my love for gory details."

"Mom..." I called out, feeling like a bear in chains.

We were all looking at Joan and even Wilma leaned forward in her chair.

"I wonder how your mom is going to do when we get to the executions?" Jeremiah turned in his chair to address Wilma and from where I stood, I could see his hand slide up her thigh. I couldn't believe my eyes when I saw her spread her legs a little, granting him access to move his hand higher. Jeremiah smirked and eagerly moved his hand all the way up to her crotch and then she closed her legs, squeezing his hand between her thighs.

He made a surprised sound and whisper-shouted, "Eager to be queen, are you?"

Wilma, who sat on his right side, lifted her left hand to his thin hair with a small smile.

He made another purring sound but then she yanked back his head and in the blink of an eye, she drew out a steak knife from her right-hand sleeve and jabbed it straight into the front of Jeremiah's throat. With his right hand locked between her thighs, his defense was delayed.

The shock in his eyes that a woman could be a threat to him was priceless and it was like time slowed down as I saw my fifteen-year-old sister with a determined expression on her face. Squeezing the handle of the steak knife that he'd been naïve enough to lay in front of her, Wilma ripped it downwards with all her might. The long cut in King Jeremiah's throat had him gasping and his hands couldn't hold back the spurts of blood that made his light blue shirt red.

"My king!" The captain tipped his chair back to get to Jeremiah.

"Behind you!" The warning from Eli came too late as Marni got up and stabbed another steak knife into the side of the captain.

Chaos erupted as the guards ran to the table to pull back Marni, who kept stabbing the knife into the captain. Starr was helping her by holding the captain down until Eli tore her back with an angry roar.

With the guards storming forward, we did the same, Frederick kicking Eli, who had a hold on Starr, while I ran to Claire at the other end of the table.

"You've got to get the keys to the handcuffs. It's in the captain's pocket."

Wilma had climbed onto the wooden table and was kicking at the soldiers who were trying to grab her by her legs. They had guns pointing at her but the idea of killing a woman was so alien to any Nman that I knew they wouldn't fire their weapons.

"Don't you fucking touch her," Emmerson yelled and tackled one of them to the ground.

Jeremiah's torso had collapsed, head down, on the table, a large pool of blood coloring the white tablecloth underneath him, but his eyes were open and blinking.

"I've got the keys," Claire said close to my ear and in a few seconds, I had my hands free again. The room was in chaos and my sole priority was to secure the women's safety.

"Get behind me," I shouted to the women and pulled my mother away from the soldier she was screaming at to put down his gun. It was obvious that the men were unsure about how to tackle women attacking them physically and verbally when they'd been taught their whole lives never to touch a woman. The soldier in front of my mom turned his gun on me for about two seconds until Frederick stormed him from behind.

Claire had managed to uncuff my father, Lucas, and Henry, and was now working on freeing Emmerson's hands. As soon as she did, Emmerson ran to the wall and pulled down an antique sword that hung as a decoration. With crazy eyes and a roar of anger, he stormed up to King Jeremiah and swung the large sword against the neck of the dying man.

Wilma, who was still on the table, jumped back but looked on with the same blood rush I'd seen in her eyes when Emmerson fought in her tournament.

The chaos and noise that had begun a few minutes ago ceased as we all stared at Emmerson decapitating King Jeremiah with the dull sword. When it was done, he fisted his hand into Jeremiah's hair and lifted his head from the table.

"Your king is dead!" He held out the head to the soldiers and pointed to the floor in front of the table. "I call victory."

For two hundred years we men had battled for control in the Northlands and it was tradition that killing a king would make you the new ruler.

"But *she* killed him," one of the soldiers whispered to his colleague.

Wilma stepped down on a chair next to Emmerson and with a hand on her husband's shoulder she challenged everyone in the room. "It's true that I wounded the king, but it was my husband who killed him."

Only the people in this room would ever know that the king would have died even if Emmerson hadn't decapitated him.

Four of the soldiers were pointing their guns at Emmerson, Frederick, Lucas, and Henry but it was clear they were unsure of how to proceed now that King Jeremiah was dead and their captain had fallen to the floor in a pool of his own blood.

"Your king is dead! Lay down your weapons," my father repeated and this time one of the soldiers lowered his gun and slowly kneeled. Like a set of dominos, the other soldiers followed while the king's friends backed away.

"Not so fast!" I blocked their way and Lucas and Frederick were quick to form a wall with me. "Didn't Jeremiah mention there were six spears out front?" I pointed to Jeremiah, "One." My finger continued to the captain who lay lifeless on the floor. "Two." My eyes came back to Eli, Carl, and Bruce, who were all pale when I counted. "Three, four, and five."

"That sounds about right." Lucas nodded.

"Detain these men!" Carl shouted to the soldiers in a last attempt at using his former power.

Emmerson roared at them. "Don't you fucking dare! King Jeremiah was a disgusting human being and these men are rats for terrorizing innocent women. Each of you knows that what happened here was a disgrace to the Northlands."

The soldiers exchanged glances and even if none of them verbalized it, it was clear that they agreed.

"I'm ordering you to put handcuffs on them, right now."

The guards followed Emmerson's order and placed Carl, Eli, and Bruce along the wall, where they were pushed to sit down.

My dad moved to the table and picked up a glass of water. "Before we leave this room, we should eat and drink. We might have to fight to convince a few that Emmerson is the rightful ruler now."

Emmerson reached up his hands to Wilma, who let herself fall into his arms and wrapped her hands around his neck. "Did you see it?"

"I saw, babe, and I'm so proud of you."

"He was going to kill all of you. I couldn't let him, so I tricked him and..."

Emmerson swallowed her last words with a powerful kiss on her forehead.

I moved to the table and began eating from the trays of food that hadn't been sprayed with blood. Around me the couples were kissing and hugging. Even Henry was holding Marni tight against his chest and placing kisses on her hair.

My father sat down at the table and pulled my mother onto his lap. She was feeding him and they smiled at each other.

"Are you sure you want to be the ruler?" I asked Emmerson while picking up a turkey drumstick. "It's a lot of work with all the people plotting to kill you to gain power for themselves."

"I'll be like Dawson McGreggor. He ruled until he was old enough to pass on the responsibility to his son."

"Yeah, but he's the only one. Every other ruler has met an untimely death."

Emmerson pushed out his chest. "Then I'll be the second one."

Taking a bite of my drumstick, I blinked at Wilma. "I'm sure that with you by his side, Emmerson will be invincible."

She raised her chin. "That's right. You men should never underestimate us women."

I turned my head to Henry and Marni, who were talking in low voices. "Did you hear that, Henry?"

He looked over. "What?"

"Wilma just pointed out that no man should ever underestimate how far a woman will go to defend herself or the people she loves."

He nodded and kissed Marni again.

The food and beer filled me up with new energy and when Emmerson led the way down to the courtyard where people had turned up to witness our execution, he walked with a swagger and confidence onto the podium built for King Jeremiah to tower above his people.

"There's been a change of plans. You see, King Jeremiah wanted to make Wilma his queen. I agree that she would be a fantastic queen but the problem is, she's already married." In a dramatic way, Emmerson held up Jeremiah's bloody head in the air.

The cameras were pointed straight at him and would be doing a live broadcast to the whole country. Emmerson pointed to them.

"I am your new ruler, and if you want to say goodbye to your old king you can find his head on a spear outside the palace where he planned to have all our heads."

Wilma walked up to stand next to Emmerson and he placed his other arm around her while still holding up the head of Jeremiah. "This is the head of the despicable, sick man who has tyrannized us for years. He hurt not just my wife, but her sisters, her mother, and Starr too. I'm fucking proud to be the king slayer."

The people who had come to see the execution were listening and moved closer.

"Wilma, why don't you tell them what happened?"

In her own words, Wilma explained how the women had been paired with new men before their first husbands were dead. She was thundering about the women being stripped of their right to choose their own husbands and how they had fought against the unfairness of it all.

"That's right. Wilma stabbed Jeremiah with a knife in his throat. That's what you get for messing with a strong Northwoman."

Wilma smiled like she had just been told she'd aced a science test.

"Jeremiah touched my woman, so I cut off his head." Again, Emmerson dangled the bloody head of Jeremiah and in that moment, I was grateful that Devina wasn't here to see it.

For a sweet Motlander like her this would all seem brutal and primitive. But there was something deeply satisfying in seeing our tormentor reduced to almost nothing.

The people had come for executions and cheered when Bruce and Eli were shot dead and decapitated. The cheers went crazy when it was Carl's turn. As the tax collector, he and his staff were disliked for setting fire to houses of people who couldn't pay.

None of the three men had any last words before they ended their time on earth with their heads impaled upon spears.

"Tomorrow you will wake up to a new dawn and a much better world than what Jeremiah had to offer you. I will lead you and care for you with my beautiful queen by my side." Emmerson held up Wilma's hand and smiled as the crowd cheered.

"Can you believe these people?" Frederick muttered in my ear. "They came to see us die and now they're cheering for one of us to be their new ruler."

"Maybe they're afraid that we'll kill them if they don't cheer."

Frederick shrugged and pulled Starr closer to him. "Or maybe they were longing for change just as much as we were."

"Hmm."

"You know what this means, right?" Frederick gave me a small smile. "You're in a good position to ask a favor of the new ruler."

I raised a questioning eyebrow.

"Is your mind clouded from this chaos?" Frederick reached out a hand and shook my shoulder. "If Devina came to this side of the border, she might be allowed to marry a man of her own choice without a tournament."

"But there would be a war if Devina came here. The Motherlands would demand her back."

Starr and Frederick were watching me with sympathy on their faces.

"You knew about Devina?" I asked Starr.

"Yes, Frederick told me after Wilma's tournament."

"It was a secret," I scolded him, but he just shrugged.

"She's my wife and I trust her."

Fuck, I wanted what they had so badly. Sucking in a deep breath, I declared, "You're right. I'm going to go after her."

Frederick gave a nod. "You do what you have to do, but just be careful."

"Will you explain it to the others? I might be gone for a while if I have to track her down in the Motherlands."

Starr stopped me when I backed away. "Tyton."

"Mmm."

"Be sure to shower first before you go after her. You all kind of stink."

CHAPTER 34
Last Letters

Tyton

When I got back to my house only the dusk lit up my path as I ran straight to the green belt behind our house hoping to find more letters from Devina. She had told me she would be back on December 30th and that was yesterday. If the stars were with me, she wouldn't have left yet.

There were four bottles with letters expressing how she wanted to meet with me and talk. Reading her letters, I felt sick to my stomach from seeing how the woman I loved had come back sooner than expected and begged me to answer her.

Did she come back because she missed me?

I closed my eyes when I read her conclusion that I was angry with her and no longer cared.

Tomorrow is New Year's Eve. I'm giving over the house at noon and then I have to leave. You don't know how much I wish I could stay and wait for your anger to cool down, so we could talk.

Noon. Dammit, it was close to nine in the evening and she would be gone now. I reread the next paragraph with my heart hurting.

Please forgive me for causing you the pain that would make you hold a grudge so deep that you continue to ignore me and refuse to write me back.

For what it's worth, I think of you constantly, and I meant it when I said that I love you.

Devina

I love you too!

I looked up at the tall wall and calculated in my mind how long a rope I'd need to get across. Flying over with my drone would draw unwanted attention so I'd better do it as simply as possible.

The thorn bushes on their side would tear at my clothes but if I wore gloves and thick shoes, I should be able to rappel down.

"Step back from the border." The voice was female and made me look around to see a small drone approaching. I frowned and shoved my letters into my pocket.

"Step away from the border, now! This drone is armed."

Two other drones came up fast and I took one step back.

"Walk away from the border. There's a twenty-meter no-trespassing zone."

I scoffed. "Maybe on your side. But on this side, the land belongs to me."

"Step back!"

I'd never seen these drones before and felt annoyed as hell. In the story Devina and I had written, Mark had used a simple rope with a hook to climb the wall. It had never been a question to me how I'd get across it since it was ultimately just a tall wall. These little drones were fucking with my plan.

"This is a no-trespassing zone."

"Where did all these drones come from?" I didn't expect the voice to answer, but it did.

Men of the North – FORBIDDEN LETTERS

"Border security has been enhanced and these drones have the means to harm anyone who tries to climb the wall."

"What do you mean harm? Aren't you people supposed to be pacifists?"

"We will numb you. It's not lethal but if you climb the wall you might hurt yourself falling down."

"Who am I talking to?"

"This is border patrol officer Tanya Banner. I'm going to ask you one last time, step back from the wall."

"All right, Tanya." I knew she could see me via the cameras in the drones. "I'm leaving."

Backing away, I headed for my loft considering how I would get to Devina. Those drones were a nuisance, but they wouldn't hold me back. I would find a way around, over, or under that wall, and once I did, I would track down Devina and convince her that we belonged together.

Coming close to death had made me sure of one thing. I would regret it for the rest of my life if I didn't do everything in my power to make Devina mine.

The dusk gave me enough light to find my way into the hay barn and up the stairs to my apartment, where I headed straight for the bathroom. My clothes were filthy and sweaty from days of wear. Stripping out of them, I walked into the shower and enjoyed the warm water falling down on me. I wouldn't give up until I'd found Devina. Worst case, I'd get caught in the Motherlands and returned to the North, but with Emmerson as the new ruler he wouldn't kill me.

If the Motlanders decided to keep me and send me to one of their places of reflection, I could always leave. According to Devina those places weren't guarded very well.

Devina's letters had been painful to read, but at least her sweet declaration of love gave me hope that I could convince her to come back here with me. All I needed was to find her among the one point five billion people on their side of the border.

Despite the daunting task, I began whistling because a few hours ago, I'd been facing death. Now that I'd been given a second chance at life, I sure as hell wasn't going to waste it worrying about all the things that could go wrong.

When I was done showering, I grabbed a towel and dried myself off while making plans for my mission. If I left now, I could steal old Hansson's boat and cross over to Devina's side. A small voice told me it would be wiser to catch some sleep and come up with a solid plan.

Walking out of my bathroom, I moved to the closet in my room and turned on the light.

A creaking sound from my bed made me spin around to see Devina sitting in my bed looking like she'd just woken up from a deep sleep.

I jolted back as if I'd seen a ghost. "What the fuck?"

"I'm sorry, I didn't mean to spook you."

Gaping, I starred at her, unable to understand how my brain was playing tricks on me.

"Don't be angry. I needed to see you." She pulled the cover higher.

"How...? When...?" I shook my head and managed to get my legs to move me to the bed.

"You wouldn't answer my letters." Her eyes fell down my naked body and color spread in her cheeks.

I was touching her arms and shoulders as if to make sure she was real. "Devina, how did you get here? Tell me you didn't swim."

"No, I climbed the wall."

"How?"

"Funny story. The Council banned our book because Motlanders have tried to get over the wall and have gotten injured. My friend Tina is a crime writer and kind of brilliant when it comes to coming up with sneaky plans so to help me, she pretended to be a reader, eager to cross

Men of the North – FORBIDDEN LETTERS

the border. First, we carried a long ladder from our house to the border. Then I hid while she took it the last part of the way and placed it against the wall. Of course, the border patrol drones showed up and warned her to leave, but Tina was amazing. You should have seen the way she began arguing with them that it should be her choice to live in a place where she was free to pursue her art."

"What art?"

"I told you. She's an author like me, but she writes crime fiction, which isn't the same after they made it illegal to portray anything that resembles horror or violence. Now the worst she can write about is insurance fraud and identity theft." Devina seemed nervous and spoke fast.

"So, after the border control ordered Tina to step away from the ladder, she jogged along the wall leading them away from me, while arguing out loud about the unfairness of it all. All the cameras and drones were fixed on her when she stopped and gave them a speech about freedom. That's when I took my chance. I've never run so fast or climbed a ladder so quickly. There wasn't any time to be scared. I just did what Tina had told me to do and used the hook-ended rope to climb down on the other side. It took less than two minutes and I could still hear Tina arguing with the border patrol further down when I released the hook and ran to your house."

"I can't believe you're here." I raised my hands to touch her hair, letting the long strands slide through my fingers, with disbelief that I was touching her. "You know the Motherlands are going to ask to have you returned, right?"

"I don't think so."

"No?"

"All the cameras were on Tina so I hope they didn't catch me leaving. If Tina's plan goes right, it will look like I killed myself. I wrote a suicide note taking full responsibility for the unintended effect my book has had on women. I apologized and said that I had tried to stop my friend, but that Tina's obsession with finding love with an Nman had made me realize that I couldn't live with myself. I wrote that my heart was heavy with grief and guilt and that I didn't wish to live without my family any longer.

"But if there's no physical body, will they believe that you died?"

Devina swallowed and looked down. "We burned down the house."

"Your house?

She nodded and the immense sadness from her made me pull her in for a hug.

"Tina prepared everything with papers on the dining table and left a short candle to burn down and ignite the spark. The plan was for her to stay and argue with the border patrol until the smoke was visible in the sky. That way no one would suspect she set the fire and it would be too late for anyone to save the house before it burned to the ground."

"But wouldn't your suicide letter burn with the house then?"

"No, because I stuck it onto a tree outside of the house."

I shook my head. "Damn, I can't believe you'd burn down your family house. I know how much it meant to you."

"It needed to look real."

"I know, but won't the police still search for your body in the ashes?"

Devina exhaled noisily. "We've had thousands of people dying this year from the epidemic. It's a rural, understaffed area of the world with little technology. I doubt they will search for my remains since no friends or family will push them. Tina will go back home unless she's forced to check in to a place of reflection."

"Shit!"

"I know, but she said that she would use it as inspiration for her next novel. She had an idea of a plot with a lazy woman faking mental instability in order to get out of working."

"Wow!" I kept touching her. "You faked your own death to come here. Just like Mark in the book."

"It was the only way. Please don't be mad at me for coming."

I had heard enough. With my hands on her shoulders, I looked deep into her eyes. "Why would I be mad? All I want is to be with you. I'm thrilled! You saved me the trouble of coming to get you."

Her brow lifted. "But you ignored all my letters. I thought you were mad at me."

"I would have answered your letters if I'd been here." Cupping her face, I kissed her. Feeling her lips against mine and knowing there was no wall between us any longer was exhilarating and better than all the food and drink I'd enjoyed after starving. "I hate that you put yourself in danger to get here, but I'm eternally grateful that you came." I pulled my head back; our eyes locked. "I've fucking missed you."

"I've missed you too." Her eyes teared up.

"Hey... shhh... what's wrong? Don't cry." I pulled her into my arms. "You're here now. We're together."

Devina covered her face, her shoulders bobbing from the crying.

"Talk to me, love."

"I've tried to be strong, but I was so scared that you'd be mad at me. I've lost everyone and I thought I'd lost you too."

I groaned and held her tight. "No. I'm right here."

"But there's something I haven't told you and you're going to be so mad when I tell you."

Chills ran down my neck and my posture stiffened. "Did you sleep with someone else?"

"Nooo..." She creased her eyebrows.

"Then what is it?"

With her eyes full of tears, Devina took my hand and placed it on top of the cover where her stomach was.

From the look in her eyes, I knew she was telling me something.

My heart rate increased to a million beats per second and I pulled the cover away to see the most beautiful bump on my woman's belly. "You're pregnant?!"

"Yes."

My eyes were staring down at her round belly. "It's mine?"

"Of course it's yours."

We had only shared one night together and that was back in August – my mind was frazzled as I tried to count.

"I'm four months pregnant."

"Why didn't you tell me?"

Her hand lifted to caress my face. "I figured we could never be together and that telling you would only make things worse for you."

I got under the cover with her and wrapped myself around her body. To feel the warmth of her made everything better. These past two weeks had been hell to me – her goodbye letter that tore my heart to pieces followed by King Jeremiah's bombshell that he claimed the right to marry any widow he wanted to; failed attempt at poisoning him, and two weeks being locked up and unable to protect our women. The trauma I had experienced healed a little as I lay in my bed listening to Devina's heartbeat and held a hand on her belly where our child was growing. "You should have told me about our baby. I almost died today."

"What do you mean, you almost died?"

I told her everything about our attempt at killing King Jeremiah and how it had gone wrong. She teared up when I explained about the small cell and the long days with almost nothing to eat.

"So that's why you look thinner. How can anyone be so cruel?"

"It gets worse," I explained about being led to the room with the long table and seeing my mother, sisters, and Starr being paired with hideous men and forced to sit next to them and listen to our last words.

"And then what happened?"

"Well, like most men in this country, Jeremiah had no real experience with women. He mistook them for innocent and weak fairy creatures that can only do good, so imagine his surprise when Wilma jerked a knife into his throat."

Devina gasped. "What?"

"We Nmen will die for our mates, but it turns out that our women are just as fierce in times of trouble."

"Wilma stabbed him?"

"She basically cut his throat from here to here." I showed from under my chin and down to my Adam's apple. "None of us men in that room will ever think of women as fragile after we witnessed five women take on five men and kill two of them. You should have seen the way Marni kept stabbing the captain like she was taking out years of pent-up rage on men."

"That's awful."

"Yeah, but it was them or us."

She wet her lips. "I'm glad you lived and came back to me. Imagine if none of you had come home and someone else had showed up here. I could have been in big trouble."

"True." We were quiet for a while before I spoke again. "I still can't believe you risked everything to come here. I was going to track you down in the Motherlands, and then

I found you in my bed. Whomever said females were the weaker sex must not have met the same women as me."

Devina narrowed her eyes. "Where did you hear that women are the weaker sex? That's nonsense. We rule most of the world."

"That you do, but not on this side of the wall." There was humor in my smile when I began kissing her jawline and moved up to her lips. "We like strong women, but we don't submit to them."

She was kissing me back and making small sounds of pleasure. "Maybe in time, you'll submit to me."

I chuckled while kissing her. "Never. That's a promise." My hand had lifted her shirt up over her belly and I pulled it higher, curious to see if the pregnancy had made other parts of her body swell as well. "You don't know how much I want to make love to you right now."

"Do you think it's safe with the baby?"

"I think so. Frederick told me that he and Starr did it up until a few days before she gave birth." My hands were weighing her breasts, which had indeed grown. "God, you have no idea how sexy you are."

"Tyton, do you believe everything happens for a reason?"

"Sure."

"What are the odds of my getting pregnant from one night of sex?"

"Well, we did do it several times."

"I know, but I still feel like this was meant to happen and that my nana worked her magic from the other side."

"Could be. But I'm happy to take it from here."

She smiled at me and lifted her face to meet my kiss. Our tongues twirled around each other as if they too were hugging a good friend. We might only have spent one night together but being close to Devina felt like the most natural thing in the world. I had played the sound of her arousing little moans in my mind a thousand times these

Men of the North – FORBIDDEN LETTERS

past months. Now that I was suckling on her nipples and letting my hands slide down between her legs, she made those same amazing sounds.

"Ahhh..."

I took time to feel and kiss every inch of her. The first time we had been together, I'd been eager to get inside her, but now that she was pregnant, I took time to investigate my mate and enjoy her soft curves. "You are gorgeous."

"So are you."

"Yeah? Are you getting used to my muscles?"

"I guess, and I always loved your eyes. They're very pretty."

A low groan sounded from me. "Don't call me pretty."

"Handsome then."

I moved up to kiss her, deep and demanding. It only made her breathing faster.

"Tyton..."

"Mmm...?"

"I want you inside me."

"Patience, sugar." I closed my eyes and enjoyed the moment when Devina pushed me onto my back and climbed on top of me. Her perky breasts were like something from an ultimate fantasy and the beautiful bump on her belly made chills run up and down my spine.

I reached up to push her hair back so I could see her eyes better but she intertwined her fingers with mine and scooted into position.

My eyes widened a little and I held my breath when Devina slid herself down on top of me. At first it was only my tip but that alone made me moan out loud.

"Fuuuck..."

I had remembered sex with Devina as spectacular, but that was before she had chosen me and my child was growing in her womb. With the way I'd come close to death today and with the fear that I'd lost her forever, this moment was pure bliss. If there was a paradise on earth, then this was it.

"Ahhh…" Devina leaned her head back and sunk lower on my cock.

My free hand grabbed her hip and I began guiding her up and down on me. The way her tits bounced a little and her pussy made slurpy sounds from her wetness just about made me come. "This is so good. Being inside you… ahhh… it's heaven."

Devina placed her hands on my chest to support herself and increased the tempo.

"Ohhh…" I groaned and feared that I wouldn't be able to hold it much longer.

"Do you like it?" she panted.

"You have no idea… to see you… ahhh… riding me like this… it's fucking amazing." All the words were pushed out as I was clenching my core muscles and trying to hold back the orgasm that was building up too fast.

With my ball sack tightening, I scrunched up my face. "I want this to last so bad."

Devina had her eyes closed and moaned, "Yeah, me too. Don't stop."

The only thing I could do to avoid coming was to pull out.

"What's wrong?"

"Nothing." With a strong grip, I pulled her to the edge and sank my head down between her legs. Devina arched up and began panting. Focusing on her pleasure gave me a chance to get myself under control. It was such a turn-on to hear my woman fall apart in my arms as my tongue and fingers took her close to her release.

"Yes, Tyton, yes."

She was holding on to my head wanting me to keep licking her, but I broke free and pushed myself inside of her again. This time I didn't have to hold back. Devina was close to the edge and moving her head from side to side with her eyes closed and her moans growing in volume. "Yes... yes... ohh, yes."

The friction of my cock sliding in and out of her took me right back to nirvana. When she grabbed on to my wrists and squeezed hard while arching and screaming out her orgasm, I let go too.

"Oh... fuuuck!!"

I could feel burst after burst as I emptied myself inside Devina's warm, tight pussy. My orgasmic high made me hold on to her and press myself against her.

I was kneeling on the floor and after a long moment, I kissed her navel and caressed her stomach before resting my torso on top of hers. Devina wrapped her legs around my hips and held on to my shoulders like she needed the closeness between us as much as I did.

"Give me a few minutes and I can go again," I muttered against her neck.

"Tyton, how is it possible that I love you so much when I hardly know you?"

"You know me!"

"I don't understand how I can feel so safe with you but it's like an instinctual thing inside me."

"That's because I'm your mate." I was trying to get my breathing to calm down.

"Whatever this thing between us is..." She inhaled deeply. "It's powerful."

I smiled and nuzzled my nose against her neck feeling like the luckiest man alive.

"Does Wilma know about us?"

I pulled back to look into Devina's eyes. "Not yet, but she will soon because tomorrow morning I'm calling her and Emmerson." I paused for a second. "At this time tomorrow, we'll be husband and wife."

"We're marrying tomorrow?"

"Yes. I know it's strange for you, but it's the only way I can protect you and our kids."

Devina looked serious. "If I marry you will the other men leave me alone?"

"Yes."

"Okay then."

When she kissed me, I couldn't help deepening the kiss. The taste and scent of her made me insatiable and on cue my cock stirred. Cupping her face, I smiled. "This is like a fantasy come true to me, you know that, right?"

She just gave a sweet chuckle and let me seduce her again.

CHAPTER 35
King Slayer

Devina

The next day Tyton and I were glued together. We both reached out and touched each other at random times as if to make sure this wasn't a dream. When he was on the phone with Frederick or Emmerson, he pulled me down on his lap and played with my hair or stroked my arm.

"We need to go and see the others. Emmerson has agreed to wed us. That way my claim on you will be official."

"And there will be no tournament then?"

Tyton's eyes dropped to my stomach; he wore a satisfied smile. "Tournaments aren't for pregnant women. It's pretty clear that you've been claimed."

"Oh..." I thought about it. "But then my fear of being auctioned off in a tournament was irrelevant. Now I feel stupid. All this time, I believed we couldn't be together because I wouldn't be safe here in the Northlands. Why didn't you tell me?"

"It wouldn't have mattered. Jeremiah was selfish and unpredictable. It's impossible to say what he would have done if I'd asked permission to marry you."

We intertwined our fingers and sat with me leaning against his shoulder for a moment. "I have a question."

"Okay."

"You tried to poison the king to protect the people you love."

"Uh-huh. We felt sure that Jeremiah was up to something and that he would kill the man of the woman he had his eyes on."

"But if I understood you correctly then the man who kills the ruler becomes the new ruler."

"That's right."

"So, if you had succeeded you would be the new king of the Northlands."

Tyton shook his head. "No. I never wanted that role. I would have let other men fight for power and supported someone more suitable."

"Like Emmerson?"

"Emmerson is young. He wouldn't have been my first choice, but from what I saw yesterday he has what it takes to stand in front of a crowd and shine with confidence."

I let my fingers play with his hand, trailing over old scars, his short nails, and callused skin. "But if you didn't want to be king, then why did you volunteer to kill him?"

"Because I naïvely thought that if it didn't work, only I would get punished. If I'd known they'd try and destroy my entire family, I would have chosen a different method."

I looked down. "You know I don't condone violence."

Tyton snorted. "Trust me. Jeremiah was so vile he could have made even you capable of committing murder. He was a menace, and many are celebrating that his head is rotting on a spear."

I lifted my gaze to meet Tyton's eyes and raised an eyebrow. "Metaphorically speaking you mean?"

"No. Jeremiah planned to chop off our heads and exhibit them on spears outside his palace for everyone to see. Now it's his own ugly head that hangs with four of his friend's heads."

I covered my mouth and furrowed my brow with disgust.

It made Tyton close his eyes for a second and sigh. "I know, pixie, but he did say he had a taste for the macabre, so in a way we're honoring him."

"You're honoring him by placing his head on a spear?"

Tyton rubbed his face. "It sounds bad when you say it like that."

"Because it *is* bad. It's barbaric and..."

Nuzzling his head against my neck he muttered, "I adore your innocence, but you're in the Northlands now. You're not going to like everything here, but I hope I'll be worth it."

My innocence was challenged when, a few hours later, we went to the royal palace.

"Cover your eyes," Tyton instructed and led me past the tall spears with the five bloody heads, but I'd already seen them from the air before the drone sat down.

We were welcomed in the courtyard by Wilma, who came running with all her youthful energy.

"I can't believe that you returned." She hugged me tight and then she leaned back, glowing with happiness and laughing. "I'll bet you never suspected that I'd be the queen of the Northlands when you saw me again." There was such pride radiating from her that I couldn't help but smile.

"I thought Emmerson didn't want to take the title of king." Tyton looked up at the building.

"No, he says it has a bad connotation after the way Jeremiah mistreated our people. He'll be Emperor Emmerson."

"Emperor?" Tyton's brow rose.

"Yes. I like queen better than empress, but Emmerson isn't budging."

I smiled at Wilma. "I'm just happy that you're all right. Tyton told me about the awful things that happened."

"Did he tell you we women saved him and the other men?"

"Yes."

Wilma's eyes swung to her brother. "It would have been your head on one of those spears if I hadn't put a knife in that disgusting pig."

Tyton took a step forward and pressed a kiss on top of her hair. "I'm glad you did."

There was a tender moment between them as they exchanged a long smile and then Wilma threw a nod to the building. "The men are in there. They've been waiting for you."

"Thanks." Moving forward, Tyton pulled me with him.

"It's okay, Devina can stay with me while you talk to them."

Tyton tightened his hold on my hand. "No! Devina and I stay together until we're legally married. No one is coming between us."

"You've seen what I can do. Don't you trust me to protect her?" Wilma asked with humor in her eyes.

"No, and I don't like that you're out here without a protector either." Tyton kept going, with me following him.

Wilma caught up and complained, "If you tell Emmerson that I ran out here by myself, I'll be really pissed at you. I saw your drone arrive and I couldn't wait to see you. All the men do is talk and strategize. Mom, Marni, Claire, and Starr are watching the children in the banquet hall, but that's boring too. I wanna go explore every room but Emmerson doesn't trust any of the guards yet, so he wants me to stay close to him. We were going to explore the palace last night together, but we didn't make it far."

"Why not?" I asked.

She chuckled. "Because we walked into a very pretty bedroom and didn't made it out of that room until this morning."

Tyton stopped. "So, Emmerson doesn't know you left the room to meet us?"

"No. Which is why you'll let me sneak back in before you knock on the door."

Tyton's low laughter rumbled from his chest. "It's too late for that." He pointed up.

Wilma and I looked up at the same time to see four grave faces stare down at us. Emmerson opened a window and with Frederick, Lucas, and William behind him, he spoke in a firm tone.

"Wilma, what are you doing out there when I asked you to stay close to me?"

"I was only gone for a second."

Slamming his hand down on the windowsill, Emmerson was red in the face. "I don't care. Do you have any idea how fast my heart was beating when I turned to see your chair was empty? How the hell did you even get out without us noticing?"

Wilma looked secretly proud of herself. "You were all distracted when you looked at that list of people you were discussing. I saw Tyton's drone and I went to welcome them."

"Don't you ever fucking pull a stunt like that on me again. If anyone gets to you it will kill me. Do you understand?"

Wilma looked to her father for support, but William's face was as stern as Emmerson's, so her head fell and she fiddled with her hands. "Sorry."

I had a feeling this wasn't the last time Wilma would get in trouble, and I didn't blame her. The thought of always having to ask for permission to go anywhere didn't sit well with me, but a quick look over my shoulder, to see the five heads on the spears outside, made me move closer to Tyton.

"This is Devina," Tyton introduced me.

Emmerson nodded to me and addressed Tyton. "Come up so we can talk.

Wilma ran up the stairs and stood waiting for us at the end of the staircase. "Holy shit, you two are slow."

I wondered why she was so eager to get back to Emmerson when he was mad at her, but the girl was fearless and ran straight into his arms and cuddled up against him. Emmerson closed his arms around her and lowered his head and whispered something to her. He looked as large and fierce as he had the time I saw him fight for her.

"Good to see you again, Devina." Frederick was the first to approach Tyton and me. He was smiling widely. "You really faked your own death to be with Tyton?"

I gave a small nod.

Frederick's eyes lowered to my abdomen and his eyes glistened. "It's like a fucking miracle."

William came over and was followed by the others in the room, who all congratulated us.

"So, you're sure you want to be with Tyton?" Emmerson had his arm locked around Wilma. "I now have the authority to wed you two, but I need to be sure it's what you want."

"It is," Tyton answered.

Emmerson ignored him and kept his eyes on me. "I'm sure you can speak for yourself."

"Yes." I licked my lips, feeling nervous with all the large men staring down at me. My hand went to my belly as I found strength in the fact that I wasn't doing this for me alone. "I want to be with Tyton."

"Why?" Emmerson's direct question surprised me.

"Because... ehh..."

"Why would you leave the Motherlands to move here?"

I swallowed hard and tried to find my words. "I don't have a rational explanation for it. It's more like a pull in

Men of the North – FORBIDDEN LETTERS

me that I can't explain with words. Tyton and I..." I looked up to meet Tyton's eyes and felt him squeeze my hand. "I don't know why, but he feels like family to me."

"Yeah, I know the feeling. That's how Tyton feels to me too." Frederick laughed at his own joke and it lightened the situation, but Emmerson wasn't prepared to back off.

"We've never had a situation like this in the Northlands and there will no doubt be protests that Tyton gets to claim you without fighting for you. Other men will feel cheated."

"But I don't want anyone but Tyton."

Lucas grinned and shoved at Tyton's shoulder while I added, "We're in love."

Emmerson narrowed his eyes. "Yeah, but that's the thing. Marriages here don't require that the couple be in love. That part comes later once the couple gets to know each other." He shifted his stance. "It's not a valid argument to marry you two and besides, from what I understand you haven't spent much time together, so how can you say that you love him?"

"We got to know each other through our letters."

"Hmm... I'm searching for an argument that will justify letting Tyton marry you without a fight."

Tyton groaned. "All you have to tell them is that I've already claimed her and that she's pregnant with my child. Now, stop grilling my woman with all your questions. She chose to be here and you can see that I'm not forcing her."

Emmerson's eyes traveled between Tyton and me and he scratched his beard.

Tyton was losing his patience. "Come on, man, just say the words that will make us man and wife, so I can relax a little."

Emmerson held up a hand. "Be patient, my friend. We have to do this right."

Tyton was jumpy and with a deep frown he got testy, "What do you mean? You said there would be no tournament."

"Will you just listen?" Emmerson arched a brow. "I mean we're going to announce it to the whole fucking country. That way no one will question the legitimacy of your marriage."

"I don't know... I mean what if the Motherlands has a spy on this side? They would find out about Devina being here and ask to have her back."

The men all laughed at Tyton's paranoia.

"Who the hell would spy on their own country for the Motherlands?"

Tyton still looked troubled. "I had contact with Devina without anyone knowing it. Someone else could be talking with people on the other side of the wall and rumors could spread."

William turned to me. "Devina, do you think the Council in the Motherlands would ask to have you back if they found out that you are here now?"

I thought about it and then shook my head. "In a way I think that they'll be relieved that I'm no longer around to stir up more trouble."

"What are you talking about?" Lucas frowned with confusion.

"It might sound strange to you people, but the Council saw me as a troublemaker because of the book I wrote with Tyton. It was a love story about a man from the North and a woman from the Motherlands and it caused quite a controversy. To be honest, I suspect they'll use my suicide note to justify why they banned my book and made it illegal to even mention you Nmen."

"They did what?" Lucas who hadn't said much scrunched up his face.

"After the book came out the News has reported about women trying to climb the wall and getting injured in falls.

The Council members know that you men are dangerous, primitive, and violent. That's why they're trying to protect everyone in the Motherlands from you."

"We're not primitive or dangerous..." Emmerson gave an offended snort.

I turned my head to the window in the direction of the spears outside. "But you are."

He shifted his weight and shrugged. "Okay. Fair enough, but we're not dangerous to women." Pulling Wilma closer, he added, "We protect them."

"Just like we protect you men," Wilma interjected.

"The thing is..." I began and avoided all the eyes of the men. "In the Motherlands there's nothing to be protected from. Crime is rare, and men are gentle and kind. That's why the Council considers anyone who wants to come here as naïve and unable to make good decisions for themselves. Right now, they're doing damage control and trying to eradicate all versions of my book and making it illegal to even mention the men of the North."

"Huh." Frederick placed his hands on his hips. "That's fucked up."

"You have no idea." Tyton nudged my shoulder. "Tell them about the ban on emotionally disturbing things."

"Ehh, yes, any movie or book that contains emotionally charged content such as horror or romance is banned too."

Tyton added, "They even have a new policy where they can't swear or they'll get reported for inappropriate speech."

"It's called improper communication," I corrected him.

"Improper my ass," Emmerson scoffed. "Now I see why you want to live on this side."

"Yeah, but mostly it's because of me, right?" Tyton gave me a loving gaze.

"Yes." I smiled back at him.

"So, let's get this party started." Emmerson clapped his hands together. "This king slayer has a wedding to prepare."

CHAPTER 36
Magic Words

Tyton

The six hours I had to wait until I could marry Devina felt like six years. Emmerson was a new emperor and we were all on edge since he hadn't established complete control of the Northlands yet. I understood why Emmerson wanted to perform the ceremony in front of an audience and transmit it to the entire country, but all I wanted was for him to say the magic words that would formally bond Devina and me together.

Frederick had been trying to calm my nerves for the last hours with little success. "Relax, brother, no one is going to challenge you for her. She might not have a ring on her finger, but her pregnancy is visible and that alone will make other men treat her as a married woman."

"I fucking hope so." I was pacing the room and kept looking toward the door. "What's taking them so long?"

He handed me a beer. "Have something to drink."

"No. I'm not thirsty." No food or beverages would ever satisfy the craving I felt. "I just want Devina back here and for Emmerson to say the words."

Frederick moved to the window and looked down into the courtyard. "The press is here."

"Good, then we can get started."

"Yeah, I'm sure it won't be long now, and don't worry about Devina; the women are taking good care of her. It shouldn't have surprised you that Mom insisted they should dress her up and do her hair. A woman only marries once, and all that."

I groaned. "We can have a wedding party later. Right now I just want to make it official that she's mine and I'm hers."

Loud steps sounded outside just before the doors opened and Emmerson strode in. "Are you ready?"

"Yes!" I was already moving to the door, where Emmerson stopped me with a hand to my shoulder.

"First, I'll speak to the nation and then I'll perform the ceremony. The press will have questions and I think it's better if you answer at least a few of them."

"Okay, can we go now?"

"Damn, you're eager."

"Hey, I saw you fall to your knees in relief when my sister picked you. What don't you understand about my eagerness?"

"But Devina already picked you. The ceremony is just a formality."

I pushed his hand away. "Emmerson, stop wasting my time. I want to marry my woman, now!"

He laughed and smacked me on my back. "It will be my privilege."

The banquet hall was filled with friends and family that had flown in on short notice. A few looked hung over because yesterday had been New Year's Eve, and many had celebrated the death of King Jeremiah.

A group of people from the press were present and filmed as the new emperor strode in with Frederick and me at his sides.

We walked up the floor with confidence and greeted people we knew on the way. There was a step up to the emperor's table, where our closest family was gathered.

The people in the room were clapping to show their excitement that Emmerson was now in charge and when he turned to speak to them, he had to raise his hands to silence the loud cheers.

"Today is the first day in the year of 2237. It's also the first day of a new era in the Northlands where I will rule instead of King Jeremiah. It's tradition in our country that we all celebrate when a girl is born because with too few women, each one of them is precious. Today I have something spectacular to share with you as we're adding a woman to our current number of two hundred and six." Emmerson paused and let the anticipation build in the room.

"She's not a baby but a beautiful and grown woman ready to marry and bear children."

Whistles and outbursts were heard in the large room and again Emmerson had to wait for the cheers to quiet down. I closed my hands into fists, not happy with the way he teased the men in the room that Devina was already taken.

"A woman from the Motherlands has chosen to move here and have a family. She made it a condition that she got to choose her own husband and I agreed. The man she has chosen is the father of her unborn child, Tyton Green."

Confused mutters filled the room.

"I know this isn't according to our traditions, but if we're lucky the child she's already carrying will be the first of many girls."

I listened to him talk for what felt like an eternity before Emmerson finally placed a hand on my shoulder and gave me a smile. "Are you ready to see your bride?"

I nodded and stood straighter.

On his signal, the doors to the back of the room opened and Devina came in with Wilma, Starr, and Claire behind her.

I forgot to breathe as I watched Devina come toward me in a dress that showed off her gorgeous curves and displayed her pregnancy to the world.

"Wow," Frederick muttered and I sucked in a breath.

There was envy in the men's eyes when Devina passed them with her sole focus being on me. My chest was bursting with pride that she had chosen me over every other man in this country.

When she was ten steps from me, her smile grew and it was like the whole room lit up with bright sunshine. It had to be the most angelic smile in the history of the Northlands and I swallowed hard to suppress all the emotions in my throat.

I reached out my hand to her when she was close. Still smiling, Devina took it and walked into my arms to hug me tight.

At normal weddings there was no hugging or kissing before a ceremony, but we weren't strangers and I closed my arms around her and kissed her.

Emmerson grinned and spoke up again. "I'll say that shows every skeptic that the bride knows this man and wasn't forced in any way."

He gestured for us to face him and then he began a speech about the joy of finding love and how hopefully the future would bring many more unions between Nmen and Motlander women. I only heard half of it because I was blinded by the beauty of my bride.

Emmerson raised a piece of paper and read from it.

"Do you, Devina Baker, take Tyton Green as your husband?"

"Yes." She smiled at me.

"Do you promise to love him for better, for worse, for richer, for poorer, in sickness and in health; to cherish, and stay true till death do you part?

"Yes."

"And do you, Tyton Green, take Devina Baker as your wife?"

"I do."

"Do you promise to honor, cherish, and protect her for as long as you live?"

"I do."

"Then give her your ring as a symbol that you will worship her with your body and endow her with all your worldly possessions." Emmerson nodded to Frederick, who stepped forward with two rings on his palms. They were simple rings that would serve only until we had time to pick out the right ring for Devina.

My hands shook when I slid the ring onto her finger. I had visualized this moment a thousand times these past six hours while waiting for the ceremony to begin.

Emmerson's voice was loud and clear. "I now declare you husband and wife."

The explosion of euphoria inside me made me lift Devina from the floor and claim her in front of the nation in a deep kiss.

In the background white noise rose from cheers, whistling, and laughter, but all I focused on was the feeling of ultimate victory, and my fist rose in the air.

I may not have fought for Devina in a tournament, but I had faced a different kind of battle in seducing a Motlander who had been brainwashed to think of us Nmen as dangerous monsters. I still didn't understand how I'd managed to make her want to leave the Motherlands and stay with me, but I would never question her choice. Miracles happened, and this was my personal miracle.

My eyes were blazing with love and devotion as I pulled back and smiled at her.

"Is it over?" She wrapped her arms around my waist and looked up at me with the softest smile.

I beamed back at her. "No, sugar, it has only just begun."

Someone pushed a beer into my hand and shouted, "Cheers." I offered Devina a sip and she drank a little before she wrinkled her nose up and shook her head.

"You don't like it?"

"No. It tastes awful."

I grinned and squeezed her body. "You're so damn pure and I love it."

Behind me, I heard Wilma praise Emmerson. "You did good; you looked so majestic."

"Thanks, babe. I'm happy I had it written down or I would have forgotten half of it."

My mother came to congratulate us. "Oh, Devina, you don't know how happy it makes me to see Tyton married. Two weddings within five months... who would have thought?" Her eyes dropped to Devina's bulge. "And to think that we'll have another grandchild soon. Yesterday I felt like the world was coming to an end but today I feel full of hope."

Wilma moved closer and snaked her arms around our mother. "All your children are married now."

"I know." My mom's eyes grew moist.

Wilma turned her face to Devina and grinned widely. "And to think you burned the motherfucking place down before you left. That's some exit."

"Wilma!" I frowned. "You're talking about her ancestral home. I'm sure it wasn't fun for Devina."

Devina moved closer to me, holding on to my upper arm while looking at Wilma. "I couldn't have done it alone. My friend Tina helped me."

"Why didn't you bring her? We have plenty of men for her to choose from." Wilma nodded to the room full of Nmen.

"Nahh, Tina liked the fantasy of an Nman but not everyone wants their fantasies to come true."

Wilma shrugged. "That's her loss, but you know everyone is curious about how you ended up here with Tyton. Will you two do an interview with the press?"

We agreed and stood close like Siamese twins when we were being interviewed by the North News.

For the most part I let Devina answer when the reporter asked her questions like how long she had known me, how we had met, and if she had ever considered marrying before she met me. I got nervous when the reporter asked her, "What was your first impression of Tyton when you met him?"

Devina bit her lower lip and my heart beat faster. If she told him that I'd been aggressive I would have a whole fucking country of upset men after me.

"At first I was scared of Tyton."

Thump, thump, thump, my heart hammered away and I shifted my weight while rubbing my forehead.

"He was much bigger and stronger than the men I'm used to in the Motherlands and he swore a lot."

My shoulders eased a bit, as she hadn't mentioned the part about my confusing her for a boy and pushing her around.

"Also, you have to understand that I've grown up hearing horror stories about you Nmen. When I met Tyton, I was sure he would hurt me."

The reporter swung to me. "And what was your first impression of Devina?"

"Well, I thought that she was reckless coming here without protection and she was stubborn as hell and wouldn't listen to my warnings. Devina is very independent and opinionated." I gave her a smile. "But I like that about her."

"Devina, the obvious question that every Nman wants to know is when will more women follow you?"

She sighed. "I don't think anyone will. The Council has increased the border control and made it illegal to talk about the Northlands."

The reporter looked disturbed but managed to finish his interview before Devina and I moved on to celebrate with family and friends. The entire night, I kept close to my wife and introduced her to a number of people.

The fear that someone would be upset with Emmerson for killing Jeremiah melted away when the twentieth person declared what a relief it was to be rid of the tyrant.

Our wedding turned out to be a wonderful way to start off Emmerson's new rule and with the way Wilma batted her eyes at her strong husband, he came across as the ultimate hero.

Frederick, who sat next to me, saw me observing Emmerson and Wilma. "Cheers."

I raised my glass. "Cheers."

Throwing a nod in Emmerson's direction, Frederick muttered, "It could have been you or me up there."

"Nahh, I'm good. Better him than me. Look at that line of people eager to lick his ass. It would drive me crazy, but Emmerson is a showman who likes attention. He seems more at ease in his new position than I ever would have been."

Frederick nodded. "I hear you. Plus, he's going to be swamped in work while we can focus on our families."

We stood for a second watching him laugh and talk with his friends while Wilma stood glued to his side when Frederick added, "We'll have to do everything in our power to make sure Wilma doesn't end up as a widow before she's twenty."

I looked around. "Look at them. They already love him. He's everything a ruler should be: strong and a superior fighter, not to mention that he's charming too. I have a feeling Emmerson will do fine."

Devina was on my lap talking to Claire, who was explaining about our customs and traditions. When Claire was distracted by Lucas and looked away, I kissed Devina's neck and whispered in her ear that it was time to go.

"So soon?"

"What do you mean so soon? We've stayed far longer than normal and I'm eager to consummate our marriage." I pulled her to the center of my lap and let her feel how eager I was.

Devina turned her head and gave me a mischievous smile. "Are you going to be like this every day?"

"What do you mean?"

"Are we going to have sex every single day?"

"As I see it the only thing that could keep me from making love to my wife would be if both my legs and arms were broken."

She raised her brow. "Or if I wasn't interested."

My smile widened. "I would take that as a personal challenge." Letting my hand slide up her thigh, I tightened my hold on her. "I bet I could find a way to wake your interest."

Devina answered me with a kiss. "I'm ready when you are."

My chair scraped the floor as I pushed it back and stood up with Devina in front of me to shield the bulge below my midsection. "We're off."

No one protested when we left, but many whistled and raised their glasses, with comments of envy.

"You lucky bastard."

"I'll bet if she had met me before Tyton, it would have been my kid in that gorgeous woman."

I pointed to the man who said it and warned him, "I heard that."

He shrugged. "You can't blame us all for being jealous. You would be green with envy if our roles were reversed."

He was right, so I walked on with my back straight from pride.

"May you have beautiful daughters and plenty of them," someone shouted from the back.

Just as we exited the hall through the double doors, I once again raised my hand in victory and led Devina out to my drone waiting outside.

I helped her in by lifting her up to her seat.

"I'm happy that I don't have to disguise myself as a boy any longer."

With her sitting and me standing, we were the same height and I kissed her nose. "Never again. From now on you never have to hide yourself or your talent."

I closed the door to the drone and walked around to the other side to get in myself. It gave Devina time to think and when I buckled up, she asked. "Do you think Nmen would read my books? Is that what you meant by talent?"

"Are you kidding me? We're all curious about the Motherlands. Your books are going to be bestsellers because you're a credible source and you're a great writer." I programmed the drone and as it lifted up, I turned to her. "I still have the last manuscript of *Forbidden Letters from the North*. The fact that it's banned in the Motherlands is going to make everyone on this side want to read it. We'll have a publishing deal before you know it."

Devina sat awestruck.

"What's wrong? Did you think you'd have to give up your writing or something?"

"No, yes... I don't know. I haven't had time to think about it."

"That's okay. I predict that you'll be the biggest author in the Northlands before the year is over."

"You mean *we*. I didn't write that book alone."

I just smiled at her.

"If we publish it here, we should do it in both our names."

"You mean that?"

Devina nodded. "Yes. I mean it."

"Wow, that would make me a published author like you."

"Yes, it would."

I scratched my stubble. "Maybe we could write more books together. I mean, Mark and Deidra still had a lot of those one hundred and eighty positions left from the Kama Sutra book."

Devina laughed. "That's not a bad idea, but all great writers take research seriously, so we would need to go over each position to better understand what we're putting our characters through."

I reached my hand out to her and when she took it, I lifted it to my lips and placed a kiss on the back of her hand. "Consider it a deal!"

Epilogue
Seven Years Later

Devina

With the garden full of people, it would look like a large party to anyone stopping by. To us it was a standard Sunday get-together.

My three oldest children were playing with their cousins and were far too busy to listen when I repeated, "Food is ready, come and eat."

"Hey, Spartan…" Marni gave a loud whistle and got the attention of her youngest son, who was still older than all of Tyton's and my kids. "Dinner is ready, tell the others."

"But we're just in the middle of a game," he protested and took up the chase to get the soccer ball from some of his older brothers.

Marni shook her head. "I swear that boy is turning out like his brothers; they never listen either."

Tyton came over with our youngest daughter on his hip. "Someone wants her mother."

Hannah was two and a half, and too heavy for me to carry around in my third trimester.

"Let me just sit down and I'll take her."

Our toddler climbed on top of me as soon as I sank down on the garden bench.

"She's so pretty." Claire sat down next to me and stroked Hannah's soft curls. Once again, I felt bad that she and Lucas still hadn't been able to conceive children of their own.

"Hey, sweetie, do you want to cuddle with Aunty Claire?" she coaxed Hannah, who reached out her arms to her favorite aunt.

"You're so lucky that you keep having girls," Marni said with a sigh.

"I had Justin," I reminded her.

"Yeah, but he's more like a bonus twin to Caro, isn't he?"

Placing my hand on my belly, I smiled. "I just hope the universe gives me one more girl so I can name her Maria."

Tyton and I had named our first daughter after my nana, whose name had been Andrea. She was six and a half now and the proud sister of our four-year-old twins, Caroline and Justin, named after my oldest siblings, and sweet Hannah, who was two years old. In three months' time, I would be giving birth to our fifth child.

"How many are you going to have?" Marni asked while gesturing with her arms for the children to come and eat.

"We both wanted a large family but I've told Tyton that after this one, I'm done."

Claire smiled. "I don't believe you. If I could, I'd have at least ten children."

Marni snorted. "Just wait until you have to push them out of your body. I swear, when I was having my fourth, I was cursing at myself for being stupid enough to let Henry get me pregnant again."

"But the joy of having children outweighs the pain, doesn't it?" Claire asked me.

I smiled at her. "Yes, it does."

"The food is getting cold." Joan came over and joined us.

"Then how about you use your grandma super powers and reeling in all the children?" Marni gave her mom a large smile. "I've whistled and shouted, but they would rather play than eat."

"So, let them." Joan shrugged. "We adults can eat and then when they complain that there's only sad leftovers for them, they'll learn. Maybe it will teach them to come when we call next Sunday."

"All right." I kissed Hannah and got up. "I'll get you a plate, Claire."

Tyton and the other men were sitting in the sun, talking. Frederick had his youngest son on his shoulders and they were laughing at something.

"What's so funny?" I asked as I passed them.

"We were just talking about how lucky we were to be born as free men." Lucas lifted his hand to shield his eyes from the sun. "It's fucking sad that the Motherland Council are indoctrinating women who believe we're monsters."

"I know, but it's not all bad in the Motherlands."

Henry snorted. "Name one good thing."

Touching my stomach, I thought about it. "Ehh... well, the Motherlands is a place of caring and nurturing. They may go overboard sometimes, but it's colorful, and no one is left behind in poverty or sickness. They care about animals and have high ambitions when it comes to cleaning up the earth."

"But you can't swear, fight, or fart." One of Marni's and Henry's sons had joined the conversation.

"Or drink beer," Tyton added and raised his bottle to his mouth.

"It's true that it's illegal to drink beer and swear, but the thing about farting is an exaggeration. It's not illegal per se... more like bad manners."

"I couldn't live in a place with that sort of mind control," Frederick declared and shook his head. "Where is it going to end? If we live our way and they continue to live their extreme way, we'll be so different that even if the wall crumbled one day, we would be like two different species."

I shifted my weight and wrinkled my forehead while Frederick continued, "Think about it. For two hundred years Motlanders have whispered about us like we're some kind of demons. What if no one crosses over in the next two or three hundred years? Imagine the culture

Men of the North – FORBIDDEN LETTERS

shock it will be? I kinda wish I would be here to see it. I'll bet in the future Motlander women will find a way to make themselves hermaphrodites, just so they won't need us men at all."

Tyton laughed. "I'll bet they would, except that they don't like technology too much and nature doesn't work that fast."

"Ah, come on, in two hundred years they could have found a way to grow dicks," Lucas postulated.

Tyton nodded. "Oh, they already have a way to grow dicks. How do you think they make Nmen? All the boys we get are made in laboratories and they control the exact number of boys and girls they make."

"Tyton, stop. You make it sound worse than it is," I protested. "Women are inseminated in a clinic, but the babies grow inside their mother's womb just like here. You make it sound like Nmen are grown in some cold laboratory and that's not true."

"For now, but in two hundred years they'll be growing children in laboratories, trust me." Tyton took another sip of his beer.

"I doubt it, and before you decide that the Motherlands is hell on earth, let me just remind you that some amazing people live there. People like me who are kindhearted and caring."

"Hmmm…" He frowned. "I don't know about that. Last night you fell asleep before we had a second round of sex. That's kind of cold." He smiled and winked at me.

I ignored his joke and pointed out to all the men. "The Motherlands is a wonderful place. Trust me on that."

Tyton got up and came to put his arm around me. "Just admit that you like it better here, my love."

A quick look around the large family I had now and my children playing, with happy faces, made it easy to nod my head. "I love it here."

Tyton broke out in a large and very satisfied smile so I added,

"For the most part."

"For the most part? What's that supposed to mean?"

"Just that there are days when I miss the Motherlands."

"Why?" Frederick wrinkled his nose. "We just agreed it's a shitty place."

I sighed. "It's not! They made some unfortunate rules that I don't agree with and it's not perfect, but neither is The Northlands."

Tilting his head, Tyton argued, "Ah, but don't forget that they banned our book, while the Nmen loved it."

That comment made Frederick scoff out loud. "I don't know about that. The sex scenes were a bit tame for my taste."

Over the last seven years I had published five books and three of them had been co-written with Tyton, who didn't take criticism too well. Flipping Frederick a finger, he squared his chest. "If you want porn, go find a book from the erotica section. Our books are fine art."

"Sure they are." Frederick rolled his eyes, but I didn't get offended because this was so typical of the two brothers, who loved to rile each other up. Frederick turned his head and winked at me with a small smile just as Wilma came around the corner of the house.

At twenty-two she was more beautiful than she had been when I first met her.

We watched her give out hugs to the nieces who ran to greet her. With the boys she nodded and smiled but avoided touch.

"Where's Emmerson?" Tyton called out to her.

"Oh, he had to go to the east coast but he'll be here next Sunday."

"What about Marshall and Czar?" I kept waiting for her two sons to come around the corner and on cue they came sprinting.

Wilma laughed. "We had a little detour because Dad took us to feed the chickens."

"Are you hungry?" I nodded to the table with food and from behind me Claire called out:

"Hey, I'm hungry and still waiting for that plate you promised me."

Hannah was playing with Claire's hair when I turned to apologize. "It's like time disappears when you people come over. I'll be right there."

"It's fine, let me," Tyton offered and walked over to pile food on a plate for his sister. After giving it to Claire, he came back to me. "Do you want me to get you something too?"

My lips pursed up. "You already did."

The look of understanding between us made me lean against him. There was no need for me to tell Tyton that he was my safe space. He already knew that our children, and the rest of the large family he had given me, filled me up and helped heal the trauma of losing my siblings and parents.

We had been man and wife for seven years and had reached a place where looks and movements could replace words.

Pulling me in for a warm hug, Tyton kissed the top of my hair. I pressed my cheek to his strong chest and breathed in his familiar masculine scent.

"You okay?" he whispered.

Pulling back to look into his eyes, I blinked away a tear and smiled up at him. "I've never been better."

**This concludes *Forbidden Letters*
– prequel to the *Men of the North* series.**

When I finished the *Men of the North* series, many readers were begging for more books in the series.
This book, *Forbidden Letters*, was meant to be a short story as a sort of bonus for my readers. But Devina's and Tyton's story unfolded and instead of cutting it short, I decided to go with the flow and make it a normal-length novel.

If this was your introduction to *Men of the North*, then you have an exciting series of entertaining books in front of you – each with a different tone and style, from humor to adventure and mystery, but always with a love story at the core. You can stop at any time because these stories don't have cliff-hangers, but to avoid spoilers, I strongly recommend that you read them in order.

After lovely pressure from readers I'm currently working on writing about the third generation. Mason's story called The Artist – Men of the North #11 is available now.

All books are available on Amazon in ebook, paperback, and audiobook. If you are a member of Kindle Unlimited you can read them for free.
If not, you can get them discounted when buying the box sets.

Books in this series

For the best reading experience and to avoid spoilers, this is the recommended order of the books.

Prequel:
Forbidden Letters # 0.5

First Generation
The Protector #1
The Ruler #2
The Mentor #3
The Seducer #4
The Warrior #5

Second Generation
The Genius #6
The Dancer #7
The Athlete #8
The Fighter #9
The Pacifist #10

Third Generation
The Artist #11
The Explorer #12
The Outcast #13
The Heir #14
The Champion #15

The books are also available in paperback and audiobooks.
For a full overview of my books and to be alerted for new book releases, discounts, and give-aways, please sign up to my list at
www.elinpeer.com

What's next?

Here's a short overview of my books.

Cultivated
Set in the USA and the gorgeous Ireland, these six contemporary romance books take on the question of mind control.
They're suspenseful, fast-paced, and full of humor. As always, they carry Elin's unique style of writing, which readers refer to as 'self-help that reads like fiction.
Find a description of book #1 called Charlie below.

Clashing Colors:
These five contemporary romance stories dive into the theme of opposites attract.
From romantic comedy to dramatic scenes offering food for thought; these books will make you both laugh and cry.

The Slave Series:
Five intense "enemy to lovers" books portraying strong women who won't be defined as victims.
Expect some dark scenes and steamy sex.

Men of the North:
One prequel and fifteen romantic sci-fi stories that take place 400 years in the future where women rule the world. Each book about a different couple with no cliff-hangers. These stories are unlike anything you've ever read and have made several bestselling lists on Amazon.
It's a tug of war between the crude alpha men on one side of the border and the altruistic women on the other side. Can they find a way to integrate?

About the Author

With a back ground in life coaching, Elin is easy to talk to and her fans rave about her unique writing style that has subtle elements of coaching mixed into fictional love stories with happy endings.

Elin is curious by nature. She likes to explore and can tell you about riding elephants through the Asian jungle, watching the sunset in the Sahara Desert from the back of a camel, sailing down the Nile in Egypt, kayaking in Alaska, river rafting in Indonesia, and flying over Greenland in a helicopter.

After traveling the world and living in different countries, Elin is currently residing outside Seattle in the US with her husband, daughters, and her black Labrador, Lucky, who follows her everywhere.

Want to connect with Elin? Great – she loves to hear from her readers.

Find her on Facebook: facebook.com/AuthorElinPeer
Or look her up on Goodreads, Amazon, Bookbub or simply go to elinpeer.com

Made in the USA
Las Vegas, NV
18 December 2020

13744361R00174